Ithaca

ALSO BY STEPHEN PEARSALL

Yesterday, A Memoir

Counterpoint

Focus

A NOVEL

Ithaca

THE LONG ROAD HOME

STEPHEN PEARSALL

Order this book online at www.trafford.com
or email orders@trafford.com

Most Trafford titles are also available at major online book retailers.

Print information available on the last page.

ISBN: 978-1-4907-8489-2 (sc)
ISBN: 978-1-4907-8490-8 (e)

Trafford rev. 10/20/2017

 www.trafford.com

North America & international
toll-free: 1 888 232 4444 (USA & Canada)
fax: 812 355 4082

For

Bradford
Stephanie
Gregory
Jennifer
Sarah

Gnossienne

n. A moment of awareness that someone you've known for years still has a private and mysterious inner life, and somewhere in the hallways of their personality is a door locked from the inside....

KYLE

Book IV

1

FOX ONE

September 1966

The platoon moved slowly through the jungle; a rushing stream provided a path along the side of the mountain. It was wild and beautiful if viewed from a detached viewpoint, but the jungle had immersed Lt. Kyle Norquist in the uncomfortable and dangerous present. It seemed that the monsoon would never end, and the rain had begun again, this time a heavy downpour pelting the leaves with a clatter, turning the path to mud. Tropical evenings were brief, and darkness would soon envelop them. Using a pencil flashlight, Kyle studied a ragged map and then handed it to his first sergeant, Red Farney. "I think we're about here," he whispered, as his finger poked on the spot on the map. "This stream should begin to fall away and feed into a narrow river about a thousand meters ahead. We should stay put until dawn."

"I agree, Skipper," Sergeant Farney muttered, looking at the sky instead of the map. "We're spread out too wide. I'll set up a perimeter, and the rest of the men can hunker down on this outcrop." They had been moving in groups of three for most of the day through a jungle that clung to the steep mountainside. Three squads, with the center team covering the platoon command center, the wireless radio, a corpsman, and Cpl. Koonce with his grenade launcher.

Kyle fingered the gold bar on his collar; the rank and file called it a 'butterbar.' He had been in Viet Nam eight months, spending most of the time at Battalion Headquarters, before his assignment two months ago to the 1st Cavalry Regiment at a new helicopter base "Jumper" situated south of the rugged mountains that lined the Laotian border. Fox One was his first command, a rifle platoon with limited battle experience. It was composed of three squads totaling thirty-one troopers, small caliber weapons, a short-wave radio operator (RTO), one Navy medic and a battle-worn four-stripe sergeant named Farney.

Kyle possessed most of the requirements to command an army infantry platoon: familiarity with every weapon available to a rifle company, map reading skills, basic medical knowledge and a textbook fluency on leadership. Combat had not tested these skills. Kyle had lucked out when Fox Company assigned Sergeant Red Farney to his platoon. Farney was a four-striper, with battle experience in Viet Nam as well as in Korea during the conflict there a decade earlier. He possessed an essential ingredient for command and survival—a natural instinct to make sound decisions. It was Farney who led the platoon, and he did it quietly without usurping Kyle's position as the platoon's first officer. The men respected Farney; and were, in fact, entirely dependent upon him.

When Kyle prepared for Viet Nam, he envisioned a jungle one would find along the Amazon River, but what his platoon was struggling through was elephant grass, sometimes impenetrable, punctuated by thick bushes and trees. The undergrowth was hard to navigate and offered exposure to an ambush. Kyle turned to his RTO, Morris—the men called him Code—"Send a short message to TIGER (Battalion Headquarters) with our coordinate 072054, affirming 'location quiet.' Make the signature Fox One Actual."

Kyle looked around for the driest spot and began digging with his small folding entrenching shovel. Sleeping would be near impossible, but the poncho liner would provide some warmth, so he rigged the poncho onto sticks for a shelter from the rain. It would not be a bunker, not even a hole, just a ditch three feet deep where he could stretch out. Kyle could hear the others digging; they were like animals burrowing for the winter. He fashioned a gutter around his shallow hole to channel the water away. The rain stopped suddenly, and Kyle headed to a log where Morris and Farney were eating their K-rations. They had a fire going in a K-ration can, and he could smell the coffee.

The three sat in silence, lost in their thoughts while watching the fog swirl up the hillside. "I'm not tired," Kyle muttered from his spot on the log. "I'll take first watch."

The sergeant agreed. "Better bring your poncho. It'll get cold and start raining again. I have an extra tarp to cover your curious looking foxhole," he said with a smirk.

Kyle grabbed his rifle and poncho and crept between sleeping bodies toward the edge of the outcrop, a location offering a wider view of their bivouac. The fog would be a problem he realized, watching it envelop the trees on the perimeter of his vision. Sitting alone in the darkness of the jungle, with the enemy somewhere close-by, causes a gnawing dread that bordered on terror. Kyle's mind drifted. He could find no meaning in this uncomfortable location; there was no purpose in the fighting and killing. To extinguish a life, human or animal, was contrary to his morality. His upbringing and education did not support it. Even the M-16, which rested on his knees and a tool he could use with precision, felt foreign. He had not killed yet. When the time arrived, could he do it?

His journey to desolation, to the very spot where he was sitting, had ruminated in his subconscious before becoming mindful. During his college years the war in Viet Nam had been on his mind, unacknowledged at first, then questioned, but it had been Catherine who had brought it out in the open. Kyle's mind drifted before settling on the time he and Cat had been drinking strong beer in one of the bars lining the Bergen Wharf. They had just begun their year-long European sojourn, and the thrill of being together on a mission of no consequence had not sunk in. They were 'in the moment,' absorbed in the joy of the midsummer revelers, the ever-present sun sitting on the hills, and the nearness of their bodies. June in Norway embodied a freshness that extracts a sense of exuberant living, of the out-of-doors, of a new beginning and an awareness of oneself. They had started talking, at first idly, but soon their chat shifted to what was really on Kyle's mind.

"Your thoughts are somewhere else, Kyle," Catherine had said, leaning back in her chair and looking at him with an impish grin. "What's bothering you?"

Kyle's California tan had darkened in the Scandinavian midsummer sun; his shaggy, thick brown hair concealed the back of his neck. He looked like he belonged in Bergen. He hadn't answered immediately, his gaze embracing the woman before him. Her scrubbed beauty always attracted admiring looks, but it was her uncanny ability to read and analyze Kyle's mind that had at first startled him and then, soon captivated him. Remembering, "You're in my thoughts again and, yes, I am thinking of a faraway place."

"The war."

"It's wrong, and yet I have this compulsion to serve my country. Many friends are dodging this responsibility. It's the less privileged who are in the battle; in fact, several from my high school have lost their lives. I feel guilty sitting here with you drinking beer and watching these beautiful people enjoying themselves while others, the same age and with the same aspirations, are dying in a senseless war on the other side of the world. You and I have talked about this for so long. I feel a need to do something about it. Something more than just talk."

Catherine had leaned forward and asked earnestly, "Wouldn't you accomplish more by remaining home working to end this useless conflict?"

"I would only be authentic if I had experienced the battle first-hand."

Catherine had turned away looking out at the water, "Then you should go."

Kyle wrapped himself in his poncho and let his eyes inspect the brush on the perimeter. Nothing, not a sound, the rain had stopped. Suddenly he heard a rustling noise behind him, and every nerve stood on end.

"Lieutenant, your watch is up, sir. I'll take your post," said a young voice with a southern accent.

Kyle could now see Corporal Koonce lying on his belly. "Come on up here."

Koonce slithered next to Kyle. "Anything happening?" he whispered.

"Nothing. Staying awake is hard. Where're you from, Corporal?" Kyle asked, turning his gaze to the young man.

"I grew up in Alabama, sir, but I now live in Chicago—South Chicago—Black Chicago," he said with a tone of ownership.

"What did you do before the army?"

"I own a 'comfort' home for men," the gleam of his white teeth broke the darkness. "Lots of beautiful 'poontang,' Lieutenant. You come to Chicago, man; I'll fix you up with some sexy 'honeys.' Ever had a black woman?"

"Thanks for the invitation." Kyle let the last question slide and headed for his fox trench. "Take care, corporal."

Kyle slipped into his now dry hole and searched for sleep. His rifle nestled next to him and the rest of his gear, ammunition, grenades, a knife, shovel, and pack, lay at his feet. He had no more slipped into an uneasy sleep when Farney whispered, "Lieutenant, time to get moving. There's coffee on the log."

In August 1966, the First Cavalry Airborne Battalion had positioned itself on the south side of the Chu Pong Massif, just below the DMZ on the Laotian border. Other battalions were there as well providing engineering, artillery, and a field hospital. On the other side of the rugged mountains, the North Vietnamese Army (NVA) had massed three regiments and was preparing to move into South Viet Nam. They would accomplish this using the well-hidden trail on the Laotian side of the border and by moving east along the Ben Hai River, which would open their access to the Quang Tri plain. Large numbers of Viet Cong had already infiltrated valleys to the East, which cut off the US Army's vital road access to their base. Now men and materials arrived by helicopter. The US and ARVIN plan to push into the mountainous area to the north the moment the monsoon season showed signs of subsiding.

On one exceptionally humid morning, Kyle's Battalion Commander summoned him to report to Battalion Headquarters. Fox Company commander Captain Gus Walton joined him, and together they stood before Lieutenant Colonel Charles Allen who was studying a table strewn with maps. Allen walked around the map table smiling. "Morning, Gus," he said in a deep voice and grasped Walton's hand. Then turning to Kyle, he stretched out his hand and said, "And you must be Lt. Norquist."

"Yes, sir. Good morning, sir."

"I understand you are good at reading maps as well as the stars," Allen said with a smile. "Come over to the table and help us with one complicated situation." The map in question covered a mountain range positioned tight against the Lao border. "Here on the north side," Allen stabbed the area with his pointer, "we know there are a couple of NVA regiments, maybe more. What we don't know is if they have moved east or are they attempting to maneuver straight south through the mountains, which would put them on the hilltops overlooking our base."

Kyle studied the topographical map carefully. His comprehension of contour maps amazed his superiors. "The quickest way to find out for sure," he said looking at the colonel, "would be to send a reconnaissance platoon up this narrow valley extending in from the east face. If they are there, it will bump into troop activity. Otherwise, those assholes will be moving through the mountains."

After a long pause, Colonel Allen turned to Gus Walton and said, "Send one of your rifle platoons up Lt. Norquist's valley. It needs to be light in weight so that it can move quickly. Keep me informed."

In the early morning light, Fox One moved cautiously along the side of the mountain they had been traversing for two days. The platoon was in its fifth day of reconnaissance. In the hazy sunlight, high mountains, steep and jagged, loomed to the west. "Maybe the monsoon has ended," murmured Code who was trailing Kyle through the tall grass.

Sergeant Farney emerged from behind a thick grove of bushes. "Our friends are probably positioned on the other side of this narrow valley, and they will see us. How far are we from the Ben Hai River, Lieutenant?"

Kyle checked his map. "Five clicks, Sarge."

"We need to cross to the other side of this valley. It's dark over there and more cover. If we move higher on that hill, we will be in an improved position to view any activity either in this valley or the big one ahead." Kyle and Farney crawled to the edge of a rock formation that gave them a view of the valley. They saw a small hamlet, maybe ten huts, and a well-tended rice field along a stream. Four women labored in the rice paddy. "Let's move closer to the hamlet, hunker down, and cross to the other side at nightfall," Farney whispered.

Fox One, in their camouflage fatigues, settled onto the hillside behind thick brush, sipped from their canteens, tapped into a K-ration and the squads not on watch, dozed. The scene seemed tranquil to Kyle, a postcard valley filled with rice patches. Open ducts fed water from the stream to the rice fields. The women had their garments hitched up as they walked through the flooded fields tending their crop. There was no activity in the hamlet; no children, no animals—nothing. Beyond, on the far edge of the fields, a dense jungle formed a backdrop. Foliage enveloped the entire far side of the slope.

Near the end of the afternoon, as daylight ebbed, a wizen old man emerged from the compound of huts and using a staff, ambled slowly to the rice field edge and appeared to signal to the women. They moved without haste to join him and together the five headed to the far side of the little valley and disappeared into the jungle. They just vanished leaving an eerie silence.

The sergeant kneeled next to Kyle. "Something's funny here, sir," his gravelly voice not quite achieving a whisper. "Where did those women go and why is there no one in the hamlet?"

"I don't like it either, Sarge. Here, take my binocs and see if you can find an opening in the jungle on the far side. There's nothing, no road, not even a path. We can't cross the valley here—too dangerous." Kyle swung around to Code. "Change your frequency and advise *Tiger* of our coordinate, 076081, and report no encounter. Close down your transmitter fast."

It began to rain again causing the men to scramble to cover their equipment and themselves with their ponchos. The thirty-one tired, hungry and dirty men of Fox One platoon each donned a flak jacket before wrapping their ponchos around themselves. Each strapped on a cartridge belt with its canteens and belt suspenders and backpack, cradled their weapons and began moving cautiously, single file, through the brush, their direction slanting ever so slightly downward toward the hamlet. Sam Collier took point, followed by Squad A, then Sergeant Farney leading Squad B in the center of the column. Kyle was the command post (CP) and brought up the rear along with the RTO, the corpsman and Cpl. Koonce carrying the thump-gun—an M79 grenade launcher. The three squads' sole method of communication was a messenger. Their mission was to locate the NVA's outer parameter, and Kyle figured they were probably sitting on it right now. Where the hell is the enemy, Kyle wondered?

The cloudburst was brief, and a mist drifted in settling over the rice paddies, providing some cover for Fox One as it positioned itself above the hamlet. Then, just before dusk, the mist lifted revealing empty fields. "Where are the four women," Kyle muttered under his breath. His platoon did not have the native scout typically provided to reconnaissance patrols, and he now realized this was a miscalculation. Kyle examined his tattered map searching for a safe route out of the valley or to a chopper landing zone (LZ). To evacuate the entire platoon at one time, they would require an LZ space for a CH-47, and there hadn't been anything close to that size on their trek so far. But the clearing in front of this hamlet would accommodate a Huey. Fox One had to clear the area to assure the copter's safety.

Their present location was tenuous; with sparse cover and a lousy back door. Kyle's mind was spinning with options and worries. His assignment was to find the enemy, not fight them. He now realized that would be impossible. They would be on the move and alert. He was stepping into the jaws of uncertainty.

If the NVA were moving south through the Chu Pong Mountain range, Fox One would never intercept them. If, however, and more logically, they were running east along the Ben Hai River Valley, the enemy could be no more than five miles away, and they would protect their flank with patrols skirting through the foothills along the valley's south side. Fox One's location lay smack along this parameter. All we need to do, Kyle reasoned, is to confirm the enemy's position, size and their direction without an encounter. Kyle looked up from his map and gazed once more at the narrow valley and the hills beyond. He needed to reach the summit of the first hill and from there he ought to be able to see troop movement along the Ben Hai Valley. Could he reach this advantage point without detection? If not, and a skirmish ensued, Fox One would be at a disadvantage with its light weaponry. Kyle made his decision. They would cross the narrow valley before them; bivouac, and he would lead one squad to the hilltop early tomorrow morning. "Koonce, find the Sarge and bring him back."

The morning's first rays caught the hillside and the rice paddies in the valley below. Kyle and Farney stood in the shadows drinking thin coffee and reviewing their plan. It would be Farney who would take A Squad to the top. He could read the troops on the move better than Kyle, and he slipped through the jungle with the litheness of an animal. His squad would mirror his movements with confidence.

"As I develop information, I'll send a messenger down the hill," Farney said, turning to Kyle. "Send it to TIGER, if you think it warrants opening up the airwaves."

"What if you don't see anything?" Kyle could sense his adrenalin surging and took deep breaths.

"Then we have gone as far as we can and would have completed our mission. If there are no gooks around, the choppers can come to the LZ over there," the Sergeant growled and pointed to the field by the cluster of huts.

"And if you run into trouble up there?" Kyle murmured, trying to control his breathing.

"We would be fucked. If you tried to come up the hill, we would all be in trouble. Sir, do not bring the men up the hill!" Farney's voice was deep and insistent. We'll fight our way out. Just get the choppers in."

With that instruction to his commanding officer, Farney turned and headed off into the brush, followed by nine men, all carrying only their weapons and munitions belts. Kyle positioned his men in three-man fire teams along the valley edge, instructing them to crouch inside the thick brush, and close enough to allow communication.

The LZ became the CP. Kyle could see through his binoculars Koonce placing his grenade launcher at the far end of the defense line where he and his squad could ambush patrols coming up the valley. Kyle's mind focused on the present and the precarious position of the platoon under his command. He tried to think of home or Catherine or anything that would ease his growing fear, but the heaviness of his situation controlled his thoughts. The minutes ticked slowly. An hour had passed and the morning was now hot and humid. No messenger. Nothing.

Cpl. Collier emerged from the brush suddenly and so quietly that it seemed he might have been standing there all morning. He looked grim. "Lieutenant. Sir, I have a message from Sergeant Farney."

Kyle took the piece of paper but looked into Collier's eyes. "What have you seen?"

We saw the NVA—we estimate a regiment—moving along the road in the valley, heading east. There were vehicles and heavy armament—anti-aircraft and 75mm cannons."

"Is your squad coming down now?"

"Yes, but there is more." Collier paused, but Kyle said nothing. "enemy troops are moving up our valley."

"How far away are they? On foot, I assume?

"Two kilometers, three at most. They're sweeping the valley."

"Corporal, go back and tell the Sergeant to move his squad down here immediately. Tell him we are calling for choppers and we will intercept the enemy patrol. Move your ass!"

Kyle turned to Code hunched over his transmitter. "Get *TIGER* on a new frequency."

Code picked up the handset and barked, "*TIGER, TIGER, TIGER, this is Fox One, come in, over.*" Morris moved the frequency dial searching for a new channel. "*Come in TIGER, this is Fox One, over.*"

"*Copy, Fox One, this is TIGER, speak, over.*"

Kyle moved Code aside and claimed the handset. "*This is Fox One Actual. Can confirm NVA, regiment size, troop movement east along big snake* (code for the Ben Hai River), *troop carriers, cannons, mobile anti-aircraft. Our mission complete. Request withdrawal ASAP.*"

"*Roger, Fox One. Wait one.*" The pause seemed interminable. "*Fox One, Tiger Actual here. Request approved. Designate LZ coordinates, over.*"

"*Huey LZ 076082 ready, between paddies and ten shack hamlet. NVA patrol two ticks north in our valley moving south, we will interdict, confirm, over.*"

"*Roger, Fox One. Estimate 30 to ETA LZ. Area must be clear of enemy fire, over.*"

"*Understood, will evaluate situation in 15 and report. Require three birds for evac and one gun, over.*"

"*Roger. Set clock zero minus 10, now. Over and out.*"

A steady wind blew up the valley. A burning hamlet would provide a fire screen to the landing site if the wind direction held. When the Hueys arrived, Kyle planned to toss a thermite grenade into one hut; the resulting explosion would ultimately ignite the entire hamlet, which would block the enemy's view of the LZ. With the rest of his Squad, he raced along the edge of the valley toward Koonce, his point man, hoping to find an elevated and concealed area from which they could ambush the approaching patrol. Kyle's mind spun. Too many questions are unanswered. Who was coming down the valley, VC or NVA? How many? What weaponry? He had twenty men, thirty when Farney returned. If the gooks were more than a platoon, Fox One was up shit creek. And, he couldn't fight and load the choppers at the same time. He had less than an hour to figure this out. Kyle felt no fear; in fact, the adrenaline surges had abated, leaving him with remarkable composure.

They were Viet Cong, as it turned out, ragged, armed mostly with AK-47s and they were moving haphazardly. NVA sent them into unknown situations because they were expendable. Farney had arrived and watched them through binoculars—they were now no more than one tick away. Suddenly they began to converge around the edge of the stream. "Fuckin-A!" Farney whispered. "They're setting up camp, the lazy bastards; they have no idea we're here." He turned to Kyle. "Lieutenant, I think you should return with one squad to CP and man the radio. The cloud cover is dropping. We need to get those Hueys on the LZ fast. If we're engaged, the gunship can cover us."

"If there is a gunship," Kyle said sardonically.

The radio crackled, and Code flipped a switch. *"Fox One, come in. This is HU10. Over."*

"Roger, HU10. We read you. Your position. Fox One. Over."

"HU10 now twelve minutes from LZ. Are you ready? Over."

"Cowboys (enemy) one tick north, unaware our position. No cigars (wounded). LZ clear. Other birds coming? Over."

"Roger. Be ready. Out."

The gooks heard the chopper about the same time as Fox One and scrambled for their weapons. Farney watched them fan out and race up the sides of the narrow valley. He turned to his squad. "When I fire, you fire, but use your ammo sparingly. Koonce, you remain with your grenade launcher. Send the rest of your crew back to the CP and set up a firewall around the LZ perimeter.

The first of the VC were now no more than 1000 meters from the LZ and moving quickly. Farney noticed a rocket launcher and focused his M-16 on the man carrying it. The thumping of the chopper propeller blades was distinct. When the rocket launcher reached about 500 meters, Farney squeezed his trigger, and the man went down. Others fell as B Squad opened fire.

A machine gun began firing from the far side, indiscriminately spraying Farney's position. He heard a scream followed by a shout, "medic, medic, Robert's hit!"

"Let's get out of here fast," Farney shouted, "The mother fuckers have our position. Hold your fire except you, Koonce. Keep slinging grenades at them and after one minute, move back and join us. Grab Robert and let's go."

The gray clouds hung like a wet blanket, bulging and ready to encompass the valley and the battle below. HU10 had flown close to the cloud's belly and then dropped swiftly to the LZ. It was a MedEvac version of the UH-1V with two pilots and no gunner and no medical attendant.

Kyle yelled through the noise. "I want eleven troopers on board. Leave your ammo belt and grenades." When the door hatch opened, the men clambered aboard. The chopper lifted off before the hatch closed.

Between the ten hamlet huts and the advancing Vietcong was an unused rice paddy. It was small and dry with a two-foot earth embankment. Fox One's headcount had dropped to twenty and the promised second Huey could only transport eleven. A cobra gunship offered no space. "Fuck," Kyle shouted to no one in particular. He could see Farney's men running along the valley edge, heading for the hamlet. "Code, get me, *TIGER* fast."

Farney raced up followed by his squad and for the first time looked at the lieutenant for instructions. "Place your men in a fire line along the far edge of that rice paddy," Kyle said, pointing to the other side of the huts. "When the second bird arrives, everyone moves to the LZ." Kyle noticed Koonce carrying the grenade launch bringing up the tail end of the squad.

"TIGER, TIGER, Fox One here, come in, over."
   "We read you Fox One, over."
   "Need third bird, urgent. Twenty remaining, one cigar, over."
   "Roger, hold one…Fox One, switch to OF-3,"
   "Roger and out." Morris Code moved his frequency dial slowly looking for "option three frequency." He found it and tapped in.
   "TIGER, do you read?"
   "Fox One, second bird three minutes to LZ. Cobra negative. Third bird has gun and medic. Ten minutes to LZ. Do you read?"
   "Roger. Setting up a smoke screen. We are ready to leave. Out."

The situation was intense. The enemy had dug in about 1000 meters from Fox One's perimeter and had begun to work their way through the brush and high grass along the valley edge. The second helicopter dropped through the cloud and dove toward the LZ. Kyle signaled for Farney and his men to move back. They were crawling and dragging one of their men. Koonce had gathered a mound of grenades and remained at the perimeter firing his launcher. "Sergeant, get your boys back here. I'm setting fire to the huts." Men were piling into the helicopter. They loaded two wounded warriors, and the platoon's one corpsman joined them. The Huey lifted and banked toward the south as Kyle tossed a grenade into the center of the huts and dove into a protective trench. The explosion demolished several huts and ignited the C-4. At first, there was intense fire and then thick, dark smoke. Just before the smoke enveloped the north rice paddy, Kyle saw Koonce turn away from his position carrying his weapon. A bullet, maybe several, caught him on his left side spinning him around in an eerie dance before he collapsed to the ground. From directly above, just away from the smoke, the third Huey arrived, and its gunner, from the open hatch, launched a lethal burst from his machine gun.
   "Man down!" a gravelly voice shouted.

Kyle, moving in a crouch, ran through the smoke toward the spot where he'd seen Koonce go down. Ten Fox One men remained on the ground, including Norquist, Farney, Code, Olson, and Koonce. Olson handed Code, who had jumped on board, the radio transmitter. Farney positioned himself to cover Kyle.

The enemy fire had dissipated because of the smoke, but some of the VC crawled toward the rice paddy. Kyle lifted Koonce's inert body over his left shoulder and headed into the smoke for cover. Half way to the waiting Huey, a grenade exploded behind him and to his left. The force of the concussion lifted him off the ground. He landed with Koonce sprawled on top of him. Within seconds, Farney had grabbed Kyle under the armpits and dragged him to the waiting copter. He and Olsen lifted Koonce aboard, then Kyle and as outstretched hands pulled them aboard, the Huey became airborne. The machine gunner opened up and sprayed the enemy who was now running and firing at the helicopter.

Kyle lay on the stretcher and felt a searing pain in his arm. Above him, a blurred outline of Farney's face appeared. A tourniquet tightened on his left bicep just below a blood drip. "Did everyone get out?" he gasped.

"Everyone, lieutenant."

"Koonce?"

"Yeah, he's over there," Farney nodded toward a body. Koonce was dead. Shrapnel wounds covered his body.

"Where was I hit?" Kyle asked weakly. He was becoming woozy.

"Your left side is full of shrapnel, Sir. They'll pick most of it out at the base hospital. We'll be there in thirty." He could see that Kyle was now unconscious from the morphine injection. He stared at the army officer's left arm. His hand was missing and the forearm shredded. He'll lose part of his arm, Farney figured, but he's one tough son-of-a-bitch, and he'll lead other men again somewhere, but there would be no more military battles for Lt. Norquist.

PART I

"...When you start on your journey to Ithaca,
Then pray that the road is long,
Full of adventure, full of knowledge..."

Ithaca

C. P. Cavafy

2

THE GALAXY

September 1973
Emerald Lake

The sky's clarity promised an explosion of stars that always filled Kyle with wonder and humility. With his deck chair tilted back, his eyes gathered in the growing display, just as he had done so many times as a youngster. The view of the heavens from his family's Wisconsin lake lodge patio offered an unrestricted observation, and now, as the amber slipped over the horizon, Venus emerged bright and clear. *The universe is indifferent to the travails of man,* he mused. *We are left to our own devices, and we look up for inspiration, not advice.* Kyle knew a bit about astronomy. As a teenager he had enjoyed touting his knowledge to his father who would sit in rapt silence, his patio chair tilted back as well. The summer evenings, when they gazed at the stars together, were a vital ingredient of Kyle's youth and an adhesive for his relationship with his father that stood the test of time.

"Kyle, are you star-gazing?"

Lars Norquist maneuvered slowly through the dusky shadows on the patio. He smiled as he held up two glasses of wine.

"I knew you would be here." He sighed and leaned down to hand Kyle his wine. "I remember how we would sit here, just the two of us, talking about the galaxy and our toils on earth?"

Kyle watched him adjust the chair—balancing his glass. He moved nimbly for someone approaching his seventieth birthday. Long walks in the Wisconsin woods had honed his lanky body. His still thick hair, now almost white, complemented his deep-blue eyes. His very being exuded vitality—a handsome man by any standard.

The occasion of Lars's birthday had summoned his son from Washington D. C. to this lodge on the shore of Emerald Lake. Kyle's wife, Holly, had retired after dinner knowing that sitting on the deck after dark with his father was a sacrosanct occasion for Kyle. There was to be a party, a grand dinner, and if the weather held, it would take place on this patio. Kyle's sister, Samantha, would arrive tomorrow from Chile with her husband and two sons. She and Kyle had been inseparable during their youth. Kyle's two brothers, Erik and Quinn, were older, and their competitiveness inhibited a close friendship. Carla Ashcroft, Lars's confidant and longtime mistress, would join the party.

Later that evening after his father had retired; Kyle edged closer to the gas fire, rested his legs on the fire pit ledge, and allowed his mind to float meditatively. Childhood memories flooded: sailing, swimming and endless days up the road at Gunnar's farm caring for his animals and crops. The farm had been the catalyst. Kyle's passion for understanding existential life found a footing there.

3

THE FARM

Summer 1952

Many years earlier, or at least it seemed so to Kyle, life had introduced itself to him on the Bjornstrand Wisconsin farm. He watched plant life sprout in the spring, grow during the sun-soaked summer months and then wither away in the autumn. Seasons—everything has a season, he had thought. And the animals had introduced him to the process of creation; birth and death and everything in-between. His elemental education had occurred there, not at home or in school.

Lucy Bell, a town girl, and the Bjornstrands attended the same church and sometimes Lucy and her family would return to the farm with Gunnar after church for a mid-day dinner. Lucy spotted Kyle one Sunday hanging around the barn and strolled across the dusty backyard to check out the tall young boy. He was several years younger than she but his lanky physique and broad shoulders, plus the thick ponytail, trumped the gap in years. Kyle had been mucking out the two horse stalls and stood in the shade just inside the barn door. He held the pitchfork inadvertently pointed outward as if for protection from the girl heading his way.

"Hi there, who are you?" Lucy said with a friendly smile.

Kyle shifted the pitchfork down a little and allowed himself a glance at the quick, dangerous eyes appraising him. "I'm Kyle. I live down the road and sometimes help Gunnar with the animals."

The pungent barn smell enveloped Lucy. It was earthy, and she wanted to get out of her church clothes and don her Oshkosh coveralls. Kyle was dirty and smelled of the barn. She asked him while he poked his boots around the dirt. "Do you milk the cows?"

"Of course. I work with all of the animals. Would you like to meet some of them? What's your name, anyway?"

"Lucy Bell. I just graduated from Emerald Lake High School. Where are you in high school?" She asked pointedly, searching for the age difference.

"I live in Elmwood, across the border, and go to high school there," Kyle mumbled, but looked again into her unsettling cyan-blue wide eyes. "I'm sixteen—almost seventeen."

Someone was yelling from the farmhouse. "Lucy, stay out of the barn. You'll ruin your best shoes. C'mon in now, we're heading home."

Lucy reached out and tugged at Kyle's overall shoulder straps. "Mine is just like yours. Sometimes my dad lets me borrow the car. I'll drive out one day and you can show me the animals?" She wheeled around without waiting for an answer and headed to the house.

Kyle pondered her request. It seemed like an order and he liked the thought of her returning.

Lucy and Kyle frequently met on Gunnar's farm. She pitched in with the farm work, learning from both Kyle and Gunnar. Gunnar allowed Kyle to drive the tractor into the fields and even work the earth dragging with the chisel plow. Gunnar was in town the afternoon Kyle took Lucy for a spin in the tractor. The seat was wide, designed for hefty farmers. Lucy enthusiastically squeezed next to him, her hip and leg pressed against him as they headed off along the narrow road toward the one hill. She talked the entire way until they reached the top of the hill and could see the lake.

Kyle turned off the engine and began to step off when Lucy reached for his arm and stopped him.

"Let's sit here. We can see the lake better and," she pulled him awkwardly, "I like touching you."

Kyle had been thinking—no dreaming—of touching Lucy for weeks, always with elaborate plans. A tractor didn't seem appropriate but by the time he had digested this thought, she had her arms around his neck and had begun to kiss him. Her probing tongue pried his mouth open and very quickly Kyle learned to French kiss. The summer with Lucy became the most exciting summer in his young life.

Lucy's abrupt disappearance from his life left an unsettling void. Her sparkling eyes would appear before him when he daydreamed and a rush of the summer's events would hold his thoughts. She had left town to study nursing in another state. She will be good at that, he thought.

4

GO WEST, YOUNG MAN

September 1953

Kyle left home and never looked back. His senior year had been incidental, a blur of people and events that barely etched his memory. He had moved beyond the standard curriculum and spent much of his time at home studying advanced subjects his teachers had supplied. He knew nearly everyone in town, grown-ups, and kids, but not many well. His best friend, Bobby Swenson, had joined the Marines and had skedaddled to boot camp back in June. In high school, Kyle had failed miserably at friendships. Painfully self-conscious, his awkwardness amused his classmates and worried his parents. Familiarity demanded sharing, a two-way street that Kyle found difficult. His mind process moved more swiftly than his dialog causing a time lag that befuddled his high school friends. They never equated his stumbling demeanor with his top-of-the-chart grades. Sports, friends, girls, even his parents, all took their proper place in his life, yet a subliminal urge to fast-forward controlled his conduct. Stanford University accepted him readily, and Kyle packed his bags.

Kyle's mother, Elizabeth, fussed with the packing and finally settled on a small trunk, which would travel separately by rail. At the airport, Lars and Elizabeth talked about the past while Kyle's mind focused on what was before him, a university in California, new friends, stiff school subjects and maybe some Lucys who would like to continue his basic training. His departure was swift; Elizabeth hugged him, and Lars offered words of encouragement. Suddenly Kyle was alone. The DC-7 lifted off slowly, gaining altitude before banking west. Kyle pressed his face to the window hoping to glimpse Elmwood and the Fox River that had been so much a part of his boyhood. He saw a river, a thin silver ribbon, and said goodbye. Somewhere over the Rocky Mountains thoughts of his past slipped away, and he began to plan for what was ahead.

Strategically placed just south of the daily fog bank, the San Francisco airport bordered the southern extension of the Bay and provided service to all of the Bay Area. Not far to the south, Stanford's enormous campus stretched west from Palo Alto, almost to the coastal hills. Palm trees, sandstone buildings and giant Eucalyptus trees shedding their large leaves lined the path from the bus stop into the campus. The grass looked baked and lifeless in contrast to the activity of students walking and biking with purpose; most in shorts, wearing sunglasses and carrying backpacks.

Kyle lugged his old fashioned suitcase and ambled with the flow of people toward a circle of palm trees and an energetic fountain. Smiling upper-classmen were greeting the freshmen and directing them to their dorms. Kyle froze and felt a flush scale his back and circle his ears. He looked out-of-place, foreign perhaps, no, worse, from Mars. His leather shoes, pressed gabardine trousers, and long-sleeved white shirt and ponytail shrieked for attention. He did not belong here.

Kyle's assigned roommate lounged on his chosen bed and eyed him skeptically before flashing a toothy smile and said, "Norquist, right? I'm Charlie Blass, and it appears we have a year to get to know each other. I claimed this bunk; hope that's ok." Charlie had been a dazzling student in Fresno and aspired to law. His family's pedigree included a long line of attorneys and Stanford men. His sideburns were substantial and looked like bookends on his square face. "How tall are you, anyway?."

With an unassuming, laid-back attitude, Charlie took charge of their new relationship. He knew the territory and the players. They marched across the campus, he wearing flip-flops, shorts and a Hawaiian shirt and Kyle still in his off-to-college garb. He was at an angle to the moment, the past obliterated. He rolled up his sleeves and smiled at the drenching sun.

They found the cafeteria and joined Charlie's friends before corralling a round table. Kyle's ponytail felt like it touched his butt and he considered stuffing it down the back of his shirt. The chatter covered first semester courses. Kyle had signed up for math and the physical sciences. No one at this table would be in his classes.

Fear of the unknown subsides when challenged, in this case with curiosity and self-confidence. The vast library became Kyle's Mecca on campus while the books became his friends. He read voraciously and indiscriminately, always his textbooks assignments first and then histories, politics, biographies, even a novel when he had time. Many days he would enter the library when the sun was high and emerge in the dark. He found the government course appealing—a seminal experience for the future.

"Norquist, I've been waiting for you." Charlie would groan when Kyle returned to their room after nine. "All this studying is only half the experience. Meeting new people with disruptive ideas is just as important. Come on. Let's go to town for a beer. There are a couple of girls waiting to meet you."

Charlie was a lucky draw as a roommate. He liked Kyle and took the time to entice his personality to expose itself. He recognized capacity and strength. And thus, under Charlie's guidance, the first year passed quickly, memorable for its innocuousness. In June everyone scattered without so much as a goodbye because the summer before them was but a pause. Kyle returned to Elmwood and began working in his father's millwork under the guidance of August Shilling.

5

CLARITY

September 1973
Emerald Lake

S ummer nights at the lake were singular. This spot next to the fire pit and under a canopy of stars belonged to Kyle. He had sat here gazing at the heavens and dreaming as far back as he could remember.

For no particular reason, he thought of that languid summer of 1954 that had unfolded with a monotonous sluggishness. He had been away at college for a year and returning home to Elmwood had given him little pleasure. He had, somehow, passed beyond the boring life of living with his parents in a small rural town.

Kyle shifted in his chair so that he could reach with his right hand for the almost empty bottle of wine that Lars had left behind. He poured the few remaining ounces into his glass and leaned back again to return to the same thoughts—to that summer in 1954.

There had been no defining moments, no fresh faces and he had retreated to books, and through them, his mind had sailed to exotic ports. He had always been clever at living vicariously.

From Monday to Friday Kyle apprenticed in his father's woodworking business, which rendered his vacation nothing more than an absence from school. The job paid well. Auggie, the plant supervisor, introduced him to every machine and to the business of honing hardwood lumber into beautiful objects. On weekends he took a family car and headed north to the lake lodge—where he was sitting right now—to swim, sail, read and visit Gunnar's farm. He had wished Lucy would be there, but she had left town for good. His sister and two brothers had all flown the coop as well; Samantha to tour Europe, Quinn to study Japanese and Erik to find himself in parts unknown. That summer had been desolate and lonely.

Only now, as he looked back, did he admit to selfishly squandering a chance to embrace his parents, to thank them for everything they had given him. As he sat on the patio his father and mother had built for their children, he understood for the first time, that maturity reveals questions that he should have asked earlier. The path each of us takes touches our first home infrequently, and usually too late to excavate truths of our youth that only our father and mother could expose. This insight had escaped Kyle during the summer of 1954.

Now, on the eve of his father's seventieth birthday, the memory of his dithering so long ago left him with a sense of loss—an emptiness. Kyle stood, stretched and looked to the heavens for insight on how to reach out to his father.

6

SOPHOMORE

Autumn 1954

The campus greeted Kyle as an old friend. The heat of a desiccated summer enveloped his senses: sunbaked brown grass, flowering maple-nut bushes lining the paths, honeysuckle, and above, a cornflower-blue sky. Little had changed. Anticipation enveloped him. His summer in Elmwood and Wisconsin slipped out of mind. The campus moved to the rhythm of bikes and returning students shouting and greeting each other—even a few professors walking briskly, ignoring the hilarity. He felt more in tempo with the school. His ponytail had disappeared; sharply edged sideburns had replaced it along with a tee shirt, khaki pants and loafers. He blended in with the rest of the returning students as he cut across the burned-out turf heading for his dorm.

Kyle functioned best in stillness. When in seclusion he could focus, and he had applied for a single dorm room. Curiously, he found studying complex textbooks easier than confronting people. He didn't think of himself as bashful; it was just that the students he had met so far succumbed to campus society, politics, sports, and dating, all of which held no interest to him although he secretly longed to spend time with a girl. Kyle had pushed aside this yearning in high school and worried that his ignorance of women might have become apparent. His sister had thrust a string of girls his way until finally, she had exclaimed that he was destined for a monastery. Samantha knew that Kyle headed to college untried, green and pretty stupid.

Two events occurred during Kyle's sophomore year at Stanford that irrevocably altered his life. Physics, math and applied engineering dominated his schedule, but the pre-engineering curriculum condescended to allow one elective subject and Kyle chose political science. His professor, William Delamere, enjoyed immense popularity among the students, to the envy of the faculty. His classes were small; he selected the students. Delamere's questioning mind and his communication skills infused his classroom with energy and debate.

Kyle arrived early for his first class and found Delamere mingling with his students. He moved casually around the angled desk gallery shaking hands and asking questions. When he smiled, fine-feathered lines stretched from the edge of his eyes as well as around his mouth. Kyle learned very soon that Delamere's expression could change rapidly, and this ability to throw a switch and change his style worked miracles and havoc on his students and, it was to have the same effect in the US Senate. The face with the smile and etched lines would put the recipient at ease and then, with subtlety; he would probe, cajole, tease, threaten, and eventually extract what he sought. The faint of heart were put at ease; the obstreperous challenged into submission. A conversation always remained in his total control. Arched under a mass of unruly white hair were dark eyebrows framing expressive brown eyes. Soon they rested on Kyle.

"Good morning, Mr. Norquist. I'm pleased to have a Midwesterner in my class. But tell me, why would an engineering student bother with politics?"

The professor had done his research. Kyle stood to shake the professor's extended hand. Kyle's voice seemed alien. "People interest me," he lied. "And it is important to understand how our government works and what motivates the powers that operate within it. What I'd like most is to be exposed to people with ideas."

"You're in the right place—may I call you Kyle? I look forward to our discussions."

The most provocative discussions occurred at Delamere's home where there was always delicious food prepared by Mrs. Delamere who shuttled silently from the kitchen with full trays and offered wine and beer without questioning anyone's age. Kyle's first invitation came mid-semester, and soon he became a regular. The sessions were limited to around ten, mostly upper-class students. The student body was predominantly white, male and well healed, but the issues of the 1960s had begun to penetrate the school profile and Delamere's Thursday night session reflected this. For the first time in his life, Kyle discussed important issues with Blacks, international students and, most importantly, women. His world began to open.

The students would congregate in Delamere's library with its floor to ceiling bookshelves, open hearth and French doors opening onto a formal garden. Frequently Professor Delamere would move along the shelves, extract a volume and find a section pertaining to the debate.

Kyle began to make friends among the political debate group. After one evening gathering, one of the girls in the class, she introduced herself as Doris, slipped her arm through Kyle's as he headed down the pathway from Delamere's home.

"May I walk back to the campus with you? You seem to understand the professor's ideas on the escalating situation in Viet Nam and I've got some questions."

Kyle had noticed Doris in class, of course, and had listened to her strident opinions during the evening sessions. They had never spoken, and he thought she hadn't noticed him. She was a bit stocky, and her breasts were large, but her height helped offset that. Her eyeglasses were in her hand as much as on her nose. She probably was self-conscious and myopic. They talked easily, exchanging details of their past and impressions of school life.

"I know I'm tall and that I tend to rush," she confided. She moved closer to Kyle, talking the whole time without stopping to catch her breath. They crossed the bridge leading to the campus. And then, she surprised Kyle by gently tugging on his arm, "Let's sit on this bench and chat a bit. We're off the beaten track and won't bother anyone."

He remembered this night very well. A brittle slice of a moon appeared on and off as it passed between the branches of the trees. For what seemed like a very long time they only looked at each other and then Doris turned slightly, leaned toward Kyle and began to kiss his mouth with fervor. Her tongue slipped into his mouth immediately. He liked it. She smelled of something—cinnamon maybe. She surprised Kyle again by moving her hand to Kyle's thigh, just high enough to cause Kyle to warm to the thought of more. But just as abruptly as she had kissed him, she disentangled and leaned back, her hand still on his neck.

"Have you known many girls?" she said more to the moon than to Kyle.

"Well," his voice held a new rasp to it, "not a lot. Why?"

"What I mean, Kyle, have you slept with many girls?"

He had long forgotten his answer. It must have been insipid and transparent. But Kyle will always remember her laughter and comment.

"Men are obsessed with virgins. Women prefer experience."

Somehow they ended up in his small dorm room without attracting attention. The dorm was unusually quiet. Doris surveyed the room, the piles of clothes on the floor, scattered books, papers and a single bunk.

"I hope it'll hold us," she mocked as she pulled her sweater over her head and folded it neatly on the desk. A mane of wavy brown hair cascaded to her shoulders. Her bra followed her sweater to the table and then she began to undress Kyle, starting with his shirt and sweater. He stood there, his eyes riveted on her breasts; his body alert to her every touch. All thoughts but those of the moment fled. She loosened his belt and unzipped his pants which fell dutifully to the floor. She glanced at Kyle's erection, reached down and cupped it gently in her hand, all the while looking back at Kyle's blush.

"I think you will pass your first test with flying colors." Doris slid off her pants and quickly ushered him into another world.

Their tryst remained a singular experience. They were like old friends when they ran into each other in class. Sometimes they would meet for lunch and chat about anything except their adventure. Kyle worried about his performance that night and wondered why she hadn't wished to repeat their liaison. But Doris began to subtly introduce Kyle to her girlfriends, some of whom he got to know very well. Doris had been a coach, not a conductor, and he thought she had derived a bigger kick out of that responsibility than their actual lovemaking. Kyle was slow in starting, but he soon sped up.

Charlie Blass slipped into the chair next to Kyle. His appearance had changed—the mustache and unkempt hair hanging over his ears were gone, but the same old impish grin creased his face.

"Norquist, I never see you anymore. You're buried here in the library grinding your days away."

"Hey, Charlie. I've got an exam tomorrow. What's up with you?"

"I hear you're one of Delamere's regulars. That's a significant honor. Have you given up engineering for politics?"

Kyle stretched his long arms toward the ceiling and then abruptly folded his papers and stuffed them into his backpack. "I need a break. How about coffee?"

"Beer would be better."

Spring had arrived early and the mild evening impersonated summer. Charlie and Kyle walked in silence, cut across the green to Serra St., crossed El Camino Real and soon landed in the heart of Palo Alto. Kyle inhaled the sweet air, and his thoughts flashed to the Wisconsin lake lodge which another winter storm had just slammed. He grinned. *I made the right decision to come here.* Instinctively Charlie and Kyle turned toward Murphy's Grill, which would provide the beer plus throngs of people. An ocean of heads bobbed on the waves of congeniality, some with faces looking their way as they entered and the rest turned away in conversation. Above, ceiling fans struggled with the closeness of air and cigarette smoke. They squeezed through the crowd searching for a remote table where they could talk. Charlie hailed many in the multitude, stopping to shake a hand or clasp a shoulder.

Once settled, Charlie ordered a beer and then gazed over Kyle's shoulder at the noisy throng. "Mid-week and look at this place," he bellowed. "No wonder the library is empty." He sipped his brew and looked back at Kyle with that toothy smile of his. "I hear you joined Alpha Delt. The ADs are mostly jocks. Is that your scene?"

"I'm not very active, but I like many of the brothers, and their social events drag me out of my cocoon. Engineering demands so much focus."

"What about poli-sci? Delamere's Thursday dinners are for those he thinks will have a future impact on politics. Where do you fit?"

"I don't, in a pure sense. Although we disagree often, we enjoy maneuvering each other around to our point of view although the Professor is more successful at this."

Charlie shifted in his chair, surveyed the room again and then leaned forward and rested his head in his hands, his elbows planted on the small table. "As you probably know, Kyle, I'm active in the student government. Hope to be an officer next year. The members represent different departments and next year the seat representing engineering will be open. I'm wondering if you'd like to run for it. It's all right up your poli-sci alley."

The offer was unexpected. Campus politics were not high on Kyle's list of interests. His stomach jerked when he thought of confrontations, yet wasn't that what political science taught. He hesitated for a long moment before asking, "What's the organization's purpose? How would I fit in?"

The din had grown so loud that it forced Charlie to lean forward to answer. "We represent the student body and work with the administration and faculty to better student life on campus. The most contentious issue is the school's involvement with the

Department of Defense." Charlie chattered on, his description lost in the noise of the tavern.

Half listening, Kyle turned his attention to the crowd, mostly students crushed along the bar. Why were they in school, he wondered: to acquire knowledge, to socialize and play or to escape something or someone. At that precise moment of reflection, destiny touched his life as his gaze stretched along a path cutting through the bodies, to settle on the back of a girl sitting at the far end of the room. Remembering that moment and the extraordinary improbability of his line of sight piercing the throng validates the existence of destiny. She stood while still talking to her friends and Kyle could see her tall, slim frame and dark hair cascading to her shoulders. He stood to gain a better view, and at that moment she turned and looked directly at him. Her eyes lingered and then transfixed upon him, her lips pursed as if to toss a distant kiss before her mouth segued to a pout and then, just as suddenly, she turned and headed for the street door while waving a goodbye to her friends. Kyle did not move and continued to glare at the space she had occupied. It seemed to Kyle that all of the conversations in the room had stopped—they hadn't, of course—and the only sound he heard was the pounding of his heart.

"Did you see that girl who just left the bar?" he yelled, turning quickly to Charlie.

"I did, but I don't know her. She's Chinese, I think, and upper class. She lives off campus somewhere. Why?"

"Oh, no reason. Let's head out, Charlie; I have an exam tomorrow."

A cynic once said, "We live and do not learn." But Kyle was learning, not just from his studies, but also about a more interesting subject—himself. His eyes no longer searched the sky for stars; they focused on what was right in front of him. Like a caterpillar, he eyed the moment and contemplated growing colorful wings. His thoughts insisted upon returning to that disquieting face he had seen in Murphy's Bar. She was an elusive student and did not seem to tread Kyle's paths. Her friends called her "Cat," and Kyle quickly learned that she hung around with international students and also, to his disappointment, a football player. She scurried past him one day on the campus, her hair tucked in a cap and a backpack bouncing on her slender back. He wanted to follow her, yet his feet were rooted in concrete. Carefully, subtly, Kyle questioned friends and began to arrange the puzzle pieces that revealed this phantom that had entered his life and did not know it. She was an exchange student from the University of Singapore studying international relations on a two-year program. Her name was Catherine Lee.

The spring months billowed with activities and headed toward exams and then, so quickly, summer vacation. Kyle's engineering course reviews were disciplined and objective whereas Delamere asked his students to write for two hours on only one subject of their choice. Kyle chose Washington D.C. lobbyists, skewering them in four blue books. After the last class, Delamere drew him aside, his dark brown eyes squinting under his bushy eyebrows, and said in a small voice. "I read your blue books—twice. I enjoyed your discourse—you nailed the subject. Good job, Kyle. By the way, I'm forming a political theory course next semester which will count for a grade, and I'd like you to join in. I look forward to seeing you in the autumn. Have a good summer." He turned abruptly without waiting for an answer and trudged across campus toward his office.

7

THE SURVEYOR

Summer 1955

At the end of the spring semester, the campus drained quickly. Goodbyes were cursory, rendered with thoughts elsewhere; everyone was intent on getting away—new horizons, to work and to play. Kyle's plans were not exotic but did involve earning some money. He stored his belongings in a campus locker facility, stuffed a few essentials into a duffel, caught the commuter train to San Francisco and then bussed his way inland to Camino, a hill station devoted to logging. He arrived mid-afternoon and found the Pickering Lumber Company office on an unpaved side street. A hitching post below the front porch suggested an earlier life. The company wanted to nail down the borders of its vast tracks of land. The parcels on which they were logging lay, like islands, in a sea of government land. A tree harvested on government property incurred a stinging penalty. Kyle signed the employment papers and agreed to work steadily for two months. The bespectacled office manager stirred from his chair and sauntered onto the deck, motioning Kyle to follow. The afternoon heat had driven everyone indoors. The Pickering office sported a ceiling fan.

"See the sign hanging above the corner building that says 'rooms'? You have one of those rooms along with Mr. Pickering's son, Rusty, who will arrive later today. Most of our guys eat there as well. The price is right. Frank, our surveyor, will meet you in the lobby tomorrow morning at 7:30 sharp. The hotel will supply you with lunch and a water flask. You will need rugged boots and bug juice." He didn't expect any questions, turned his rotund body slowly, headed back to his chair and left Kyle holding his duffel and job contract.

Rusty arrived energetic and curious about his adventure. His hairless face, tufts of unruly sand-colored hair and blue, open and worry-free eyes belied his age. He was a typical callow seventeen-year-old about to head off to college. As the summer unfolded, young Rusty and Kyle became easy friends. Rusty's inquisitiveness dominated their conversations; he talked incessantly and peppered Kyle with questions on every subject, which Kyle sagely answered even though some of the areas of interest were new to him as well. His status as the 'older guy' was flattering after a life lived with two older brothers.

The rooming house provided dinner for the lumbermen staying there. Near the door, sitting on the table, an enormous bowl of soup surrounded by loaves of bread greeted the hungry workers. Oscar, the manager, hoped his guests would fill up on soup and not eat so much of his more expensive meat dish. The Pickering workers were either married and lived in dilapidated houses near the railroad track or, in most cases, were single and spent their free time in the local bar telling stories, arguing, singing and drinking copious quantities of whiskey.

Each morning at precisely 7:30, Frank would collect Kyle and Rusty in his aging Ford truck. They looked untested in their new bush boots and floppy wide-brimmed hats. The hotel kitchen boxed a lunch, and in the early days of their surveying, they would nibble so that by mid-day little remained. Frank scheduled the surveying sites on the edge of Pickering parcels bordering federal government land. Some were located deep in the woods with no road access. They would drive the truck as far as possible and then tramp into the forest of towering Douglas firs, probably planted by Chinese immigrants at the turn of the century. Thick brush encroached on the trails that eventually would disappear entirely from disuse. Although there were animals, they never encountered anything more dangerous than raccoons, skunks, and the ubiquitous rattler. The most feared pest was the Manzanita bush, an unforgiving, strong as a rope, waist high, unattractive growth with branches that would slice clothes and skin. A patch of Manzanita was impenetrable. Rusty did battle with the many branched bushes—technically a tree—hacking at it with his hatchet and was usually bloodied by the encounter. In the forest, Kyle quickly learned the art of surveying while Rusty spent most of his time clearing brush and searching for border markers. It was hot work, enervating and mostly boring. Kyle came away with one entrenched thought—*whatever he did with his life; it had to be interesting and enjoyable.*

There wasn't a hell of a lot to do in Camino. A century earlier, Tuolumne County had been a mecca for gold miners and many of the buildings from that period remained. Wood was an essential building material for gold mining devices such as sluice boxes and flumes, and with plenty of timber available, lumber companies moved into the area. The miners eventually disappeared, but the timber companies stayed and expanded. Camino remained a small lumber town, overshadowed by more developed towns along the railway.

Usually, after dinner, the two young surveyors would begin their evening in the bar across the street from the hotel, drinking with the loggers before heading out to wander and inspect the aging red-bricked buildings from the gold mining days, many on back streets. During their evening walks and when they had moments together in the forest, Rusty would endlessly question Kyle on college life. Kyle had not forgotten his immaturity when he left home for the first time and happily walked Rusty through the gauntlet of a freshman year.

On weekends a short bus trip took them to glamorous South Lake Tahoe where they could dust-up—a term covering drinking beer, casino shows, and ogling girls.

Rusty haunted Camino's ramshackle movie house where first run films arrived at the end of their life cycle. One evening, while Rusty settled in the movie theater, Kyle decided to explore the newer section of Camino and, to his delight, he found a small, one-story building ablaze with lights. A library! A sign on the door announced it would be open evenings until 9 PM. The single room boasted of five rows of bookshelves, several tables, two cushioned chairs and a pretty young librarian who watched Kyle intently as he inspected the book gallery.

Kyle noticed, and since there was no one else in the library, he spoke to her from the book stacks. "I'm looking for a history of Camino and the logging activity around here."

"We have a couple of books on that subject on the far wall. Let me show you." She was tall and walked with a steady stride to the wall shelf and found a thin book with a tattered cover. She turned to Kyle who was now standing near, admiring her. "These are all old books donated by the locals. No one seems interested in this collection; everyone makes a beeline for the fiction section—crime novels mostly." Presenting the book to Kyle, she smiled, "Hi, my name is Alison. You must be working for Pickering Lumber for the summer?"

Kyle extended his hand. "And my name is Kyle, and yes, I work for Pickering as a surveyor. What a lucky night for me—to find a library and someone my age who likes books. Do you live in town?"

"I live with my parents just up the street. I finished college last month and am home for the summer."

Kyle smiled and thought to himself—*I may have met an older woman.* "I'd like to sit and read for a while. When you close-up, will you join me for a beer? You must know a spot that's not full of loggers."

"I do, and I would like a beer," Alison said readily.

The summer drifted aimlessly; days clicked off and weeks meshed into each other. Tomorrows resembled yesterdays. Rusty and Kyle tempered the monotony with weekend sprees at Tahoe. Kyle's new friend, Alison, had the use of her father's car and offered to drive Kyle and Rusty to Tahoe's South Shore.

"My family has a weekend cottage on a small lake near Lake Tahoe. If you could do without the bright lights and shows, you are welcome to stay with me on Echo Lake. We could hike, swim and if you are adept at fixing old boats, we could sail through the portage to a string of connected lakes. You buy the food and beer; I'll spring for the gas."

Rusty almost fainted with anticipation. "Yes, we accept."

The very next weekend, the three headed up Route #50, passed through Pollock Pines and then into the Eldorado National Forest. At the top of the mountain, just before the highway dives perilously down the side of a cliff toward Lake Tahoe, they cut left on a dirt road which deposited them at the tip of a long narrow lake.

"The cottage is at the other end. We hike from here," Alison advised, as she slung her backpack straps over her shoulders. She was taller than Rusty who was struggling with his pack. He had brought too much stuff.

They hiked in silence for over an hour along the wooded cliffs sheltering the east shore. The area was exquisite, remote, silent and no motor boats to disturb the peace. Kyle gathered in this peacefulness. His body moved in harmony with the trail; his mind captured only the moment. He watched Alison leading, her body moving effortlessly as they climbed higher, her long legs lithe and beautiful. He wished the trail would never end.

Alison pointed out her cottage as they descended from the cliff path down toward the lake. The faded yellow sideboards glistened in the afternoon sun. Kyle could see a short pier and around the corner of the land in front of the building was the connecting portage to the next lake. They could sit on the broad deck and check out the boats passing through the connection.

Echo Lake was cold. Alison entered the water as if it were a bathtub, swam swiftly to an outcrop of rocks, some of which were flat and perfect for sunbathing. Rusty sat on the pier edge, legs hanging into the water. Kyle followed Alison. Later, as the sun headed for the rim of the mountains to the west, Kyle began to work on the old, dinghy sailboat. The repair would take all weekend, in fact, several weekends. Alison sat on a log stump watching.

"You've worked with sailboats before," she said as an observation, not a question.

"I grew up sailing scows on a Wisconsin lake, one larger than Echo and not as cold," Kyle replied, keeping his eyes on the chisel in his hand. "My father loves sailing as do my sister and brothers." Alison and Kyle talked easily, like childhood friends. Together they lifted the boat to turn it bottom-up, and their bodies touched. That too seemed natural, and Alison began to sand the gunnels without looking at Kyle.

Dinner on the deck was delicious in its simplicity. Rusty had not tasted wine before, and he was beside himself with excitement and awe. A chill in the air drove them inside. Kyle stoked the fireplace and then turned the lamps off to save the generator fuel. The three talked into the night.

"I'm heading for bed," Alison murmured, stretching her long arms. "I will take the master bedroom over there," pointing to the door on the far wall, and you guys are in the loft."

Once settled in the loft and after a long silence, Rusty whispered, "Will you go down to see Alison when you think I'm asleep?"

Kyle snickered. "No, I will not visit Alison in her bedroom and don't get any ideas."

"She's sort of old, anyway," Rusty whispered, his eyes searching the ceiling for answers.

Around the second week in August the survey project concluded, and Frank left town abruptly without a farewell. A Pickering Company car arrived to take Rusty to San Francisco to join his family; Kyle hitched a ride to the Sacramento railroad station, and several days later he arrived in Chicago. His memory of Alison never faded. They had spent much of their free hours together that summer of 1955, returning to Echo Lake several times to complete the repair of the sailboat.

At the end of their last evening together, Alison came to Kyle, embracing him with a lingering kiss. "I loved spending the summer with you, Kyle. And I'm glad that...we didn't mess up our lives."

Kyle leaned back, his arms still encircling her waist, and smiled into her lovely face. "Years from now, in our rocking chairs, will we think back and wish we had?" he said in a soft voice. Alison rolled her eyes, smiled and disappeared into the library, and Kyle strolled back to the rooming house. It would be his last night.

Kyle didn't forget Alison. Does anyone forget an infatuation in their early years? Alison wrote to him once, after he had become a Senator, congratulating him. He had smiled while reading her letter because she began as if they had just said goodbye. She lived in Marin County with her doctor husband and three sons. They never saw each other again, but the pleasure of his memory of her remained.

8

SOLAR SYSTEM

September 1973
Emerald Lake

Time had vanished into the stillness of the night as midnight approached, and it left the world in silence. Kyle reached for the wine bottle only to find it empty. *Well it was time for bed anyway and Holly would be wondering what he was doing.* But certain moments are too precious and his memories were so vivid and delicious; to break the spell would be a mistake.

He turned toward the lake, stepped off of the patio and headed to the pier. He was not tired and as he walked his mind drifted back to that summer in the Sierra Nevada foothills when he had discovered so many new things: the stillness of the forest, being alone and enjoying it and Alison. Camino had been a mellow interlude, a hiatus from both school and home. Kyle made a mental note to include the Placerville area on his next political swing through the foothills above Sacramento. Maybe he could squeeze a day out of the schedule to visit Echo Lake. Would the house on the portage still be there? He'd never worn the boots and hat again, yet they rest in his closet, a physical connection to that summer in 1955.

Kyle had arrived home that year in August at the peak of the summer heat. The home of his childhood in Elmwood was familiar, of course, but seemed a stranger, a real but diminished part of his past life. The university had swept him to sea, like a giant ship, bearing him away from familiar shores. In a few years the ship had carried him to distant places and new horizons. His home had become a burial-ground of yesterdays. The house in Elmwood was abstract, vacant of character and silent. The shouts of his brothers, Samantha's infectious laugh and the chatter of friends were gone. Dad seemed to have notice this atmosphere too, so the three of them loaded up the station wagon and headed north across the Wisconsin border to the lodge on Emerald Lake.

Kyle spent the remainder of that summer with his mom and dad, here where he was standing—at the lake lodge. The August weather had been on its best behavior, cleansing rain squalls splashing the afternoons, usually too late to disrupt a golf game. Most days he had sailed the E-boat with his father, exchanging duty at the tiller, barking orders and enjoying the challenge of the elements. It had been great fun. Later, Kyle joined his mother while she prepared dinner, a culinary learning expedition and a perfect place for a conversation—Dad rarely visited the kitchen.

For two weeks Kyle had been alone with his father and mother. They had hiked together along the lakeshore at sunset, had long dinners with banal conversation, and later quiet togetherness sitting on the patio watching the sky. He had probed gently for their inner thoughts but learned little.

Now eighteen years later he smiled at the thought that his parents would divulge their innermost feelings to their nineteen-year-old son. Both were quiet, introspective persons, unwilling to discuss much of the lives they had lived. *And if they had spoken to me, I likely would not have comprehended it. I think about it still and worry that the fabric of my father's and mother's existence had escaped me. Mom is gone, taking her secrets with her. She had worn them on her sleeve, and I had failed to grasp them.*

This weekend will be an opportunity reborn. It will be difficult to find time one-on-one with Lars with so many people here, but

Kyle felt a sense of urgency, almost dread, that little time remains and that he needed to talk with his father one last time.

Dad has flaws like everyone, and he has paid no heed—like everyone. He loves his children fervently, and without preference, of that Kyle was confident, and Lars was kind but stingy with his thoughts, his passions, and his affections. Had Dad experienced pure joy, Kyle wondered? Is he pleased with his life or had he missed some things? *Would he tell me?* A father should, eventually, confide in his son. A father and son's relationship is a compelling journey, and when openness evolves, pleasure emerges.

Kyle asked the universe for another chance as he retraced his steps along the pier. He was ready for bed now and Holly would be there.

9

AWAKENING

Autumn 1955

The division between the sophomore and junior year in college is enormous, and Kyle noticed it immediately upon his return to the Stanford campus in September 1955. He felt he belonged; there was a kinship to the school, comfortableness, a proud ownership. His curriculum altered as well for his subjects were now his selections, and he knew in his heart that the school work would offer not only great joy but also that he would excel.

His new home base was on Douglas Street, a short walking distance south of the campus where he and two friends had rented a cottage with a back garden and a hot tub. He'd met Colin Wellesley during his freshman year in a calculus class. Both were well over six foot tall, and Kyle admitted that Colin's math ability exceed his. Colin was British; his family lived in Kent, and he had rejected Oxford for schooling in the United States in deference to his American mother. Kyle didn't know Al Silberstein as well but trusted his instinct that he would fit. The three had much in common. They were serious students, relished their subjects, loved books, were independent and insisted upon privacy. Only Kyle belonged to a fraternity. The three had sufficient spending money to pool their resources and bought a 1950 Ford Deluxe Country Squire Woodie station wagon that had spent most of its life in a garage looking pretty. They called it "Bessie" and all three smothered it with care.

Kyle divided his attention between pre-engineering classes and political science. After settling in on Douglas Street, he sauntered across El Camino Real into town and turned on Delamere's shady street.

Madelyn Delamere opened the door and smiled. "Well, Mr. Norquist. Bill has been asking about you and wondering if you would show your face. Come on in. The professor is in the back."

William Delamere rose from his desk and reached out to shake Kyle's hand. "Welcome back, Kyle. How was your summer? Sit down over here." He then turned toward the kitchen and yelled, "Maddie, any coffee left?"

Their conversation quickly turned to current events; civil rights in the South and the looming war in Viet Nam. "I'm offering a course on current events and thought about you. I'm wondering, Kyle, if you would assist me by taking on the situation in S.E. Asia?"

Kyle shrugged and pursed his lips. "I'm not so stridently anti our involvement in Viet Nam or anywhere in Asia, for that matter. As you taught me so well, there are always many sides to an issue."

"I'm not asking you to take sides. You have studied most of the players and the US's dilemma. Let the class make the decisions. We'll teach it together."

Kyle watched Catherine Lee stride across the campus, her slim body moving easily under the weight of a packsack bulging with books. He had thought about her during the summer yet, now, back on campus, he still had no strategy for meeting her. She was a senior and ran with flashy friends; well-known students on the campus. Without disrupting his routine or juggling his walking routes, he had developed an awareness of Cat's presence on campus, a sort of extrasensory perception and this desire had subtly and discreetly placed him where he could see her. She had never glanced his way.

One autumn Saturday, after a football game, and for no good reason, Kyle wandered into his fraternity house looking for a beer and distraction. The crush of students and noise made it impossible to hear the jazz music coming from a five-piece band in the corner. Kyle somehow put his glass under the keg spigot and then pressed his way to the edge of the throng. Their introduction was abrupt and unobtrusive. The mass of humanity had shoved Catherine into Kyle as he stood alone. Her eyes were light brown, curious and mesmerizing as she looked up at him. Her hands had pressed on his chest to resist the crush of the crowd. She had smiled slightly. "Well, here we are—finally. I've wanted to meet you for some time. I guess it took all of these people to introduce us."

Catherine took over Kyle's junior year at Stanford. She dropped out of the fast set and joined Kyle in his campus life. They studied together in the library and spent long evenings in town talking about books, films, politics and her home in Singapore. Colin and Albert enjoyed Cat and frequently joined them for supper. Subtly her influence expanded Kyle's perspective of life. He spent almost no time protesting the possible U.S. involvement in Viet Nam and more time talking about world events. They spent Saturdays in San Francisco at the de Young Museum, art galleries and small bistros in the Marina.

Kyle asked Catherine if she would join him at a poli-sci class at Delamere's home. He neglected to tell her that he was the teacher and that the subject was political affairs in S.E. Asia. Delamere's elite thinkers packed the room, and the conversation quickly became intense. Catherine settled in a back row, her eyes surveying the crowd before resting on Kyle. Her grasp of the rapidly unfolding events in Asia was profound, and soon Kyle asked her to stand with him and Professor Delamere. The questioning was passionate and sometimes personal.

Catherine discussed her Eurasian background; her British mother and a father connected to a well-known Singapore family. She felt confident that Singapore would become independent in a few years and that her uncle would ultimately end up as the prime minister.

"One last question," Delamere shouted over the din.

"Catherine, what will you do after you graduate this year?"

"I'm not sure, probably return to my home in Singapore and find a job. If we achieve independence, I'd like to become involved in the government. Although small, we could become a laboratory for wise and fair governance."

Catherine and Kyle became lovers not long after that fateful fraternity party. With Kyle's one-third ownership of Bessie, they could plan on at least one monthly foray to the many greater Bay Area attractions. Their first weekend trip would be to the coast north of the city. Cat arranged the three-day adventure and would not divulge the details to Kyle. "Consider it one-step away from camping with chilly nights," was all she would reveal.

The late October weather remained clear and warm. The Ford Woodie headed north on Highway101 in light traffic, and an hour later they were skirting the west edge of the elegant city of San Francisco, along 19th Street and onto the Golden Gate Bridge. In Marin County, they turned left on #1 and began to wind their way past Mount Tamaulipas toward Muir Beach. The foliage was bursting with color variation and as the road narrowed, became dense. Kyle talked as he drove; Cat listened intently. Soon she was immersed in stories of sailing on a Wisconsin lake, working on a farm, bright and aggressive siblings, a dominant father and insight into the vast galaxy above.

They turned sharply into a small farm, so abruptly that Kyle missed the welcome sign. They passed a series of small gardens with a few people bent over rows of vegetables. "Park here and keep the motor running. I'll be just a minute," Cat said as she headed into a dark-stained, circular building that hinted of an Asian influence. She returned in a flash and pointed up the road. "We'll park up there and begin our climb." They had stopped for provisions, so their packsacks bulged. They began to climb with Cat leading. A light rain hampered progress and conversation. The hill became steep and Kyle wondered how a car could navigate the road. When they emerged onto the field at the top, Kyle bellowed "Wow!" There was a bare-bone cottage with a bench in front, and far off, beyond the field and piles of rocks, was the Pacific Ocean where he could see a line of ships heading to or away from the San Francisco Bay.

The cabin was basic. Nailed to a windowless wall was a double deck bunk, probably built in a high school shop class. Sanded two-by-fours held it together and a narrow ladder ran up one end. The occupant of the small top bunk could lean over and view the double bed below. If someone slept on the worn-out couch facing the wood-burning stove, the cabin could lodge a family of four. A row of hooks just inside the front door provided the closet and in the far corner was a basic kitchen with a short counter and two wall cabinets—no appliances since there was no electricity. A crusty loaf of French bread with a note of welcome sat on the table. The firewood beckoned from a ledge that fronted a hatch opening to more wood piled outside under a tarp. Kyle added paper and stoked the steel stove and set it ablaze. A water closet appendage protruded from the back wall; the kitchen sink had running water from the tank above the cabin, and a showerhead hung from the cabin wall—outside.

Night had descended, and a thin rain splashed at the windows. Only then did they realize there was no electric power; the stove, which was now blazing, and a kerosene lamp provided light. Cat settled on the couch with a tray of cheese and a bottle of red wine. "So, what do you think? Pretty rustic, huh?"

"I like this place very much—especially because you're with me and we have the top of this tall hill to ourselves. You said you would introduce me to two surprises. I'm ready to be surprised."

Cat moved closer to Kyle, wrapped one arm around his shoulder, then leaned toward him and began to kiss his ear. Her tongue slowly worked the folds before whispering. "One surprise is called 'Zazen,' and that will come tomorrow. The other surprise, colloquially known as a 'Singapore Fling,' I will initiate now."

Kyle felt her hand move to his thigh as she began to kiss his lips and then their tongues touched. This measured petting sparked an arousal that was more intense than anything he had known; his entire body seemed hot. Cat's hand briefly rubbed his erection as she tilted her head and a sly smile crept across her face. "Get rid of your clothes and head for the bed where the 'Singapore Fling' awaits you," she murmured as she began to undress.

Kyle had lost control of this tryst and he knew it. Catherine had taken charge with an assurance that hinted at experience, but he was too excited to consider this deeply. He was tall and muscular, and he worried that his weight might be a problem. She, too, was tall for an Asian woman; her long legs emphasized her height. Kyle lay on his side on the narrow bunk and watched Catherine move to the bed, only a silhouette in the darkness.

She moved him onto his back in the center of the bed and then swung one leg over him and sat on his groin with his erection between her thighs. Her thumb knowingly massaged the sensitive tip of his penis before she gently rolled the condom onto it. Kyle watched with an erotic thrill as she lifted herself, letting him enter her slowly. The sensation created by her movement blotted out all other feelings. Kyle leaned forward and grasped her hips. She too leaned forward and jammed her tongue passionately in Kyle's mouth and whispered between kisses, "This, my lover, is called a 'Singapore Fling.'" Her hips and buttocks now swayed with a determined rhythm, and the two lovers lost themselves in an ocean of sensations. Somewhere close to climax, Kyle lifted Catherine, without losing her, onto her back, shifting her legs to his shoulders and as they moved together, both exploded in ecstasy.

The morning broke bright and warm. The sun inched over the top of the hill leaving the cabin in the shade but bathing the field and the ocean in its rays. Kyle, still nude, stretched and swung his legs over the side of the bunk. *It would be a good day*, he thought. He dressed and opened the cabin door to look for Cat. The world was serenely quiet. He finally spotted her sitting on a ledge up the hill a bit. She was motionless and in the shadow of the hill, her form blended with the rocks. Finally, she saw him, waved, collected her mat from the ground and walked down into the sunlight to him. And then, for the first time in his life, Kyle kissed a woman as his first act of the day, and he loved it, and just maybe she loved it as well.

Breakfast, coffee, a three-hour hike to the cliff and onto a trail that led to adjacent fields full of grazing horses and llamas. They kissed, held hands, laughed but talked little. After lunch, Kyle napped, while Cat stretched out on the couch with a book. A little after mid-afternoon, Cat suggested they sit on the bench in front and watch the sunset. It was almost November, and dusk would arrive soon. Kyle grabbed a bottle of wine and two glasses. Both sat, lost in their thoughts. The wine heightened the moment. They sat perfectly still, listening to the silence and focusing on the golden ball dropping out of the sky to the west.

Finally, Kyle turned and asked, "what about my second surprise? My first surprise, was, well—ah—memorable."

"My two surprises complement each other," Cat replied slowly, weighing her response. "Our fling last night was wonderful, for both of us, but, it was, in essence, a temporary gratification, as you Americans like to say. I want to introduce you to something more enduring and complicated in its simplicity. It is a way of life woven into the very fiber of my mind and body. It has several names—we call it Zazen. It is a form of Zen meditation, Japanese, but not too different from Chen, the Chinese way of practice."

Kyle's mind was alert. His brother, Quinn, had spent several months studying in a Japanese temple and practiced Zen meditation. "Tell me about it."

"My parents are Buddhists. We would attend retreats together, which not only illuminated my knowledge of myself, it tightened our family bonds. One summer they sent me to a temple in Northern Japan for two months."

"And Zazen, what is it?"

"It's a sitting meditation. It teaches you to bring quietness to your body and mind and think about nothing. You just let your thoughts pass through your mind and eliminate all judgmental thinking. And soon you begin to look inward at yourself—and that takes a lot of practice and a long time."

"According to Quinn, enlightenment is the ultimate quest."

"Yes, and along the path, you acquire a balance and clarity that will enhance your life and that of those around you. I haven't known you for very long, but I think you have the patience and tenacity to give it a try. We can do it together. Tomorrow morning, before we leave, let's sit on that crest up there and clear our minds. Are you up for it?"

"I am," Kyle said, leaning over to kiss Cat. "I'm up for another 'Singapore Fling,' as well."

Everything that occurred on that mountaintop weekend remained stamped indelibly on Kyle's mind. It sometimes interfered with his studies. This woman, who came out of nowhere and from afar, foreign and curious, had affected him in so many ways. Even his roommates commented on his new 'being.' "That Chinese girl has you by the balls, Kyle," Colin said, laughing. "Don't get me wrong, old chap, she's beautiful, and I like her too, but she's very much—perhaps too much—in your mind. Maybe you, Al and I should head for Sugar Bowl for the weekend."

November slipped by; exam finals arrived, and Christmas vacation loomed. Kyle hadn't seen Catherine for several days; both were busy with finals, but this evening they had decided to walk to town to one of the many Palo Alto restaurants.

"Vacation starts in a couple of weeks," Kyle said as if he had just thought about it. "Going home for you wouldn't be worth it. Why don't you come with me? I'd like you to meet my family."

Catherine looked up from her dinner, searched Kyle's eyes for a long moment, and then returned to her nasi goreng without responding. Finally, she answered in between bites. "Unfortunately I can't, but what a beautiful thought. Thank you."

"What will you do?"

"I'm flying to D.C. next week. My father is there for some meetings. We'll probably hang around the city and then when everyone leaves for the holidays; we will rent a car and visit your Civil War battle sites. It's something Dad has always wanted to do."

Kyle tried to hide his disappointment. He had assumed she would accept. Catherine acted differently than the other girls Kyle had met on campus. She wasn't frivolous, more evolved; she was someone going somewhere. Kyle admitted to himself that he didn't know her at all; she had been reticent about her background. Kyle plunged.

"Well, maybe next summer. Come for my birthday in June before you head home."

"That won't work either, Kyle. I graduate in mid-June, and my mother will be here. My birthday is in June as well—we're Gemini's—maybe we're twins. How old will you be? Twenty is my guess."

"Yep, no longer a teenager. You will be twenty-one, right?"

"Ah, no. Twenty-four."

Kyle's two affairs, one with Catherine and the other with his studies, had blended perfectly during the spring term. Meditation had helped to bring the two obsessions into balance. Zazen had become a habit. His grades were excellent, indeed good enough to guarantee acceptance by an engineering school. He and Cat had spent a weekend at an ashram in Big Sur and another long weekend in Mendocino. They traveled well together; both seeming to know when to talk and when not to. They had become comfortable with each other, like a seasoned married couple, who retained the passion of their early years. When they did chat, Catherine questioned but was adept at not revealing her most private thoughts.

On a Saturday near the end of the semester, they returned to Marin County but this time headed out a peninsula to Tiburon and 'Sams,' a restaurant hanging over the water. Packed tables crowded the weathered deck, and impetuous seagulls sat on the railing and sometimes moved to a table. A light breeze raked the bay providing perfect sailing conditions. Cat and Kyle sat in the sun watching the sailboats emerge from the Belvedere yacht harbor, rolling beyond the breakwater to fasten the rigging and set sail. "Does this setting whet your appetite for your summer at Emerald Lake?" Cat had never sailed, and she wondered how she would handle the pitching and rolling.

"Colin has invited me to visit his home in the UK. Apparently his father is an avid sailor, owns a forty-two-foot sloop and spends much of the summer ocean racing. He has challenged us to sail with him out the English Channel, around the Cornwall peninsula and then to the Irish Sea and the Isle of Man. I've heard Colin talk about this voyage many times. I guess the sea is rough and the ports hospitable."

"When do you leave?"

"I'll fly with Colin in early June and return home in late July. But what about you? I have no idea where you are going and when I'll see you again."

The wind caught Catherine's long dark hair and swept in around her face forming a mask as if to hide her thoughts. She pushed her hair back, looked at Kyle with furrowed eyebrows bridging an intent gaze. "I'm returning to Singapore with my mother immediately after graduation. My uncle has offered me a job, and he's insisting I start immediately."

"Where will you live?"

"At first, with my family," she answered. "My sister lives in Australia, but my brother is still at home."

Kyle looked back to the bay. He was wondering about her male friends, and his thoughts were transparent. "Do you think you will ever return to America?"

Cat smiled and reached for Kyle's hand. "Kyle, this past year, our relationship, our weekends together and long chats about so many ideas has been extraordinary—at least for me. Our time together is not something I will forget. But your life is so full of possibilities—mine too—and we should take the time to pursue these opportunities. You have another year before graduation, and then there is graduate school."

Kyle interrupted. "All of what you say is true, but to have had this incredible connection, this affinity—call it infatuation—for each other and then to merely say goodbye and sail off into the sunset leaves me with a feeling of…dislocation. I don't want to lose you."

"You don't have me to lose. I have responsibilities, promises to fulfill, and my life to lead which offers no space for a love affair if that's what you are hinting. We had an affair, a beautiful one. Let's not ruin it with remorse or hurt feelings.

Kyle sat stone still, his heart pounding, and his mind awash. He had fallen in love with this woman, never realizing that it was just an affair for her. He signaled for the check and said, "Come, I have another spot I want you to see."

Old St. Hillary's Chapel roosted halfway up the hill with a splendid view of Tiburon, the Bay and San Francisco in the distance. A non-denominational church, its one room tried to remain all-embracing—not committed to any specific sect. Cat and Kyle sat on the steps of a long flight leading up to the door and looked at the garden before them. Small colorful flowers—especially blue and whites covered the stone steps. "I read somewhere that the flowers growing on the grounds surrounding St. Hilary cannot be found elsewhere. They are unique to this spot." Kyle continued, without taking his eyes off of the flowers. "And you," he abruptly turned to face Catherine, "are a unique flower in my life. I will find you again, and soon, but as you have said so clearly, we need to get on with our lives—unobstructed. You have been a teacher and a friend. You have opened windows to view the world, honed my ability to judge and understand, and you have exposed my soul. Somehow, I feel our connection will not end."

Catherine returned home, and Kyle went sailing. Time seemed suspended, directionless, something to savor. By Christmas, the Stanford School of Engineering had accepted him. His senior year was bountiful.

"Hey, stud," Al yelled at Kyle as he approached their off-campus cottage. "You have a blue envelope postmarked Singapore." Colin stood behind Albert waving the letter and smiling.

"I suppose you jerks have read the letter," Kyle said as he snatched it from Colin's hand. He moved to the refrigerator, found a beer, and headed to the back garden for some privacy. Cat's handwriting and a colorful stamp with a tropical bird stared up at him.

> *Dear Kyle,*
>
> *You are back on campus after your Christmas holiday. I can picture it all, palm trees, Colin polishing Bessie and especially you. I sent you a card last month full of questions about your life and senior year. You're busy, I know, political science ala Prof. Delamere, skiing and probably some girlfriends.*
>
> *My job is going well and absorbing. I'm learning how governments run, or ought to run, and my mentors are the best. Yesterday my uncle gave me a new and exciting assignment. He wants me to spend the better part of a year in Europe beginning around June and gave me several projects. He thought it would be prudent if I traveled with someone. I don't believe he was comfortable with his niece wandering around Europe alone. I'd like it to be you. It would be a great adventure, new frontiers, and challenging ideas. Most of all, I miss you—in many ways. So think about it. My schedule is somewhat flexible.*
>
> *Love,*
> *Cat*

10

ITHACA

March 1957 - June 1958
Singapore

A man with a high forehead and scowling eyes stood in the center of the large room. The ceiling fans twirled slowly sixteen feet above him, moving the languorous air and offering little relief from the humidity and heat. He was accustomed to the weather, which varied little throughout the year. Only the rain punctuated it. White dominated the room; the cushions perched on rattan furniture, the walls, and the man's starched long sleeve shirt. All of this was normal for him having lived in Singapore since his birth thirty-four years ago. The years had been full, including time in prison during the Japanese occupation and a university education at Cambridge. Of the indigenous population—Chinese, Malay, and Tamil—he was the most widely known and respected person in the city.

The giant double doors were slightly ajar, and Catherine poked her head in, smiled broadly and asked, "Hello, Uncle. You invited me to come around for a visit. Is this a good time?"

"Catherine, my favorite niece," he said with a slight chuckle. "Your timing is perfect. Come in, come in. Let's sit over here by the window and hope for a breeze. You know, people wonder about our relationship when you call me your uncle. I'm not old enough to be your uncle, and for that I'm thankful."

"You and my father are such good friends. When you visited our home, Dad asked me to call you 'Uncle,' and it stuck." Catherine smiled, "I promise not to call you 'Uncle' in public."

"You have been working in our informal ministry of foreign affairs for seven months. Are you learning from Keng Swee?"

"He is fascinating. I'm now studying fifteenth-century Italian city-states. I'd like to visit them some day."

"Maybe you shall." He rose and marched to the big doors and murmured to someone standing just outside. "I've asked for some ice tea. I hope that will be alright for you." He began to shuffle some papers on the table, studied one for a moment and then sat back in his chair and studied Catherine. "You are a beautiful and accomplished young woman, and I will again compliment your mother and father. How are your language skills?"

"I studied Spanish at Stanford, and my accent is tolerable. My Mandarin is fluent, not so for Cantonese and my Hokkien is rusty. A childhood girlfriend insisted that I speak Hakka with her family, but a test wouldn't be welcome," she laughed.

"Yes, Cantonese is difficult, with all of the tones. What about Malay?"

"My conversational Malay is fluent. But, my English is best of all. I love the language. Its depth of words and subtle meanings offers so many options when defining something. I've been reading almost exclusively in English."

"As you know, our little operation runs on the sly—by that I mean it's covert. There are only ten or twelve people who are familiar with our work and our objectives. The British suspect, I'm sure, but they're interested in leaving here unscathed, and if we behave ourselves and mark time patiently, they will leave us alone." He looked out the louvered window and spoke to the sky as well as to Catherine. "The British will depart in a few years, and we will be left surrounded by hungry wolves. We're a small island with almost two million people. We'll need to manage ourselves like the Viennese and Genoese you are studying. It will be exciting and dangerous, but we are preparing for whatever comes our way. I need you and want to enlist your help."

"Of course, Uncle, I will do anything to help. My work is exciting, and Singapore is my home—I want it to prosper. What can I do?" Catherine studied the man while he formed his thoughts. His head was larger than she remembered and his dark eyes unrevealing. He was a force, and she could sense his energy.

"I would like you to take a hiatus from your work and spend a year in Europe. We have several projects which are both dangerous and secret. They will require patience and astuteness. And, also, I'd like you to study French. I didn't when I lived in Europe, and I've always regretted it. It's the diplomatic language, and I want you to point in that direction. Would you be interested in this?"

"I'll go home and pack now," Catherine said eagerly, her body language tense.

For this first time, the man offered a beaming smile. "I have in mind next June. Here is a preliminary brief and you will see that we have a lot of work to do before you leave. For simplicity, let's call this home office Unit-G, and you will be dealing directly with it, never with me. In the meantime, I will mention this adventure to you father, and I bet he will be more comfortable if you can find a friend you can travel with but who won't ask questions.

He stood and extended his hand. "We'll talk more before you leave." They never hugged. He had always been somewhat distant.

Kyle's life pivoted the moment he read Cat's letter. She had told him once to grasp opportunities as they rarely linger and this was a significant one. Graduate school could wait a year, and the Viet Nam war across the ocean would rage on. He would roam Europe and, perhaps, learn a language. But at the core of his deliberation was the thought of the woman who monopolized his feelings.

He had replied immediately and accepted categorically. "Where shall we meet and how will we travel?" he wrote.

Catherine's answer was swift. "Mid-June, anywhere and you choose. You arrange all of it, and I will repay you when we meet," she wrote. "I have the funds to cover all of this."

His parents adjusted reluctantly to his change of plans. Lars had briefly commented that Kyle had a huge appetite for living beyond his means. They had flown west for his graduation; even his brother, Quinn, had shown up.

"Where are you going in Europe?" Quinn asked. "Will you live in one place and use it as a base?"

He had not told his family about Catherine; that would have to come later. Traveling for a year with an older Chinese woman would be too much for them to grasp; well, maybe not Quinn. Colin was his main crutch, plus an unknown number of other supposed classmates. He shipped his belongings home, sold his share in Bessie and like a shadow, slipped away from campus life and into a new world. Delamere blessed his decision and wished him well.

Lars contributed to Kyle's war chest and made one request. Norway had to be a 'must' stop. Kyle arranged with Cat to meet him in Bergen, Norway and suggested a date soon after June 15. The flight from Singapore would cross six time zones, make four stops and three plane changes. Cat agreed without comment.

Bergen, Norway

It had been one year, almost to the day, since they had said goodbye and gone their separate ways. Now, in the small Bergen air terminal, they stood looking at each other, diffidently, before embracing like strangers. It was after 9 pm and still light by the time they reached their mountainside hotel. The small balcony offered a view of the city, the docks, and the bay. The activity below their balcony on the wharf resembled a Brueghel painting, even at this hour. They sat in silence sharing a beer while watching the shadows play on the hillside across the bay. The mid-summer sun moved low in the sky with no intention of resting and would reappear in the east a few hours into the morning. Finally, they began to converse, randomly, about Kyle's senior year, their respective school friends, his classes and plans for the future. "Have the Viet Nam War protests become more aggressive?" Cat asked.

"Yes, and they have moved across the country onto most campuses. The administration in Washington thinks it's doing the right thing, but students everywhere know better. No one wants to fight." Kyle took a long pull on his beer bottle and asked, "What are they saying in Singapore?"

"People take both sides. Most trust the strength of America and are comfortable that it has moved into the void left by the French and British. Most, also, think the war is unnecessary."

Catherine rose, leaned down and kissed Kyle on his nose, and his lips, then yawned and stretched, stripped naked and said lazily, "We have so much to talk about, but it can all wait—love making too. We have months to be together, but I need sleep. She eyed the curiously designed Scandinavian bed composed of two narrow single beds pushed together, each with a bottom sheet and comforter. She shrugged, slipped under one comforter and quickly was in a deep sleep.

In the morning the wharf bloomed with activity: food stalls, fresh fish, flowers and a line of café's offering breakfast along the quay. They had hiked down the hill, and both were ravenous. The sun's rays highlighted Cat's thick dark hair, which she had woven into a braid that made her look like a teenager. "We are now in the moment," she said with a broad smile.

They dawdled, enjoyed being with each other until the late-morning sun drove them to seek shelter inside the café. They planned their day and arranged to attend a Philharmonic concert the following evening. It had to be Grieg, of course. They avoided discussing the year before them. Kyle had decided not to probe and to allow Catherine to reveal her intentions when she wished. They left the café, which had become crowded, briefly strolled the wharf and then boarded a streetcar that worked its way up the hill, tacking several times as the grade was steep. It was midafternoon when they arrived back at their hotel, and they peeled back the comforters, slowly removed each other's clothes and finally settled on one bed to make love. Cat uttered one brief sentence, "I've missed you more than I thought I would—especially in bed."

Their journey began in Bergen a few days after midsummer. They set out cautiously and unhurried, with a curiosity about everything: the people, countryside, food, birds, smells—and each other, as well. They had the better part of a year, so why rush. Life is transient and should be savored. They stood on the top deck of their steamer watching the brightly colored city slide away off the stern. The wind picked up, and the passengers headed to the cabin for coffee. By midmorning they were moving up the center of the Sognefjord where granite cliffs shot straight up from the water's edge, marking endless tundra and small villages. The stoical Norwegians sat quietly reading their morning newspaper and drinking strong coffee, oblivious to the stunning landscape that was theirs. The ship slowed and turned toward Balestrand, a tiny village on a point separating two fjords. "This is perfect," Kyle said. "Let's jump ship and find a hotel. We can continue to Oslo tomorrow."

They sat on the hotel deck drinking beer and watching the sailboats on the fjord, cutting the waves and causing the water to blink in the sunlight. Cat studied Kyle while he gazed at the boats. He had matured during the year they had been apart; his self-assurance surprised her, he seemed relaxed and had become even more attractive. "I'm still on Singapore time, and this constant sunlight confuses my body," she murmured as she moved to his lap, the beer bottle still in her hand.

"I'd like to devour you," he said pulling her close.

"Before or after dinner," Cat questioned coyly.

"Both."

It had been awhile since Catherine had felt her adrenalin surge. *Feels good*, her mind reflected—and she replied without hesitation, "Let's head to our room. We can have supper later and discuss our plans."

In the morning they returned to the hotel deck and ordered everything on the breakfast menu—they had skipped dinner the evening before and were starved. Catherine had anticipated impetuous questioning and was almost disappointed that Kyle had asked nothing of her plans. Catherine chuckled to herself. *I wonder what my uncle would say if he could see his new 'agent' right now? I'm going to let the year before me unfold at a slow pace. I'm so glad Kyle agreed to join me.* "Hey, where do we head after Oslo?"

Kyle shrugged. "Don't know. Where do you want to go?"

"Well," Cat casually said as she signaled for more coffee, "I need to be in Amsterdam in July. How we get there and where we live are up for grabs. I have the funds; you handle the logistics."

Delamere once told Kyle never to accept anything at face value. "Dig deeper," he had urged, and you will find layers of deviations and variations that conceal the core truth. But digging renders the subject more challenging, sometimes dangerous and often fascinating.

In Flåm, at the end of their voyage, they boarded a train with old wooden coaches, and like a corkscrew wound its way up the mountain to Myrdal to connect with the express to Oslo. Catherine watched the stark land flash past the train window, endless trees, rocks, and roaring streams. Her eyes moved from the window scene to the man sitting next to her reading the *Harold Tribune* English edition. Kyle sensed her gaze and said, "I booked our Oslo hotel. When we arrive late this afternoon, we should look into a car rental, one that will allow a drop in Amsterdam. I think we should drive down the west coast of Sweden, catch a ferry to Denmark, pause there for a week, and then head south to the Netherlands.

"How long should we stay in Oslo?"

"My brother married a Norwegian girl from Oslo, and we are duty bound to visit her family or Quinn would be upset. They are expecting us tomorrow for dinner. You'll enjoy them. Tonight we'll visit the giant ski jump at the Holmenkollen and find a restaurant nearby.

Amsterdam

The rain had carried a scent of the sea; fresh and invigorating. Catherine leaned on the houseboat railing distractedly watching the canal activity, which included early morning sightseeing barges and a flurry of small boats darting between them. Her mind hovered elsewhere, and the object of her musing demanded attention. Unit-G had asked for an update on a man in London that she should have contacted weeks ago. Time had run on—and now, as the sun's light pierced a break in the clouds, she made her decision and swung into action.

Kyle sat on the edge of the bed, his long legs stretching, and watched Cat writing at their all-purpose table. "What's up?"

Catherine had not revealed to Kyle the details of her assignment in Europe and, to her infinite surprise, he had never asked. Her mind contained compartments that were off-limits, a prudence developed by her uncle's training last year. Divulge what is necessary to achieve your mission and do that sparingly. But here she was—traveling with, daily conversing with and sleeping with a man who knew nothing of her inner thoughts and exhibited little interest in probing for them. And to make it more bizarre, she wasn't sure what lurked in his mind—if anything worthwhile—he was barely twenty years old! Cat looked up from her notebook, studied Kyle as he dressed and made her decision. "Kyle, you and I are going to London on business. I need to meet with a man, who lives there, and you might want to meet him as well—you would find him stimulating. I'll make some phone calls while you book tickets on the channel ferry to Hull."

Kyle and Catherine stepped out of the London cab into a light drizzle, popped their umbrella and headed down Regent Street. When they reached number 57, Catherine pointed down the street and said, "Why don't you head toward Piccadilly Circus, check out the shops and art galleries. There is a respected gallery two blocks to the right," she smiled and continued, "it's called the Royal Academy of Arts, and I'll meet you in the Keeper's House at one o'clock. If my meeting goes well, I'll invite this gentleman to join us for dinner. I suspect you will find him interesting." Without waiting for a response, she entered the lobby and took an iron-grilled elevator to the second floor.

Alan Fong's small outer office accommodated two desks and a row of metal file cabinets. A young woman greeted Catherine diffidently, pointed to a straight back chair in the corner and then strode to an inner-office door and entered it without knocking. A thin, well-dressed man with Asian features immediately appeared in the door and smiled.

"Miss Lee, I've been looking forward to our meeting. Come in. Would you prefer tea or coffee?"

They sat facing each other on the same side of a desk, the top of which was barren. A telephone hugged one corner in isolation.

Catherine studied Alan Fong as he arranged the tea serving. Did the immaculate office reflect this man's thought process? He looked older than his twenty-nine years and his quick smiles failed to mask a melancholy countenance weary of the world. Not unexpected, she thought, because she had read his dossier. He had killed men at an age when he should have been in a university. Catherine belatedly realized that this meeting could be tricky and that she had not prepared adequately. Her stomach tugged.

"How is Singapore these days? Prospering and growing I wager. And your Mr. Lee is already recognized as a burgeoning force. Is he a relative of yours?"

"No, there are lots of Lees in Singapore," Catherine said smiling. "Although I have met him, he is not in my circle of associates," she lied smoothly. "The city is still a colony, very British in nature and bustling with activity."

"Bustling with intrigue, as well," Fong said between sips of tea. "The British have committed to leaving soon. Then what's in store for your city?"

"We are preparing for several possibilities, and it is because of this that I telephoned you. I work with a small group of individuals who would like to have a plan in place that would protect and benefit Singapore when the British do leave."

Fong sat very still and appraised the attractive woman before him. Catherine allowed the ensuing silence as she knew he was debating her veracity. Her new business was all about trust.

"I'm not sure how I can help you," Fong said abruptly. "My company specializes in land development, mostly in Malaya. We work in close collaboration with the Hong Kong Shanghai Banking Corporation (HKSB); they introduce the clients and supply the money, and I provide knowledge of the land and people. My specialty is rubber plantations and oil palm estates, although we have developed some mining activity."

"What will happen to your business when the British depart?" Catherine asked.

"My clients will need me even more. My connections are not only in Kuala Lumpur but at the grass roots as well. I was born in Malaya. My mother was Malay. And, as I'm sure you already know, I worked for the British and the Malayan security forces during the 'emergency.'"

"That is why we would like to have an arrangement with you for the development of intelligence in Malaya, Sabah, and Sarawak. We are small, and we need to anticipate the desires of our neighbors."

Fong rose from his chair suddenly and said, "I have to rush to another appointment. Let me think on this and why don't we met for dinner this evening and talk more?"

"I am traveling with a friend who has nothing to do with what we have discussed. Dinner sounds perfect, and you will be our guest. You select the restaurant."

Fong rose to greet Catherine and Kyle when they arrived at the Indian restaurant on Soho Square. Kyle rarely wore a tie and jacket, and he felt vaguely uncomfortable when Cat introduced him to Alan Fong. Her elegant black dress and one pearl dangling from her long neck caught glances from the diners as she slipped into a chair next to Fong. Their conversation was polite and ranged from art to horse racing, a sport Fong liked. He directed his attention to Catherine, rarely looked at Kyle, who felt out of place beside the two of them. Catherine orchestrated the conversation adroitly, accepting Fong's keen attention without any promises. Finally, he began to talk about his upbringing in Malaya and the 'emergency.'

1948 Northern Malaya near the Thai border
The road from Penang east to Kelantan proved impassable for the British Marines for several reasons: parts poorly maintained, parts washed out, it threaded through a dense mountain range and sections were no more than a trail. For the entire way, it passed through the thick jungle and over marshy waterways. As if this were not enough, most of the territory along the road belonged to the Malayan National Liberation Army (MNLA), a guerilla army supported by the Chinese Communist Party. The guerillas were mostly local peasants, battle worn from the Japanese occupation when the British supported them with arms and supplies. After the Japanese had left and the British colonialists returned, the Kuala Lumpur government tolerated the MNLA. The Japanese had been cruel and controlling; the British were officious and controlling. Nothing had changed. The peasants were still dirt poor, uneducated and lived in bleak kampongs located tight against the jungle and along narrow rivers. Small gardens and hunting provided the bulk of their food supply; tin goods would trickle in on barter. The British planters returned quickly to claim back the land they had occupied before the war. The mining companies, rubber, and palm oil plantations began to clear vast tracts of land, which pushed the indigenous people further into the interior. It didn't take long for the Communist Party to exploit the natives' restiveness.

By 1948 there were disputes over land ownership, so the guerrillas reformed and the killing began again. The settlement of old grievances occurred first, usually violently: a villager who worked with the government or a colonialist employee on a rubber plantation. Soon it escalated to ambushing police patrols and random assassinations of the white manager on remote palm oil plantations. The jungle war began again, and this time they called it 'The Emergency,' a technicality to circumvent a clause in the planter's insurance policies that excluded coverage during a war. The Malayan police couldn't cope and quickly asked the British to help.

The first regiment of marine commandos arrived by sea—the South China Sea—and offloaded into small river boats with outboard engines that could transport them up the Sungai Kelantan River to Pasar Mas, their predetermined headquarters location. Sergeant Major Hogg was the first British soldier to plant his foot on Malaysian soil for the mission of eradicating communist guerillas. Several town council members were at the dock to welcome the expeditionary force. One spoke English.

Hogg came right to the point. "We will need the services of a trustworthy person from your town who speaks English and is familiar with the bush area and the guerrillas' locations. Once we set up camp and have our scout, we will begin our search operation."

The head councilman turned and waved to a young man standing on the dirt road leading to the dock. Looking back at Hogg with a smile, he said confidently, "We have a man for this job.

His name is Fong—look, he is coming along the dock now."

"He's just a boy," Hogg said with surprise.

"In the jungle and after the Japanese, our boys are men. Fong is already twenty. He will help you." He turned to a tall and rail-thin young man who now stood before them. "Fong, you will help this gentleman and his troops settle and then lead them north into the bush."

Hogg studied his new scout. "Let's hear you speak English."

"My name is Alan, sir," Fong said evenly. "I learned English in school in Tanah Rata, a hill station where I spent my childhood. My father worked for the government as a forest ranger in the Cameron Highlands. In 1938 he was transferred here as the senior government land manager."

"Do you know the area where the guerrillas operate?"

"They are everywhere," Fong said with a shrug. "Even in this town, there may be a few."

"And how do I know we can trust you?" Hogg asked, leaning into Fong's face.

"I hate them. The guerrillas killed my father. I want them gone."

The British began their search-and-destroy operation with one company of Royal Marines. They were a battle-hardened group of professional warriors, graduates of the war in Europe, skirmishes against the Turks in the desert and even the Burma campaign. The first day, Alan led them north along rivers and through leech infested swamps. The insects were relentless. They would bivouac near a village where food and water were available.

"Do the rebels know we're here?" Hogg asked Alan.

"They knew about you the moment your motor boats arrived at our dock. They are waiting for you to push further into the jungle and then they will ambush. We must be very careful."

The killing began the following morning. The point man in the lead platoon never sensed their presence. A single bullet caught him in the chest, near his heart and he died on the spot. The platoon pushed on, spreading men on both wings of the column. They moved swiftly and soon blundered into the rebel's sparse campsite. Alan hung back while the butchery took place. The Marine's superior weapons killed many rebels before they fled. As final evidence of triumph, the Marines collected the decapitated heads in a box to display in villages on the way back to camp.

Kyle remained silent as Fong spun a web of violence and sadness. For four years he toiled as a scout for the Marines. After weeks in the jungle, leading men through constant danger, Alan would return to his village, Pasar Mas, exhausted and restless. The killing had desensitized him. His sentiment for the communists and the Marines was the same—he felt nothing. He wanted to sleep and to dream of leaving this desolation. Fong drained his wine glass and looked at Catherine. "I've talked too long. It's a part of my life that won't go away and becomes more vivid when I return to Malaya on business. The people haven't forgotten the wantonness, and a few would like to cut my throat."

Kyle's thoughts were in Viet Nam. He asked, "Was it all worthwhile? Could the same ends be accomplished by other means?"

Fong looked at Kyle for an eternity. "Yes, is the simple answer to your question. The complex answer is to solve the root causes of the issue, which are more complicated than killing the consequence."

Catherine said, "We are returning to Holland tomorrow afternoon. Would you have an hour in the morning to finish our discussion?"

"How about ten o'clock?" Alan rose, shook hands, first with Catherine and then with Kyle. "The food here is delicious. Thank you." He left without looking back.

Catherine posted a detailed report on Alan Fong to Unit-G from Amsterdam. He had agreed to become a covert source of intelligence regarding Malaya in return for a considerable amount of money deposited to a numbered checking account in a Singapore bank. The secrecy of his mission and the position and number of people who would be privy to his activities concerned him. For the present, he would report to the Unit-G committee.

Kyle and Catherine took a break from their life on the Amsterdam houseboat. They rented bicycles and, each with a pack on their back, headed west on the many bike paths leading to the coast. The paths took them past harvested tulip fields to the beckoning sea. They cycled through fertile farmland, reclaimed from the sea, and verdant forests, before stopping for the night in small villages. An irritating wind swept the coast driving sun seekers from the beach and cold water. They lingered for several days and then headed south to The Hague. Neither was interested in sitting on a beach, and Catherine especially wanted to visit the museums and art galleries in the attractive city that is the seat of the government but not the capital.

After a week at The Hague, Kyle surprised Catherine with a suggestion she accepted immediately. "Let's move to Bruges. I understand it is one of the most beautiful cities in Europe, and everyone speaks French. We could begin studying the language and continue our bike exploration."

Before folding their Amsterdam tent, Catherine had one more task. Autumn loomed, and Unit-G was pressing for reports on her assignments. How could she delay; they were paying all of her bills with no questions asked. Unit-G had provided a dossier on a man living in Amsterdam along with his picture. Geert Mertens, a Moluccan. The sheet said he emigrated from Indonesia to Holland in 1950. Most Moluccans in Amsterdam live in a cluster east of the Amstel River. The file did not give a birth date, address or family connections. A needle in a haystack, she groaned to herself. She wondered if Kyle could handle rijsttafel.

"Kyle, how good is your knowledge of South Pacific geography?"

"Lousy, why?"

"Indonesia, for example."

"It's an archipelago that stretches for thousands of miles. You should know. It's right next door to Singapore."

Without thinking through her decision, she asked, "Have you wondered about who is paying for our European odyssey?"

Kyle turned on his side and adjusted the pillows as a headrest. "It's not your family," he said impassively. I think you are working for some agency in your government, yet you don't have a government, so I don't know."

Catherine thought for a moment and then continued. "You're close. Friends of my family who may someday want to be involved in the government have asked me to research and interview people who could be of help to them. I'm telling you this because, at times, I may need your help and advice. May I have your confidence?"

"Of course and I would rather enjoy it. Just caution me if I slip over a boundary."

They discussed Catherine's dilemma and arrived at no solutions.

Kyle swung out of bed and sat at the table. "This guy, your Mr. Mertens, is past fifty, has no family we know of, and lacks the contacts you seek. My older brother, Quinn, knows this part of the world well and speaks Malay. I have listened to him many times describe the deep ethnic conflict between the Chinese and the Indonesians. Since Singapore is Chinese dominated, I would think that you would look for a well-placed, disgruntled Indonesian-Chinese person living in Jakarta. Shouldn't be too hard but you'll not find him here in Europe."

In 1957 Singapore was not particularly significant internationally and not even regionally. As a crown colony of England situated on a small island occupied by almost two million people, it had little significance except for its location. The British were preoccupied with their departure, vacillating on the timing and extent. To the north, Malaya grappled with similar problems except its shoes of independence were much larger. And to the south, across the Straits of Malacca, spread the Indonesian archipelago. The Dutch had left; the Chinese had not, leaving President Sukarno with internal unrest. The Singapore Chinese were diligent and kept their eyes on the moment.

The clandestine Unit-G committee worked diligently on strategies for the future, consumed with the knowledge that not planning would doom the island's future. The issue of how to establish, quietly, a viable military presence presented severe problems. In the end, the Committee reached out to another small, isolated country surrounded by enemies—Israel.

Kyle and Catherine settled on a furnished apartment in Bruges, not far from the center of the city. The cobbled streets, the canals, and medieval buildings swept visitors back in time to the 17th century. It was a city painted in beige, fawn and various shades of burnished brown; all encased in the velvet French language. They immediately hired a tutor and began what would become a lifelong romance with the language. Both loved to spend weekends along the nearby seacoast. They learned to bike in the rain in the Flanders fields or south in the numerous national parks across the French border.

On a rainy day in October, a letter arrived, postmarked London. Catherine let it sit unopened while she finished her language lesson. She didn't recognize the return address, but she intuitively knew that the letter contained a new assignment from Unit-G. Kyle was out which allowed her time to study and to speculate about the envelope's content. Finally, she read the letter—three times, each time more slowly, letting the full impact of the Committee's request sink in. She decided that she needed to keep Kyle out of this caper, at least in the beginning.

She walked the three blocks to the telephone exchange, found the phone number in the Brussels directory, set a column of coins on the ledge of her booth and placed the call.

"Israeli Embassy. How may I help you?" the gruff female voice said in thick French.

Cat had only one name and one reference. "Mssr. Allon, s'il vous plait."

"I will ask him to return your call," the thick voice said in a rush.

"That will not work as I am in a phone booth," Cat said in English. "My name is Catherine Lee. Ask him to speak with me briefly."

After a long pause and many coins, a soft whispering voice said, "Allon here."

"My name is Lee. Mr. Isaac Redstein referred me to you." Cat said quickly. "I live in Bruges and would appreciate a meeting with you at your earliest convenience."

Allon didn't hesitate and responded in English. "I will be out of town through the weekend, Miss Lee. How about early next week? Say, Monday at 2 pm."

"I will be there. Thank you, Mr. Allon." She hung up but remained in the phone booth thinking. How did he know to switch to English? My French is poor but why English. And he didn't ask about my connection to Radstein. Still wondering…, she turned and headed out into a thin rain.

The Israeli Embassy occupied the first two floors of a narrow three-story building, inconspicuously positioned between an appliance store and a medical supply distributor. Cat studied the building from across the street and wondered who occupied the third floor as the entry directory only listed the Embassy. The receptionist on the ground floor escorted her immediately up a stairway to a small office. Allon, a short, stocky man looked up from a messy desk, stood indifferently and gestured to the lone chair. His dark eyes followed her, and Cat wondered what he was thinking about—her purpose or her figure.

"I've never visited Singapore. It's on the equator, isn't it," he said gesturing to the wall map. "Must be hot." His hands were in constant motion, moving desk papers or waving in the air. His actions preceded his spoken thought as if his body worked slightly ahead of his mind.

"The weather is constant, day in and day out—always hot and usually humid. The locals tell me the moisture is good for one's skin," Catherine added, almost as an afterthought.

"I am not the person you seek," Allon said, breaking the trend of conversation, his hands in the air shrugging. "I'm a political officer and have little or no experience with the military. Isaac sent you on a wild-goose chase."

"Could you direct me to a MOSSAD office in Europe?" Cat asked boldly.

Finally, Allon's hands folded together quietly on his stomach as he tilted his chair. "You are very young for this type of work, Miss. Lee. Be careful as it has some rough edges. But I have a thought. I know what you are looking for, and MOSSAD is not your answer. My country has a larger agency called AMAN which is the intelligence division of our military. They do not have an office in Europe," he lied, "but there is a man who frequently visits us who probably can help you."

"How do I contact him?"

Allon stood and circled his desk. "Please communicate to your superiors that the State of Israel is keenly interested in the well-being of Singapore, and we are ready to help where we can. As you know, we have our hands full at home." He opened his office door and motioned that their meeting had finished. "Leave your contact information, and we will reach you in Bruges. Be patient." Without a handshake or goodbye, he turned back to the mess on his desk.

A month slipped by without a message from the AMAN agent or the UNIT-G office. The weather in Bruges had turned cold accompanied by low hanging, dark clouds, and intermittent rain. Kyle and Cat spent their time indoors: restaurants, art galleries, and their sparse apartment. They had become veteran lovers: spontaneous, meticulous and selfless. Sometimes after breakfast, when the rain pelted their glass balcony doors, Cat would shuffle past Kyle, letting her hand move across his shoulders and then stand before their bed, which was visible from the breakfast table, and slowly shed her clothes. In sex she was the motivator, the alpha and still the most experienced. At times she startled herself by her decadence, her animal hunger to touch the body of this quiet, well-built man. This hiatus from ordinary life, this bliss, would end soon, and she wondered if she could return to her other life. She suspected Kyle could with little hesitation, and that bothered her. As a result, she tried to ignore the thought and stay in the moment.

Kyle had become restless with the weather which precluded cycling or simply being out-of-doors. "Cat, let's move on. It will be Christmas before we know it and it's snowing in the Alps."

"What do you suggest, Mr. Marco Polo?"

"I'm told that Vienna is the place to be for the holidays because of its music and pageantry. Visiting the art galleries alone would consume a week. Some of the best ski resorts in the world are just down the road from Vienna."

"I'm not a skier, Kyle, and I didn't bring appropriate clothes for the mountains in the winter." Catherine didn't look up from her book and dismissed Kyle's suggestion with a seeming lack of interest.

Unphased, Kyle persisted in promoting the Austrian caper: during walks along the canals, or in a café and even in bed. On one such occasion, as they lay in bed, Kyle abruptly stopped his idle caressing of Cat's body, tossed off the cover and swung his feet to the floor, "I purchased a travel book on Austria. Wait till you see the pictures."

Cat grabbed him by the arm. "Get back in here and continue what you started. I will go to Vienna but only with your promise that afterward, we will visit Paris and then move to the south of France."

As if their travel arrangement required confirmation, near the end of November Catherine received a long distance call handled by several operators. After static, pauses and brief conversations in several languages, a soft voice asked if he may speak to Miss Lee.

"This is she," Cat said, suddenly very alert.

"Miss Lee, my name is Levi Berkowitz. The man you met in Brussels last month asked me to call you. I have a general idea of what you are seeking, and there is a possibility that I can help you. I'm calling to ask if you would like to meet in early January either in Brussels or preferable in Bruges as I have always wanted to see that beautiful city."

Cat interrupted him before he launched into a discussion of Belgian architecture. "Mr. Berkowitz, I'm happy you called. I've been waiting to hear from you. We or rather, I am leaving Belgium next week."

"Where are you going?"

"Austria. I will be in Vienna for the holidays." She thought the plural "we" would confuse him.

"I don't like Austria and never go there. Would you be willing to cross a border for a day or two, say Switzerland?"

Catherine shuffled some papers looking for Kyle's travel arrangements. "I will be skiing with friends in Gargellen, which is close to the Liechtenstein border. Could we meet in Vaduz sometime around the 20th of January?"

Cat heard a rasp in his worn-out voice before he almost whispered, "Yes, I will meet you in Vaduz. Give me your hotel and dates, and someone will contact you."

"I will be at the Hotel Bradabella for two weeks beginning on Jan 5th."

"Thank you, Miss Lee. We will be in touch. Ski safely." He rang off, but the static remained.

Gargellen, Austria

Cat learned to ski and to love fresh snow in Gargellen. Kyle insisted she join a ski class, while he spent the day challenging some of the best pistes in Austria. The cold weather provided Kyle something he was unfamiliar with—whipped cream snow. While ski instructors were vying to become Catherine's teacher for the day, Kyle would catch the lift to the top right after breakfast and spend the day skiing back basins. After a week, the instructors reluctantly released Cat from their school and she skied with Kyle. Both had attained a level of competence that allowed them to take untracked powder runs. They screamed with joy and excitement on their descent, always finishing with the promise—"Let's ski here every January. I've never felt so free and in touch with a place." They would laugh and head back up another lift.

Kyle had given Cat a black, mink, Russian-looking cap, tall on her head with a visor, to match her ankle-length black coat. Her boots and hat added height, which complemented her lissome figure and luxurious cascading hair. Conversations invariably stopped when Cat entered a restaurant in her all-black outfit. She and Kyle combined to revel in each other's company: skiing together, inquisitive conversations, and satisfying lovemaking.

A call from Berkowitz interrupted their idyllic life. Catherine agreed to meet him in Vaduz in three days.

"Our meeting may go down in the annals of meetings as the most...now, what's the word?—oh yes, I looked it up...bizarre." Levi Berkowitz said this with a smile as he settled himself on a pillow atop the chair seat.

"Why is that, Mr. Berkowitz?" Catherine asked. She and Berkowitz were alone in a hotel room which overlooked the Rhine River and Switzerland beyond. Cat's light brown skin tone had darkened from the Gargellen sun. Her body movements reflected a relaxation gained from a fortnight of physical activity.

Berkowitz surveyed Catherine from his perch across the small conference table. "You are so young and, I might add, very attractive. I would judge that you are scarcely out of school. And here I am, nearly eighty, having lived beyond my usefulness. There is over a half a century gap between us. I know my associates would think our meeting is bizarre." He paused, "By the way, please call me Levi."

"And I'm Catherine," Cat said. "I'm in my late twenties," she lied, "which seems like mid-life." Cat opened her notebook and leaned forward to emphasize her point. "The importance of our 'bizarre' meeting is that you have a wealth of knowledge that Singapore needs. I hope I can convey the trust we place in you."

Levi sipped his coffee and gazed at the Swiss mountains. "Let me begin with some background." His voice wheezed signaling a breathing disorder. The softness of his voice caused Cat to hang on each word. "I'm a Latvian Jew, born in the last century in the beautiful river city Riga. It was a time of joy, music, art and a liberal tolerance of Jews. Latvia maintained a small army, which I joined as a young man and with a name change and diligent effort, my background became lost in the culture. I became a specialist in weaponry. I won't bore you with the intervening years. I lost my wife to cancer in the 1930s and our only child, a son, graduated from a university and ran off to the United States to study medicine. I tried to follow, but US immigration would not accept me, and so I drifted east, ending in Russia. They didn't realize I was Jewish and readily accepted me into their army as a weapons consultant. Their antiquated weaponry put the Russians years behind Germany. After those brutal years, the war finally ended, and I fled to Israel in 1947. As this fledgling country grew and developed its military, I ended up back in weapon development. I'm now an *ex officio* officer of a small army operation whose sole objective is to study the munition industry worldwide and to purchase the weapons we need." Levi sat back in his chair as if his monolog had exhausted him. "Israel understands and appreciates Singapore's position, perhaps better than anyone, and would like to offer assistance in any way that would help you and not breach our security. Where should we start?" he wheezed.

Catherine tingled with excitement. She was talking with the only person she thought could supply the information she wanted. What luck, she thought? "Our belief is that we will not need a standing army. It would not be appropriate and would frighten our neighbors. If and when we become independent, we would like you to help us organize and train a citizen's army much like Israel's which has performed so well."

"I will give you contact information," Levi said evenly. "When that time arrives, we will quickly dispatch a unit that will train your officers, who in turn will train your militia. You can count on our help."

"Our second request is more complicated. We would like to begin soon to explore weapon sources. As you can appreciate, it would be unfortunate if other countries became aware of our activities so we need discrete contacts."

Levi moved off of his pillow and sauntered to the window where he made a production of cleaning his reading glasses.

Catherine patiently waited as she knew he was contemplating her request.

Levi returned to the table and extracted a file from his briefcase. "I have a plan which I will present to my colleagues. My idea would deliver what you want without exposure. In the meantime, here is a general list of munition manufacturers that we use. Most are in Europe, but you will note that the US is our primary source of weapons."

Cat perused the list and looked up when she saw the GDR. "You are dealing with the East Germans?"

"Yes, but reluctantly. GDR has one rifle we like to use."

"Continue with your idea?"

Levi returned to his perch, folded his hands on the table and said, "What do you think of an arrangement where we secure your weapons and have them delivered directly to you. We would have to charge a small handling fee and would insist that you pay up front. Everyone knows we are buying weapons so there would be no raised eyebrows. We would ship most of the items you will require by air. Even the United States need not know about our arrangement.

Cat grinned. "I like it, and I believe my superiors will also."

At the door, as Levi took his leave, he held Cat's hand in both of his and looked at her. "We shall not meet again, my dear. I wish for you a wonderful life and may it be safe and rewarding. I have enjoyed our meeting." He turned and stepped out into the hallway where two men, much taller, joined him, and they quickly vanished.

Later that evening Kyle studied the list of munition manufacturers with rapt attention. He had become a full partner in Cat's activity, rarely questioning. Kyle found the quantity and variety of weapons Israel sourced in the US alarming. "Cat," he said without looking up, "selling arms to foreign countries is a poor substitute for food and medical supplies. Is the money worth the killing?"

"If you don't do it, others will," she replied.

"Delamere and I have talked about this many times. This obsession with guns and bullets are antithetical to a safe and caring world. They will destroy us."

"Forget about all of this, Kyle. Remember, you don't know a thing about my work. You promised never to reveal our activities. And, you will be happy to know, I've finished my job in Europe. We have four months left. Let's head to Paris and then to the south of France and immerse ourselves in the language."

Two weeks in Paris and a month attending a language school in Pau slipped by in no time. The days were long and laden with study and a desire to capture everything 'French,' from all forms of art to every culinary taste. The sun followed them south and ultimately pushed the two lovers to the Riviera where they settled in a small apartment in the hills overlooking Antibes. Their fluency in French allowed them to communicate with the French who were already arriving for their summer vacations. The April rains cleansed the city.

Kyle and Cat's relationship had reached a point of coalescence. They influenced each other in everyday activities: foods, hygiene, books, art, music, even how they wanted to spend the day. Their lovemaking had reached what seasoned married couples longingly refer to as a zenith. Their desire for each other bubbled. They never talked about the future, and yet their 'future' would begin in two months. Perhaps Kyle's ingenuous youth prevented him from a confrontation with reality. Cat's prescience enabled a reluctant understanding that time was running out for the two of them and that they would soon head down different paths.

One day in late May, they sat on a café deck overlooking the beach, lingering over chicken salad and cold white wine. The sun had started to push through the washed-out Mediterranean sky, and the concessionaires were returning to the sand to arrange their striped chairs in perfect rows.

"I've booked my flight home," Cat announced suddenly.

"When will you leave?" Kyle asked without taking his eyes off of the beach activity.

Cat searched his face looking for a hint of emotion and found only acceptance. "In two weeks—it's a Thursday. You should be heading back too. What are your plans?"

Kyle pondered the conversation; so cold and matter-of-fact. They had been together for ten months, had become wonderful friends—and more—and now this separation without any commitment for the future. He remembered his father's saying, "The choices we make mold our life, and today, my boy, our decision is to go sailing." His wisdom resonated. Kyle admitted to himself that he had known from the onset that this sojourn had a beginning and an end, and he had planned to tap it for every drop of joy and involvement. Cat was a mystery, so open, unselfish, fun and intelligent, yet there were times when she withdrew. Why he wondered? *Perhaps she still considered him an ingénue.*

He turned and looked into her beguiling eyes which were studying him intently. "I've not made any plans. I've meant to discuss it with you, but instead of doing so I just kept putting it off. I think I'll take the train to London and visit Colin before flying home. I must be back at Stanford by mid-August to begin my engineering program. Prof. Delamere has some ideas up his sleeve, as well. I'll book a ticket tomorrow and leave when you do."

"And the war—what will you do about that?"

"As long as I am in school, I probably will not be drafted. After that, I'll have another decision to make. I hate the thought of killing—and here you are buying guns."

"Yes," she said in a quiet voice.

They took a taxi together to the airport; Kyle's train departure was later in the day. They stood on the curb, oblivious to the throng of travelers, kissed gingerly but unwilling to relinquish their embrace. For Kyle, time stood still. Cat titled her head back to take in Kyle's face one last time. "My father frequently visits the US. I'll come with him sometime and find you. Be safe. You are my love." And then she was gone and time began to move again.

PART II

"You will never meet the Lestrygonians,
the Cyclopes and the fierce Poseidon,
if you do not carry them within your soul,"

Ithaca

C. P. Cavafy

11

A MISSION

January 1967

Two feet of snow draped the nation's capital when the Delamere's arrived there by train in early January. The blizzard had swept up the eastern seaboard with howling winds, drifting snow, and freezing temperatures that caused crippling chaos in D.C. Madelyn huddled inside the railroad station while Bill searched for a taxi that could navigate the snow-laden streets. Both began to doubt their decision to leave the warmth of California.

The storm had disrupted plans for a demonstration in front of the White House. The outcry against the war permeated all levels of society on a national scale, not just on the Berkeley and Stanford campuses. Delamere carried this message and looked forward to stirring the cauldron of discontent in the Senate. The next six years would be, Delamere told himself, the summation of his ambitions. His affable nature concealed a rebel, a man who had an agenda, a commitment to his belief that the world could be a peaceful place, prosperous and equitably balanced if wisely governed. He intended to begin that process in Washington D.C. where a government in disarray and discord deliberated.

"I'm not sure I want to live here," Madelyn almost whispered as she watched the swirling snow from the hotel window.

"We've never lived apart, Maddie, and now is not the time to start. I need you more than ever."

"Where will we live? Washington looks so gray and inhospitable. There are no trees."

Bill moved from unpacking and joined Madelyn at the window, his arm circling her shoulder. "Tomorrow we have an appointment with a real estate agent, and if the snow storm will allow, the agency promised a tour of the city. I think you will love the brownstone apartments. We'll find one with a garden."

It took two weeks of trudging through the snow before they settled on a small apartment in Georgetown. Bill wanted proximity to universities, Maddie liked the gardens—a small patch with potential in the back of the apartment and public parks within walking distance. After signing a two-year lease, they boarded a bus that took them down Pennsylvania Ave., past the White House to the Congress Buildings and to what would be Bill's office. Bill Delamere would now, at age 58, begin to do something about the imbalances in a public theater rather than influencing young minds as a university professor.

On his first day, Senator Delamere found an office that looked as if his predecessor had walked out the door minutes before. It displayed the stillness of a library. He stood in the entrance like an intruder, letting his eyes wander over the desks piled with folders and papers. Then, Mary Alice appeared, introduced herself as the office manager and immediately began to show Delamere around. She was the sole occupant as the original staff had decamped. "I didn't attempt to dissuade any of them," she said as she escorted Delamere to what would be his office. "I thought you might want to begin afresh and, to tell you the truth, none of them were worth salvaging."

"How large of a staff will we need to run this office smoothly?"

"Five or six would be a start. You could delay hiring a receptionist until you settle in. I'd like to stay if you wish."

Delamere wasted no time and quickly hired two clerks, both native Californians; one a young man with five years of experience working for the French Embassy and the other a twenty-five-year-old, slender brunette, just back from Peru where she served with the Peace Corp. Holly Saddler was attractive, poised, and a Stanford graduate.

Kasper Wilderman grew up in California where his father had settled after fleeing Germany. His Irish mother provided him with his loquacious nature. His friends at Cal Berkeley called him "Wild" and wild he was at fraternity parties and in the streets protesting the country's growing involvement in Viet Nam. In 1961, he graduated and headed to Washington D.C., to find a job. After five years with the French Embassy, Kasper returned to school and earned a Master's degree at John Hopkins. Delamere hired Kasper right out of graduate school.

Holly required only one interview; Delamere skimmed her resume and hired her on the spot. She exuded a fresh enthusiasm, yet answered the Senator's questions thoughtfully. She knew what was going on in the world, had lived abroad, spoke a foreign language and appeared eager to dive into Washington politics. In addition to all of this, Holly possessed an ability to speed-read with remarkable mental recall. She was smart, wanted the job and accepted Delamere's offer immediately.

Delamere's cheerful smile and non-threatening bearing put people at ease. He developed this technique with students at Stanford and applied the same friendly, smooth approach with his collogues in the Senate. Kasper and Holly soon fell into his positive attitude and became devoted to and inspired by Bill Delamere.

12

WILLIAM DELAMERE

1925 - 1965

D elamere's deep-seated antipathy toward guns amplified during
his years at Stanford University where he taught both political
science and modern European history. Both disciplines laid bare
human duplicity that inevitably resulted in war. His attitude
toward weapons had evolved slowly.

In Nebraska, where he spent his youth, hunting was an
ingredient of life. Frost and blazing sunsets heralded the hunting
season as well as Bill's father's retreat to the basement to oil and
clean his arsenal of shotguns—10 gauge, an over/under 12 gauge
Remington, a double-barreled Winchester and Bill's 4-10. Pheasant
season opened in November. The hunt would begin at 5 a.m. at
Angelo's café where his dad's buddies huddled around a large table
laden with scrambled eggs, hotcakes, sausage, and coffee, swapping
stories of other hunts and smoking cigarettes. By dawn, the hunting
party, which included a Springer Spaniel named Jasper, parked in a
farmer's yard and began to fan out into the cornfield. In those days,
the 1920s, farmers harvested corn by hand. Some of the husks were
on the ground and the stalks, brittle, creaking and rustling in the

wind, stood naked in rows. Scurrying about were large pheasants, and it was the colorful cock that was their quarry.

"Keep your rifle pointed up toward the sky," Bill's dad coached. "And another thing," he added, "never fire at a bird running on the ground. Your buddy, Jasper, is out there in front of you working his way back and forth looking for your bird. Wait until the bird is up and flying. You will hear him; they make a racket."

Hunting with his Dad was the best part of the sport. His father treated him as an equal, one of the buddies. Just walking along the rows of corn in the cool of the early morning with his dad talking to him from three rows over was thrilling. The kill may have provided a quick rush—not much more. And cleaning the birds was a smelly task. The first time, his father worked him through the removal of the feathers, the gutting, and the cleaning. Bill's mom would secretly watch him at work on the back porch stoop, peaking out of the kitchen window, chuckling.

In high school, Bill had little time for guns and hunting. He liked everything teenage life provided: school work, baseball, and girls. He could whiz through books at twice the speed of other students and retain what he read. English, history and social sciences were his passion.

The University of Nebraska in Lincoln offered more of the same. Bill's passion for history reached to the four corners of the world. He excelled and as an upperclassman tutored and assisted professors in grading and preparing lectures. He met Madelyn on one of his political science department forays. Both loved politics, debate, and current events. Bill graduated on the eve of the great depression, moved to an apartment near the campus and accepted a teaching job at the local high school. He settled in to wait the two years for Madelyn to graduate. When she did, they married immediately and settled down in Lincoln.

In 1940, Bill turned thirty-one. Before the US involvement in the hostilities raging elsewhere, the US Army recruited him, offering a commission as a First Lieutenant. The army wanted him to teach European history at West Point, a prestigious appointment for so young a man. West Point knew with certainty the country would soon be caught up in the conflict and that the cadets would need an understanding of recent world events that precipitated the war. The cadets loved Delamere's class for the scope and passion that the young teacher provided and the free-range debates that were born there. Soon, other faculty and administrative officers began to audit the course. The insightful discussions so captivated one officer, Col David Warren, that he became a regular visitor. Warren had graduated from West Point eight years earlier and had become a specialist in weapons—arms of all types, and taught battle strategies.

Bill and Madelyn regularly dined at the Warren home. They became good friends, and in 1943 when Warren transferred to the War Department, located in the recently completed Pentagon building, Delamere moved with him as his assistant specializing in the procurement of small arms. Delamere defined this as any lethal weapon that could be hand-carried by a soldier. The war in Europe and the Pacific had reached its zenith in ferocity. Delamere lived in his office grappling with the complexity of selecting the right weapons, orchestrating the production and delivery with time constraints previously unknown. It was during this period of his life that he learned about guns, which company produced them and their deadliness if they were not in the hands of "a well-regulated Militia."

While at Stanford, Bill Delamere mellowed. He and Madelyn put roots down in the sandy soil, husbanded a small orchard in the rear of their Palo Alto home and raised two daughters. The Delameres were a popular couple with the faculty and students, and their involvement in campus activities gave Bill significant exposure. He taught history and political science, the latter hesitantly until his courses became trendy and oversubscribed. During his thirteen years as a Stanford professor, Delamere quietly endured the Korean Conflict, but when the country's involvement in Viet Nam expanded, he became the voice of opposition—of discontent. In the mid-1960s, he frequently joined the student protests to the astonishment and dismay of the administration. Secretly, some of the faculty admired his courage.

For students embroiled in controversial events on campus and those wishing to debate contentious issues, the Mecca to do this was Delamere's home on Thursday evening. An invitation was necessary. The gatherings achieved an élite status, much coveted and included some of his brightest political science students. Delamere's popularity and passion for understanding the historical roots of current politics provided exposure in the political arena. He was a sought-after speaker and a confidant of the governor, Pat Brown. His views on weapons became national news, and in 1965, he began to ponder running for political office. He threw his hat into the 1966 Democratic primaries and ran for the open Senate seat. Delamere won handily and joined Brown's third term ticket. Pat Brown lost by a large margin to a new politician on the scene, Ronald Reagan; Delamere, to the surprise of the old-line politicians, won. In January 1967, he and Madelyn rented their Palo Alto home and headed for Washington D.C.

13

GRACKLES

March 1967

The grackle stalked along the roof ledge of the large white building. He paused to survey the activity three stories below, noted there were cars and people milling around and that the evening shadows were expanding rapidly. He began to chatter with his friends, all of whom were standing around near a corner of the perimeter wall—they all sensed it was time to move on. Flying north to the horse farm would take less than an hour, and they would arrive at dusk.

A solitary human figure marched slowly around the edge of the roof of the same building. A large instrument rested in the crux of his left arm. He was smoking and humming to himself. The grackle fluttered down to his friends hoping to avoid the smoke. He then gracefully leaped off of the ledge, and flapping his wings vigorously, gained altitude and banked east toward greener pastures. He knew the direction; he had been there many times, and his friends followed. The Maryland countryside soon appeared on the horizon.

On the second floor of the large white house that the grackles had abandoned, two men hovered over a map spread out on a coffee table. Both were sipping whiskey and one puffed on a cigarette.

The President muttered, "We're getting our ass kicked. The daily reports are depressing, especially the body count. How in hell does the press get this information?" He sat in shirtsleeves and had kicked his shoes under the table. His face appeared desiccated, his eyes weary.

"They're all over Saigon, and many are in the field with our troops," replied the other man, still studying the map. He looked like a professor with his small, round, rimless glasses, immaculate dark suit and tight hair combed straight from a clean part.

The President rose and began to stalk the room in his stocking feet. "The country hates this war, and the people hate me for persuing it. Students are protesting on campuses, in some cases rioting. Look out the window; they're marching on Pennsylvania Avenue as we talk. You know, Robert, I may not run for office next year. The fire isn't in my belly anymore. I can't sleep. The killing won't leave me alone."

"Yes, I feel the same way. I'd like to bring this war to a close quickly, but for the first time in my life, I'm not sure how to do it." He took off his glasses and cleaned them absentmindedly, then stood, walked to the window and looked across the vast lawn to the activity in the street. He had already decided to resign from his office; he just wasn't sure of the timing.

The President headed for the toilet, kept the door open, and continued to talk. "Congress seems steadfast in their support of the war. They represent the people, and the people don't want this war. Why the duplicity?"

"Money and power, Mr. President."

"Is there anyone on the hill standing against this onslaught of money?"

McNamara had been Secretary of Defense for six years, appointed by President Kennedy in 1961. He spent his time with senior military officers although he knew his way around Congress as well. His supporters in the Senate were usually conservatives, war hawks and were, he suspected, well connected with the industries that prospered from the war. There was one man who did not fit this profile. Recently, at a large dinner party, McNamara and his wife had joined a table of ten, which included an influential and unpredictable senator from California. McNamara remembered him clearly because he was straightforward, well-informed and thought-provoking. Yes, what was his name—Delamere, William Delamere? His staff called him B.B.—symbolic because he was the embodiment of hostility toward the munitions industry, yet his opposition had about as much punch as a BB gun. He had been a professor of political science at Stanford and because of his fervor to end the country's adventure in Viet Nam, had run for Congress and won handily.

"Have you met the new Senator from California? He's against our involvement in Viet Nam and is making a lot of noise."

The President returned from the bathroom adjusting his pants and muttered. "Why don't you go ahead and meet with him on the quiet. I'm too visible. Let's hear the other side of the debate. Let's find his soft spots. You never know, he may have a withdrawal formula we should look at."

"I'll call Senator Delamere in the morning," the Secretary of Defense replied, as he folded the map of Viet Nam.

The grackles found the horse ranch easily, for it was their home. The wild brush on the ranch perimeter provided hideouts for their nests. The Chesapeake Bay headwater lay just to the East, which is where the valley watershed pointed. Lots of water and fertile earth provided abundant food for the flock of grackles. They even liked the horses and sometimes sat on their hindquarters while they grazed in the meadow.

Lyme, Maryland, and the surrounding farmland had supported European settlers since before the American Revolution. Oddly, the town's proximity to D.C. had not altered its posture. The wooded countryside surrounding Lyme attracted expensive, secluded estates. The small farms along the rural roads provided a camouflage, a suggestion that this is all there is and there's no point in looking on the other side of the trees. The estates were either renovated colonial homes or immense, new construction occupying a spot where an old farmhouse once sat. The occupants commuted to D.C., their teenage children were away at boarding schools, and they alternated their leisure time between horses, tennis, boating, and intimate dinner parties.

The buildings on the grackle's horse farm were relatively new with clean, rectilinear lines. The six thoroughbreds lived in a double roofed, white stable with mughal green window trim. A swimming pool and a tennis court graced the elegant split-level home. A high front double-door and a stone porch greeted visitors. Tall windows stretched up from the flagstones that circled the lower portion of the house, the rest of the siding being cedar. Two black cars sat in the drive; one a limousine and the other a late model Mercedes Benz sedan.

The owner of this pretentious home, Clifford Williamson, had purchased the twenty acres a decade prior when he served as one of Idaho's senators. For more than a year, he had spent his weekends driving the Virginia and Maryland countryside looking for a property that fit the image he had created in his mind. The land he wanted had to be within an hour's drive from D.C., relatively level, mostly wooded, secluded and inconspicuous, with operating farms on the perimeter. He sought two features: total privacy and horse trails. Once these twenty acres became his and the buildings were under construction, he immediately introduced himself to his three neighbors, farmers, all growing corn, two with dairy cows and an assortment of barnyard animals. He could talk the farmer's language with a naturalness that put them at ease.

Cliff had spent his youth on a ranch where he learned to ride horses and rope cattle at an age when most kids were on bicycles. When weather permitted, he would ride his buckskin Quarter Horse five miles to high school, played sports after school and returned home in the dark. Ranchers in the west, by nature, were conservative, preferring to run their lives with total freedom from government intrusion and Cliff's roots were deep in this culture. By the time he graduated from high school, he had hunted and killed many deer, a moose, and several wolves. He could gut and dress the deer, hoist the carcass to his horse's hindquarters and lug it home to the smoke house. Following in the footsteps of his father and grandfather, he entered the University of Idaho in Moscow, a town that touched the Washington state border, where he breezed through the curriculum in three years. He entered Harvard Law School, became an editor of the libertarian-leaning *Harvard Chronicle,* graduated with honors and selected to the *Harvard Law Review.* It was 1930, and the terrible decade had already inflicted pain on his home state. Clifford Williamson headed home by rail, with his fancy diploma and some small change in his pocket.

It never crossed his mind to return to the ranch. He found an opening with a large Boise law firm and began as a mere clerk. Eleven years later, when the United States entered World War II, Cliff had become the managing partner and a confidant of most influential business people and politicians in the state. Cliff joined the Army as a major and served as a legal adjutant to the Secretary of War. During his four years in Washington D.C., he tasted the excitement of government affairs and the political instincts of his forbearers quickened in his veins.

The Williamsons were a politically powerful clan in Idaho, and although ranchers, many had also been elected politicians—one a governor. Cliff returned home once again from the East and this time he knew what he wanted to do. He won a congressional seat in 1946 and returned to D.C. the following year. In his fifth year as a congressman, the senior Idaho senator, who should have retired years before, died at his desk and the governor quickly appointed Cliff to replace him. Thus began his twelve years of extraordinary influence in the Senate. He became a staunch conservative and was the darling of the farm lobby, the chemical producer's lobby and, of course, the munitions industry's lobby.

Cliff purchased the Maryland property in 1957 and began to lay plans for his retirement from Congress. He was well-connected in D.C. and enormously wealthy. In 1962, as the Viet Nam War quickened, the ever-reclusive munitions industry asked Cliff to manage their government affairs. Cliff was eminently qualified; he could walk the halls of the Pentagon with impunity, he was a confidant of many in both chambers of Congress, and he periodically visited the Oval Office. It was this man who sat before the roaring fire, swirling his whiskey, the ice cubes clicking, in this elegant home near Lyme where the grackles lived. Two men sat with him, sipping their drinks, quietly watching the fire in the hearth.

Bobby Steed suddenly began to chuckle. "We slipped Defense's contract for fighter jets to the Saudis into a farm bill, and there wasn't a whisper."

"There was one," muttered the third man in a light tenor voice—a surprise as he was tall and robust. He continued, "The new senator from California."

"Old B.B," Bobby snickered. "He's been a surprise to all of us. Delamere arrived in our chambers talking and has been talking ever since. We figured it was hot air, but many are now beginning to listen to him. He's a cunning old cracker. He doesn't belong to anyone, and that bothers me. And he's smart—oh, so clever. He wants the war over and done with and our troops out."

"Is it the war and the killing that pisses him off or is his antagonism broader? The tall man turned to Cliff with this question, not Bobby.

Cliff studied Sumner Boynton's countenance looking for a deeper meaning in his question. It was a Nordic face, maybe German, with the graying, bushy eyebrows shielding his summer-blue eyes. The face showed none of life's tread marks, no revealing emotion, nothing at all except a coolness that Cliff found unsettling. "If you mean, does he have his eyes on us—yes, he does. By now, Delamere has already found the jet fighters in the farm bill and is barking at the press."

Boynton left the subject unsolved and quickly moved on. "I've been thinking about a new opportunity for us, and I'd like to run it by you. There is an enormously profitable market in this country staring us in the face. We spend our time selling big stuff to the military and dictators abroad, and that's good, don't get me wrong, but I want to back this with a bread-and-butter business that is immune to the vicissitudes of war."

"Are you talking gangs or the Mafia?" Bobby blurted out, now very alert.

Boynton continued, without responding to Steed. "I want a business that attracts no government entanglements, one that is lucrative, steady and self-perpetuating."

Cliff took Boynton and Steed's drink to the bar, freshened them, then poured whiskey into his glass and moved to the side of the hearth. He gazed at Boynton who had settled back in his chair. "I'm all ears."

"Our Constitution has provided us; I'm sure unintentionally, a market for weapons right here in our backyard. Our friends at the NRA vaguely refer to the Second Amendment and place their emphasis on gun safety, training, and hunting. Their publications support our gun laws. Now I understand from a reliable source that the Bureau of Alcohol, Tobacco, and Firearms will expand its enforcement of all gun laws."

Boynton nipped at his whiskey letting his thought linger before continuing. "I think there are a lot of folks out there who would like to own a pistol or two for their protection. The libertarian element in the NRA is growing bolder and driving this need. We represent several famous names—handguns and rifles—designed for the individual, not the military, and these manufacturers are pressing me to open this market for them."

Boynton let this idea float for a moment as he sipped his whiskey. "Cliff, why don't you visit with our NRA friends in D.C. and subtly begin to expose them to this idea. They are already receiving contributions from our clients, and we would sweeten the pot for them. They would need to move slowly through gun clubs, gun shows and expose the idea in their magazine. You would continue your relationship with Congress."

"My God," exclaimed Bobby, "this could be huge. I know exactly where to start with this concept, and I'll begin immediately."

"No," Boynton interrupted, "say nothing about this idea to any of your friends. The idea needs to grow from the bottom up, and it eventually will reach a point where your friends will support gun legislation. At that point, you go to work."

The three conspirators thrashed the scheme until the fire died to an ember and Steed announced that he was heading back to D.C. Cliff walked him to the front porch and watched him slip into the black limo. The night was chilly. He could smell the horse barn a hundred yards off. It was a good aroma, healthy somehow and it shuttled his mind to Idaho.

Boynton was now standing. "The Senator from Alabama is a loose cannon. Keep him reined in Cliff, or we will be in hot water. He's living way over his income. Perhaps you could have a friendly chat with Bobby."

"I'll do that, Sumner, and soon. Let me show you to your room. I'll set up the coffee pot now, so you will only have to push a button in the morning."

"Thanks, Cliff. I have an early flight, so I'll be out of here before dawn. Why don't you plan to come to Connecticut? Come for a weekend in late spring—and bring a friend. If the weather is kind, we can sail to Block Island for lobster and strawberries. I just acquired a 37' Hallberg-Rassy sloop, a Swedish beauty and she needs some exercise. Oh, one last thought. What are we going to do about Senator Delamere? He needs to be hushed, somehow."

14

CONSPIRACY

February 1967

Senator Delamere dove into the business of legislation quickly, brushing aside the superfluous, ignoring nonsense, delegating what was possible and focused on the issues which troubled him. The war was pumping vitamins into the munitions industry whose hydra extended to the four corners of the world. *Where do I begin, he wondered.*

He decided to start in the heart of the federal government, the Senate. Gregarious as usual, Bill introduced himself to colleagues on both sides of the isle. He appeared malleable, and his peers accepted him into their web of influences and intrigues. His committee assignments, surprisingly, included the Armed Services Committee and the Judiciary Committee. By early spring he was ready to make a move.

"Good morning, senator. I'll put you through to General Warren."

A deep husky voice came on the line. "Bill Delamere, is it really you?"

"Hi George, it's good to hear your distinctive voice after so many years. And yes, I have a new job in Washington, and I need your advice. Can we meet soon?"

The Pentagon housed many dining rooms. Brigadier General George Warren and Senator William Delamere sat next to a window overlooking an inner courtyard in a private general staff dining room. A steady rain pelted the windows as the two old friends leaned forward in a conspiratorial conversation. They had covered preliminary formalities over roast beef, and now, with coffee, Bill began to zero in on his subject.

"Are you familiar with Defense's sale of weapons to foreign countries? My Senate source, and it probably isn't accurate, claims that last year it exceeded $450 billion."

"Military toys have gotten expensive, Bill. But to answer your question, no, I'm not in the loop. My concentration is elsewhere."

"I remember your curiosity well, George, when you were stationed right here in the Pentagon during the war. You must have some idea of how the orders are submitted and approved and how the Pentagon supplies the weapons?"

George shifted his gaze to the window and the rain. "This is a serious storm," he mused, postponing his reply. He looked back to Delamere. "Requests for military equipment flow to the Department of Defense (DOD) through many channels. Of course, the State Department receives voluminous requests for weapons, which it passes through our military officer posted to the embassy. But other sources are more interesting, some will make you smile, while others are outright pernicious. The White House calls—usually after a visit by a foreign dignitary. Surprisingly, some countries, usually dictatorial, small ones, approach US AID through wily methods, rarely official and involving several intermediaries. Our intelligence community provides a steady source of inquiries, typically submitted with strong supporting data. And, as you should know, Congress is always pestering us with requests, sometimes demands. There is a well-known lobbyist, Cliff Williamson, who represents the munition industry. He used to be a senator—Idaho I think. He would know a lot more than I do."

Delamere smiled and shook his head. "You know more than you think you do—you're an encyclopedia of information. How does the Pentagon process all of these inquiries?"

"Bill, our focus is almost entirely on Viet Nam. Anything not related to the war we farm to quasi-military agencies, organizations loaded with civilians and quietly embedded in remote sections of Defense. Start with the *Foreign Militarily Sales Act of 1968, public law 90-629.* Look for the word 'benevolent.' Your reading will lead you into the abyss."

The following morning Delamere assembled Holly and Kasper in an office at the far corner of the Senator's suite. A window nestled between bookshelves which spread to the other four walls. "Wow!" Kasper exclaimed, "I wondered about this room. Just look at the reference books."

Delamere closed the door, and the three settled around the center table. "I have a challenging project for you two. I'd like you to research a suspicious activity, an interesting one you will soon discover, and most of the information will be available to you right here in D.C. We do not have a timetable so you can blend your research with your other duties. And finally, I wouldn't want you to discuss your work and results outside of this office. It's a sensitive project. Here's what I want each of you to do."

15

MOUNTAIN GIRL

When Senator Delamere interviewed Holly Saddler in January 1967, she described her life as a book with three chapters: Truckee, Stanford, and Peru. Truckee was a cocoon; a small world, safe, with family love. The University presented mental challenges and an introduction to a world of dissimilar people. Peru offered a time to live humbly and to help someone else lead a better life.

Spring 1959
Chapter One: Truckee, California

The postman shoved a fat envelope into the Saddler's postbox and swung the red flag up. Margret Saddler watched from the kitchen window and then opened the screen door and walked down the path to the street. Uncertainty caused her to pause and stare at the wooden mailbox. Perhaps she should wait and let Holly discover the envelope. Curiosity prevailed, and she opened the box and extracted the mail. Her eyes went to the prominently displayed Stanford University seal on the top left-hand corner of the manila envelope.

The high school kids loved Mr. Saddler's classes; he could breathe life and meaning into events that occurred long ago, and he carried his enthusiasm home and regaled Margaret, Holly and his son Peter with historical events. By the time Holly graduated from high school, and probably one of the reasons Stanford offered her a scholarship, she could have taught her father's class. She could recite US Presidents—and vice-Presidents—backward and forward. Her knowledge of history stretched from the Bible, through Greece, Rome to the Renaissance and WWII. Her memory harbored a treasury of dates and names.

In those days, Truckee was a railroad town devoted to milling and the shipping of timber. The surrounding forest provided hunting, fishing, camping and spectacular skiing, both cross-country and downhill. Holly began skiing as a child, and by high school, she was winning slalom races on the Northern California circuit. Returning home from the Sugar Bowl ski hill one afternoon, she found her dad deep into a book. "You know Dad, our team coaches have been talking about a ski complex on Donner Summit called ASC. They say there is a trail where you can ski and shoot a rifle. Can we go over and check it out?"

At age sixteen, Holly began her biathlon training. The coach, Joe Harmon, had asked her to take a complete physical, and if fit, she could practice firing a 22-caliber rifle on the 150-meter range. Harmon knew he had found a girl with great potential when he checked her targets. Holly was a crack shot. She possessed the three essential ingredients: controlled breathing, stamina, and focus. The following autumn the Sierra snow arrived in November and Holly returned to train in earnest. By the end of 1957, Harmon allowed her to ski and shoot in competitions.

On a sunny spring day, Harmon and Holly were chatting over sandwiches in the clubhouse. The snow was melting rapidly, and the biathlon course would close at the end of the week.

"Holly, you know you're a natural at this sport, and I hope you'll train during the summer and return next season. The Squaw Valley Olympics does not include a women's biathlon event, but there will be a 15K demonstration women's race right here on our course. The best athletes from around the world will be here to introduce the sport. You could qualify."

"I love the sport, coach, but I graduate next year, and plan to go to college. I would be away in school when the Olympics are here. I'd have to think about this and talk with my dad."

The thought of having a student compete in the Winter Olympics intrigued the Stanford athletic department. Not only did the school agree to allow Holly to miss some classes in the autumn of her freshman year, but they also arranged transportation from the campus to the ASC training site on Donner Summit. The women's illustration biathlon event took place in the middle of February 1960, and Holly competed with the US team. The Europeans were far superior, but public enthusiasm for the sport propelled the biathlon sport onto future world ski competitions.

Chapter Two: Stanford

Holly's Winter Olympic appearance gave her celebrity status on campus. Although pleased with her success, she left her biathlon experience in the mountains and applied the sport's discipline to her studies. The path at school was no different from the one in the snow—long, up-hill challenges, competition, stamina and never-ending practice at gun ranges—which compared to her exams, and demanded the same focus. The complexity of her new environment added zest and incentive to her life. She wanted to become a teacher like her father and chose history as her major. But foreign languages attracted her as well, and her retentive mind made language study easy. She began with Spanish.

Reflecting back on her college days, Holly could only vaguely remember her suitors, and there had been a few. Her good looks and Olympic notoriety attracted attention. Boys had not been a part of her high school life; she had arrived on campus inexperienced. That changed as she joined off-campus gatherings and fraternity parties. To her surprise, she found herself responding to intimacy and by her junior year, she had spent the night with several of her boyfriends. She had enjoyed the sex but found it transient, a necessary experience. She understood that sex had a connection with a relationship, but the boys were inexperienced and took their pleasure quickly without returning the joy.

Once a friend took her along to one of Professor Delamere's group discussions, and the debates immediately hooked Holly. Ideas were flying around the room, and her mind burned with excitement. The morality of war and killing was the common thread of the discussion. The students argued, and Delamere arbitrated. Holly came away wondering if she would miss the future by studying the past.

In 1963, she graduated cum laude in her major, history, and with a good grasp of Spanish. She had also arrived at the decision that a teaching certificate could wait and that she needed to do something entirely different. President Kennedy's fresh idea of going abroad to serve those in need intrigued her, and she applied to the Peace Corp.

The tech industry was in its infancy just south of the campus and jobs were plentiful. Holly moved off campus with two friends and began working for a startup company that paid next to nothing. The two owners, young and unseasoned in business, pranced around the office as if the company was in the Fortune 500 and, to her further disappointment, treated the female employees with indifference. And their arrogance added to her negative experience with boys during her college days. She didn't want to play on a tilted playing field.

Chapter Three: Peru

The phone call came through to her office in October. "Holly, good morning, my name is Raul Novara, and I work for the Peace Corp. Your father gave me your phone number. Do you have a minute to chat?"

"Of course," Holly replied. "I've been waiting to hear from the Peace Corp and thought maybe they weren't interested."

"Ah, we are interested. I have your application before me. My job is to interview applicants. I'm in San Francisco for a week, and

I'm wondering if we could meet somewhere convenient for you if I drove down the peninsula?"

They agreed on a Palo Alto café for lunch later that week.

Holly spotted Raul at one of the front tables. He wore the only coat and tie in the restaurant, and the table held a stack of papers. When Raul rose to greet Holly, he slid his glasses down his nose, looked at her quizzically, held out his hand and smiled. *Is he an American, she wondered.* He looked to be in his early thirties.

"Hi Holly," he said, clearing the papers. "Should we have a sandwich before our business?"

Raul explained the Peace Corp's operation. "It is still in its infancy and periodically flounders. Attracting volunteers has not been a problem. It's the foreign lands that offer obstacles which delay progress. Some countries embraced our concept, and we have people in many villages now. Others, typically countries that urgently need our support, are suspicious, and throw up roadblocks."

"Where are you operating today?"

Raul removed his round rimless glasses and looked off in space. He then reeled off countries in East Africa, Central and South America and a few in East Asia.

"If I'm accepted, do I have a choice?"

"No, not really, but I see you speak Spanish," he said in Spanish.

Without hesitation, Holly replied in Spanish. "I studied it in college, but my spoken Spanish needs polishing. May I ask where you learned Spanish?"

"My parents are Mexican, now naturalized US citizens. I've visited Mexico only once. My Spanish came from my home and probably needs as much polishing as yours." Raul continued to speak in Spanish and spent an hour examining Holly's resume. He questioned her interests and activities at Stanford, her reading proclivity and her knowledge of activities such as plumbing, cooking, and first aid.

Just before parting, Holly asked if he discovered anything that would evoke reservation.

Raul scooped up his papers and pocketed his reading glasses. "You are the perfect applicant: bright, curious, healthy and full of energy. All of this will be in my report. I hesitantly add, and unofficially, you are a very attractive woman and depending upon your posting, you must be vigilant because where the Peace Corp does it's work, Hispanic men are known to degrade and sometimes abuse women. And of course, your assignment will be to an underdeveloped country, and you must possess the ability to adapt—seamlessly."

Autumn had arrived in the Sacred Valley, and the mountains overlooking Urubamba, topped with fresh snow, enhanced the mystic. Holly stood by Pidru's battered Plymouth station wagon eyeing the wooden shack that would be her home for two years. The corrugated steel roof glistened in the afternoon sunlight. A water tank sat on a raised platform in the rear. A wooden fence surrounding the cabin touched the outer edge of the platform which allowed a water truck to park close enough to pump into the tank. *Good grief, Holly, you sure have come a long way from Truckee, California.*

Pidru carried her two duffels to the door, turned the latch and nudged it open with his shoulder. Holly peered in and sighed with relief. The freshly painted room was clean as a whistle. There was a bed, one chair next to a standing lamp and an open shower in the back portion of the cabin. She walked to the sink and turned the knob. After some puffing, cold water trickled out.

"I'm going to town to tell the council that you have arrived," Pidru announced, and I'll bring back a propane tank for your stove and heater. You will need candles and a flashlight as the electrical power often has tantrums," he said grinning. "The council will want to meet you, and they'll bring food and blankets. Then I need to return to Cusco, Senora. It might snow at the top on my way over the mountain."

"Gracias, Pidru. How do I find you in Cusco?"

He dug into his pocket and found a slip of paper. "Here is a phone number at a café where I eat dinner. The main store in Urubamba will let you use their phone."

Holly stood where Pidru's car had parked and felt loneliness envelope her. *You wanted a new experience, and here it is. So now show that you have the guts.* A short distance down the road there were homes, more substantial than her cabin, and several people stood to watch her. Holly waved, and they smiled. The two trees near her offered some shade, and she noticed a spot of earth for a vegetable garden.

Soon two cars and a pickup arrived. Holly's neighbors began to stroll toward the gathering. Pidru introduced her to Llari, a stout middle-aged lady. "La Senora is in charge of all activities in Urubamba, and she will help you get settled. I'll come back for you in two years, he said with a horselaugh and headed for his car."

Five council people would influence her stay in Urubamba although she didn't realize it at the time. Llari immediately took charge by directing her cohorts to carry in the boxes containing food, bedding, dishes, pans, soap and even a rug. "March is a kind month," she said, "but soon the winter wind will arrive followed by more snow in the mountains and a cold you may not have experienced." She turned to her son, Puric, and asked him to bring in their surprise.

The bicycle had seen action but was in decent shape. "Tomorrow, you and I can talk about your plans and how the town can help you. We have heard about your Peace Corp, and everyone is excited. We hope you will work in our school, helping Suyana teach the children how to study and about the world of which we know nothing."

Holly greeted each one of them with a handshake. Both Puric and Suyana were about her age and in their brief conversation seemed eager to help and to know her better. The tall lady's name was Chio. She was the town's midwife, and she received Holly skeptically. She provided the only medical help in the town; the nearest doctor lived in Pisac, 40km away. Holly's primary assignment in the early months was to make house calls to teach family planning. Chio did not accompany her or offer encouragement. It took several months for them to strike a relationship and to understand that they could learn from each other and accomplish more. Holly encountered stiff resistance to her message because of the church's teaching and male attitude. It took a year to establish a clinic, and by then, Holly was delivering babies with Chio at her side. The first time she helped a newborn emerge from a womb, gray and bloody, the cutting of the umbilical cord became a moment of magic she never forgot.

The fifth person standing before Holly's cabin that first afternoon in March was Sonco, the area Shaman. It took him surprising little time to accept Holly once he understood that she had not come with medicine. In time, he would visit her cabin bringing herbs for her to grow and to know.

As the days disappeared into weeks and then months, Holly immersed herself in the Sacred Valley life. Her diet changed, selfishness evaporated, and the Peruvian quality of kindness took charge. She spoke English at length only three times, once when her dad and Peter visited. They hiked into Machu Picchu, a thrill her father never forgot. Pidru fetched her twice for Peace Corp meetings in Cusco. Beyond that, she had gone native. Puric and Suyana became fast friends, and together they hiked the mountains, biked the trails, swam in small rivers and shopped in Pisac for fresh food.

Holly knew that someday she would write a book about the Sacred Valley and the people that lived along the banks of the Urubamba River. In March 1966 she left with sadness, speaking perfect Spanish, a lean and healthy young woman, wiser to the world.

16

THE PLOY

March 1967

THe room was silent except for the occasional rustle of paper or a book closing. Holly flipped through the pages of a file Delamere had given her, devouring the content and then cross checking her notes with another open book. She had been engrossed in her search for over an hour without looking up.

Kasper walked in disturbing the silence. "Holly, let's talk," he said, setting two chairs at the conference table. "I have some thoughts on where we can gather information and how we should divide up our assignment."

Holly leaned back in her chair and eyed her colleague. He was so brash and exuberant; she wondered if he possessed the insight to do this job. "Ok, I'm listening."

Kasper swung his feet up onto the polished wood conference table and tilted his swivel chair back, his eyes resting on the ceiling. "The munitions industry is harvesting enormous profits from three major markets," he announced as if giving a lecture. "The most obvious is the supply of weapons to our military in Viet Nam. The Senator could obtain details of these transactions from his contacts in the DOD. But this would not be a good starting point as the

Senate would vote down any attempt to reduce the flow. So this market is not of interest to us, at least in the beginning. Do you agree?"

Holly had moved from her desk to the conference table with her pad. She wrote a brief note before looking at Kasper. "I agree. In fact, I've begun researching our laws governing weapon exports."

"We should focus our investigation on that market and another. The United States is selling or giving vast amounts of military weapons to foreign countries and organizations. Although laws and rules cover these transactions, the interpretation and execution are blurred, and I suspect the profit gain for the handlers in the middle is enormous."

Holly began to reassess the young man before her. His mind was calculating and organized. "What should we be looking for?" she asked. "Most of that information is readily available, particularly concerning the country and the type of weapons."

"Yes and no. The procurement is circuitous and involves many government agencies, both here and abroad. And, as always, there are pockets in-between."

"And what's the third market?"

"Senator Delamere is most concerned about the sale of weapons to the general public in this country. Although insignificant today he senses that it is on the brink of an explosion and the motivation comes from a few who stand to make a lot of money."

Holly wrote quickly, her head bent over the notepad, her reddish-brown hair cascading around her face. "This is a big task, Kasper. How and where do we start?"

"Follow the money, of course."

Holly was not a devious person. She saw the bright side of circumstances, always leaning to the positive. Her life so far had been one of achievement and adventure. Her DNA contained a zest for excitement and challenge, and her new job was beginning to live up to her expectations. "How should we start?"

"Let's visit some gun outlets; there are plenty in Virginia, and perhaps a shooting range. We need to hear the pop of a handgun firing and smell the gunpowder. I'd like to know the type of weapons they are selling and a profile of their customers. If Delamere agrees, I'd also like to meet with the gun manufacturers."

"Senator Delamere already has a reputation for anti-guns, and the suppliers will not welcome you," Holly interjected. "You should talk with their lobbyist."

"Yeah, you're right," Kasper said, astonished that Holly picked up on the drift so quickly. "My story will need to be tight. While I'm in the bush, may I suggest that you begin our research into US weapon sales abroad? The data we are looking for is available but probably well hidden."

"What am I looking for?" Holly asked as her pencil hovered over her notepad.

Kasper answered quickly. "Who is receiving the largest quantities, which companies are the beneficiaries and who in Congress is involved. Following this vein of inquiry will open a treasure chest of information and lead to more interesting questions."

Holly's usual demure countenance melted into a glow of excitement. "I'm free this weekend. Let's hit the road and find a shooting range. I've fired rifles before but the current breed of handguns will be new for me."

"I've never held a gun so you'll be the leader at the gun range," Kasper replied as he headed for the door.

Holly lifted the nose of the Glock 38mm, aimed at the silhouette's head on the target, held her breath and pulled the trigger. The bullet tore through the target where the right arm connected with the shoulder. "I got him," she yelled.

"You wounded him," said a deep voice. The instructor, a muscular middle-aged man with a mustache, smiled and resisted an urge to reach around Holly's waist to hold the gun for her next shot. "Don't jerk the trigger, Holly, just squeeze ever so slightly. Try again."

In the next alley, Kasper stood wearing goggles and sound muffs, ready to fire his Glock. Holly's excitement surprised him. He watched her fire again and heard her shriek. He turned toward his own target and prepared to fire. He hit his mark, about twenty feet away, but the outlined individual on the target escaped with peripheral wounds.

Holly and Kasper spent two hours with their instructor. They had begun the morning reviewing the five weapons Glenn had selected for them to try. They ranged from a Smith & Wesson 38mm revolver to a small pocket pistol to a semi-automatic Colt .357 magnums. Holly was eager to try them all; Kasper attempted to hide his nervousness.

Glenn insisted that they help him clean each gun and carried on a friendly banter, mainly directed toward Holly. "I can see you're comfortable with weapons; you've shot at targets before. You caught on quickly, Holly, a little faster than your boyfriend."

"We're just friends," Kasper said. "We're in the same office."

"Why are you two so interested? Most of our customers grew up with guns."

"I bet shotguns?" Kasper questioned.

"We practice with shotguns out-of-doors and have a skeet range east of town. It's a rifle target range as well. This indoor range is for handguns."

"Which are more popular?" Holly casually asked as she oiled the Colt.

"Our rifle range has operated longer. Several skeet clubs compete at our facility. But recently there has been an increased interest in learning about handguns by people with no experience, like you. They talk vaguely about protection, yet most do not own a gun."

Kasper interrupted. "Where does the NRA stand on handguns? Aren't they a rifle association?"

"We are a member of the NRA. They hold schools for our instructors and recently have begun to emphasize handguns. You probably saw our retail store when you came in."

Glenn looked a bit suspicious with the questioning and Kasper backed off. He paid for the session and found Holly in the store standing in front of an AK-47. She looked at Kasper, raised her eyebrows, and they walked to their car.

They headed back to D.C. just as the rain began. The rental car's windshield wipers struggled to cope. "Now that you can pull a trigger, what's our next move?" Holly asked.

"I'm going to ask our boss for a week to drive around Maryland and up into Pennsylvania visiting gun shops. I want to know what disciplines the NRA is preaching and where the stores are buying their handguns. I suggest that you stay away from gun ranges—you're too cute—and start to research our sale of weapons abroad."

Holly smirked. "I grew up with rifles, Kasper, so you go to Maryland and I'll visit the library." She was beginning to enjoy her new life.

17

ARM THE NATION

April 1967

Two men, both politically potent, set out to meet with the junior senator from California, each with a different agenda and motive. The Secretary of Defense moved swiftly; he instructed his secretary to invite Senator Delemare to visit him at his earliest convenience. The other man, a lobbyist who represented the bulk of the US munition industry, moved circuitously. Williamson preferred caution; his years of practicing law and as a US Senator had taught him to research a subject thoroughly before making a move. He cradled his phone and dialed the CEO of the National Rifle Association, Rex Sloan.

"Good morning, Cliff. You must be reading my mind as we were just talking about you and planned to ask you to visit us."

"Hello, Rex. Who were you talking with?"

"We have a new director, Cobb O'Malley, and I want you to meet him."

"I'd like to," Williamson answered smoothly. "What will be his mission?"

"We would like to expand our presence nationally, do more for our members and in turn increase our revenue. Right now we're stagnant."

"How about tomorrow?" Cliff suggested quickly." I'll drive out mid-morning, the three of us can chat, and I'll buy lunch." Cliff rang off, swiveled his chair to face the large window which framed a maple tree and smiled broadly. "*Perfect, absolutely perfect*," he muttered to himself.

Fairfax was about thirty-five miles west of D.C., and Cliff figured he would miss the commuter traffic if he left his apartment at 9 am. A warm, bright day greeted him, and he sensed that the morning's pleasantness presented a good omen. For the past few days, his mind had thought of nothing else but Boynton's idea of pumping more guns into domestic distribution. Sumner was shrewd, Cliff admitted, and also ruthless. He had amassed a fortune, probably derived from the sale of weapons, yet Cliff didn't have a clue as to Sumner's business operation. Sumner's intense light blue eyes never divulged his thoughts; he was a cold Scandinavian, very private and short on pleasantries and casual conversation. Maybe he should accept Sumner's invitation to sail, although he preferred horses to sailboats.

A young man with tattoos on his visible muscular arms led Cliff to Rex's office. The few people working in the office were casually dressed, young and mostly male. Cliff wore a suit, and he felt vaguely out of place. The office walls were bare and revealed nothing of the business they harbored.

Rex Sloan waved and smiled when Cliff entered. He bounded around his large desk and greeted Cliff effusively. Always congenial and gregarious, his friendliness concealed shyness and his questionable leadership skills. The NRA under his guidance had not deviated from its historical concentration on rifle marksmanship, competency, and safety. A lifelong duck hunter, Rex's business activity in the field usually concentrated on visiting hunting clubs. The NRA's plan of activities included liaison with law enforcement organizations and marksmanship events for youths.

It was the lack of involvement with arms manufacturers or the total absence of liaison with Congress that bothered Cliff. He guessed membership to be under one million and funding the operation from membership dues was insufficient.

Rex turned to the other man in the room. "Cliff, I'd like you to meet Cobb O'Malley, our new Director of Development."

"Hello, Mr. Williamson. I've been looking forward to meeting with you and the chance to give you some of my ideas."

Cliff felt the strength of the man when they shook hands. He noticed that when O'Malley smiled, his eyes did not; they were wide open, intelligent, curious and unrevealing. He had a large head topped with thick dark hair showing the intrusion of gray flecks. O'Malley apparently paid attention to his appearance, a pressed three-button suit plus polished shoes. Handsome, Cliff thought, and probably attractive to women. He would be an infusion of ideas, energy, and style to a somewhat stuffy organization.

Cliff settled in a chair, cradled his coffee cup and exchanged pleasantries with Rex. Finally, he turned to O'Malley, who had been absorbing the banal chat quietly. "I'm Cliff, by the way, and I hope I may call you Cobb?"

"I'd like that very much," Cobb replied as he moved his chair to face Cliff. They had subtly pushed Rex to the perimeter of their conversation.

"Tell me a little about your background before we get to your ideas," Cliff probed gently.

"Well, I'm a Missouri boy and grew up near the Arkansas border. My father loved hunting and took me to bird hunting grounds throughout the state, in fact, all over the south, so I have always been comfortable with guns. I graduated from the University of Missouri, majored in government and marketing and after graduation immediately joined the Marine officer cadet program at Quantico. I arrived in Korea in 1952 and saw action on the Demilitarized Zone (DMZ). After leaving the Marines and with their financial help, I got my law degree from Washington University in St. Louis. My luck continued when I met Rex at a gun club, and he persuaded me to come to D.C."

Cliff smiled and nodded to Rex. "I couldn't have written a better bio for your development job. Cobb, you are uniquely suited. So, where do you plan to begin?"

Cobb handed Cliff a thin file. "Here is a summary of what I plan to do initially, and Rex supports the ideas. We want to expand the hunting clubs, both in number and in size. We hope to accomplish this by attracting young people to our target-shooting ranges. I'd like to start by involving high schools in the program. And naturally, if membership expands, our revenue increases."

Cliff skimmed the file, nodded occasionally and then looked up into Cobb's questioning gray eyes. "I have a suggestion I'd like to have you consider and, of course, we would need Rex's support." He turned so that his eye contact would include both men. "There is a new mood sweeping the country, an attraction to guns, a subliminal need for personal safety and a masculinity laced with jingoism. We have many veterans from your war, Cobb, and more arriving every day from Viet Nam. Most are comfortable with guns, and many are suspicious of government. Both world wars misled them."

A silence enveloped the room. Cobb began to sense what was to come; the suggestions would blindside Rex. Cliff continued in a steady conversational voice. "This country is the largest producer of handguns in the world. Some of the models are the very best available, and the pity of it is that the market in the US is rather small. The companies I represent would like to sell to the gun outlets, the very ones you work with, and we think they will jump at this opportunity."

Rex interrupted Cliff, almost shouting. "This is crazy. You want to provide pistols to the general public! There would be mayhem. Criminals and violent gangs would be the first customers and then those living on the border of unpredictability."

"Hold on, Rex. What I'm suggesting is a long-term program. You, the NRA, would take this concept to your gun store clients.

They would need to be trained and, in turn, their customers as well. Gun stores could invest in target ranges set up for handguns. I might add, this would be lucrative for the stores and the manufacturers would financially support your market and training programs."

Rex spoke up again, this time in a hushed voice. "The government and the various law enforcement agencies would not support this. In fact, it's not legal."

Cobb finally spoke and joined with what Cliff would have added. "If I remember my constitutional law correctly, the second amendment succinctly states that citizens have the right to keep and bear arms."

"Right," Cliff said. "This program would require us to work with various legislatures. My hunch is that once they feel the force of the public demand for guns, they'll jump on board."

"Gentlemen," Rex said as he got up, "may I remind you of what the letter R stands for in NRA."

Cliff stood as well. "What we have touched on this morning will happen. The question is how the NRA will participate. Why don't you think on it and let's agree to meet again within a month? Where shall we lunch? I've worked up an appetite."

Bill Delamere, a humble political science professor, contemplated the looming meeting as he marched down a long corridor to Secretary of Defense McNamara's office. He had studied the Secretary's background, both at Ford Motors and here at DOD. The man he soon would meet was famous for his stern demeanor and mathematically oriented and concise thought process. His "critical path" analysis was in use throughout industry and government. But the calm and controlled manager was overwhelmed with the military struggle in Viet Nam. The door opened and a well-dressed man, his hair carefully combed straight back from his forehead, looked up reluctantly from a stack of papers and rose to greet the senator.

"Let's sit over here," he suggested, pointing to cushioned armchairs facing a small table. "Thank you for coming over on such short notice."

"I'm delighted to meet you, Mr. Secretary. I have admired you for many years and frequently used your concepts in my class at Stanford. I'm guessing, but I bet both of us are ducks out of water here in D.C."

McNamara uttered a short laugh and took off his small rimless reading glasses and began to clean the lenses. "You are so right, Senator. The President and I are exhausted from the enormity of the task and the dreadful consequences of war. In fact, it was President Johnson's suggestion that we meet."

"How can I help? I've only been on the job for a couple of months and have not caught up with several of the committees overseeing the DOD."

"I have a question or two which are off the record. I'll pass on the results of our discussion only to the President. We have now reached a decisive point in the fighting, an impasse actually, and to continue assertively would require more troops plus the use of appalling weapons."

Delamere glowered. "Such as what, if I may ask?"

"We are exploring the use of chemicals delivered from the air."

"The use of gas as a weapon was banished after the WW1."

"This chemical, which is called "Agent Orange" would be used to defoliate the terrain, depriving the enemy of both food and concealment."

Coffee arrived in mugs, and Delamere fed in a little cream into his. His mind was entirely clear on this subject, and he had no difficulty expressing his position. "I speak not for the Senate, but I believe the majority of my constituency in California agrees with my point-of-view. Some brilliant men in our government perpetuated a series of mistakes and involved us in a horrible and useless conflict. The countries south of Viet Nam do not subscribe to your "domino theory," colonialism is over, and the French should have left after the close of WW II. The government we support in the south is inept and corrupt and the government in

Hanoi, who, by the way, helped us fight the Japanese, is a genuine representative of the people. I doubt if the US has the patience to last and ultimately this conflict will be a disaster for America."

McNamara sat staring at Delamere in silence. He hadn't expected this vitriolic response.

"Also," Delamere continued, "the use of the chemicals you described will haunt America for years."

"Will you express your opinion in Congress?" McNamara asked hesitantly.

"No, but I'll not support the war in any fashion."

"On what issues will you focus?"

"Weapons, Mr. Secretary, weapons of all types. Americans are buying handguns for no good reason, and the proliferation will eventually inflict the country with enormous problems and grief. Additionally, foreign customers are maliciously using the military weapons we ship them."

McNamara rose and walked Delemere to the door where he paused before opening it. "I agree with many of your thoughts, and they will be passed on to the President. Good luck, Senator, I hope we meet again."

18

RIPTIDE

April 1967

The winds of change in the United States were gusting in many directions. The popular senator from California had given his maiden speech, a logical and peppery soliloquy admonishing his colleagues for their lack of commitment to control the proliferation of weapons among the civilian population. Delamere foresaw this as only the beginning of an armed society, and he urged them to create legislation which would prevent this.

Simultaneously an attractive and persuasive young man from the NRA was assiduously working his way through Washington's elected community. Cobb O'Malley's sermon included two hooks: the constitution granted the citizens the right to own guns, and the NRA would work in unusual ways with senators and members of Congress who were open-minded on this cause.

Cliff Williamson considered himself a scrupulous attorney. During his lawyering days he always painstakingly prepared his case before entering the courtroom. Although articulate, he kept his dialogue simple, professing to be a common man interested in justice. The success of this approach led to Congress, then to the Senate and now to his position as perhaps the most influential lobbyist in D.C. This trail of success accumulated for him a personal fortune and a network of connections. Considering this history, he wondered why his stomach churned as he drove toward Bill Delamere's office building. After studying Delamere's record, reading his speeches and talking with fellow Senators, Cliff concluded that Delamere's convivial façade concealed a steely determination to succeed in whatever he set his mind to.

"Ah, Mr. Williamson, I've been anxious to meet you for some time." Cautious eyes peering out from under a frown accompanied this friendly greeting. "Do you drink coffee in the afternoon? I nip at my cup all day, but it probably doesn't add up to more than a couple of cups." Without waiting for a reply, Delamere launched the conversation into the subject of gun control. "What is your opinion of my proposal to create a law that would regulate the sale and ownership of weapons?"

Cliff didn't answer the question and maneuvered the conversation to less adversarial subjects. "Have you and Mrs. Delamere settled in? This bruising winter must be difficult after living in Palo Alto." The talk drifted briefly to Delamere's brief experience in the Senate and finally returned to the subject at hand.

"I would suspect that a gun bill will die a quiet death before reaching a vote. I know the nation is still stunned over President Kennedy's death, but you will remember that the assassin used a rifle, not a pistol."

Delamere interrupted. "The rifle was purchased by mail order. How can you justify that?"

"True," Cliff replied, beginning to feel the cutting edge of Delamere's mind. "The fact remains, owning a gun is a right granted by the Constitution. I feel that it's the government's job to protect that right, and the courts will wrestle with the interpretation."

"Can you recite the Second Amendment, Mr. Williamson?"

Cliff began to fish in his breast coat pocket.

"Let me help you," Delamere said with a ready smile.

"A well-regulated Militia, being necessary to the security of a Free State, the right of the people to keep and bear Arms, shall not be infringed."

"The Amendment was ratified in 1791. That's 177 years ago, and a lot has changed since then. In those days our fledgling country did not have a standing army. Hence the operative words "regulated Militia" and "Bear Arms" are military terms and refer to rifles. For our citizens to own and carry handguns would be outright dangerous and certainly not offer security. Today we have an army, we have various branches of police and, of course, there is the FBI." Delamere took a nip of his now cold coffee and without missing a beat, continued with his opinion. "This Amendment is about as relevant as the Third Amendment. Have you read that one?"

Cliff sat very still and replied slowly and carefully. "What you have just dressed is an old salad. The courts have studied the Amendment many times and have always come to the same opinion. This country won the freedoms we enjoy with guns, and the people have a legal right to have them now as they did in bygone days."

19

SOUNDINGS

July 1967

The Swedish-made sloop sliced through the choppy sea with elegant grace; its mainsail stretched to port capturing the aft breeze. The spinnaker billowed, its blue and gold sheet waved at the thin sun breaking through gray clouds, as the 37-foot Hallberg-Rassy healed with each gust of wind causing Cliff Williamson to grip a handrail tightly. He knew now, with certainty, that he belonged on a horse and not on a sailboat.

Sumner Boynton sat coolly behind the wheel, his blue eyes shifting from the sail to the sea, with one hand on the tiller and the other concealed behind the bottom of a woman who claimed to be part of the marine package provided by the Stockholm broker, from whom he bought the boat. The fourth passenger, a young man, lounged on the cushioned bench near the cabin seemingly unaffected by the events surrounding him. Sumner had introduced him briefly as they boarded; apparently his son from a forgotten marriage. The boy was thin and tall like his father but diffident, unlike his father.

"Cliff," Sumner shouted, as he pointed off the bow of the boat. "That vague outline is Block Island, our destination. The entrance is spectacular, a narrow channel leading to an enormous harbor crowded with sailboats. We will lunch at a little beachside café, which has strawberries picked daily. We can chat there."

Sumner's new sloop raced through the island's entrance slot and burst into the harbor, the boat's graceful lines caught the attention of the moored sailors. Sumner's son and the Swedish woman elected to remain on board on the promise of strawberries and cream when Cliff and Sumner returned. An outboard skiff collected them and soon they were on the café's deck eating freshly caught lobster. In the restaurant, Cliff felt more at ease with the sailing adventure because mother earth did not rock.

"We discussed several ideas last month," Sumner muttered as he sipped his wine. "Please bring me up to date on your progress."

"We have encountered several complications," Cliff replied.

Sumner looked sharply at Cliff and interrupted him. "Problems seek solutions."

Cliff Williamson's personality was Alpha to the marrow of his bones. Boynton's propensity to talk down irritated Cliff but his many years as a trial attorney had trained his self-control. He made a mental note to find out more about Mr. Boynton. Cliff smiled. "Yes, let me describe the problem areas, and then we can mutually explore possible remedies. I've met with Sloan at the NRA. He is uncomfortable with our idea of expanding their outreach to promote handguns."

Sumner cut in. "He's old-school and should be replaced."

The carcass of the lobster tail seemed symbolic of Sloan's future—empty. "I think we are in luck on that score. He's hired a man who possesses the leadership qualities we would like to see in the NRA hierarchy. His name is Cobb O'Malley, and he's already in the field working with gun shops."

"What's the problem?"

"The NRA has no connection with the munitions industry. They do not receive financial support from gun manufacturers and depend entirely on membership dues and magazine subscriptions. We need to quietly maneuver our friends to support the NRA without upsetting Congress."

Sumner peered at the blue bay beyond the beach and then signaled for the strawberries. After a long pause, he spoke without looking away from the water. "You are our lobbyist, and you're paid handsomely. You need to work your way through both houses, every level of Congress, seeking active individuals to spread our gospel. Many have, how shall I express it, a proclivity for the fast life and their salaries do not support it. They will welcome you. Your task, Cliff, is to preach the gospel."

"And what is the gospel, exactly?"

"It's the second amendment; the last clause to be precise."

"I called on Senator Delamere and delicately explored his position on all of the issues we are discussing. He recited the amendment from memory."

Sumner swiveled his chair to face Cliff. "For a brand new junior senator, he has quickly become a thorn in our side. My contact in the DOD reported that McNamara invited him for a one-on-one and that they talked for over an hour—a record for the Secretary. Delamere's strident position apparently made a strong impact on him. How did he receive you and what did you talk about?"

"The Senator indicated he would spend little time opposing the war in Viet Nam. He considers it senseless, a miscalculation, the loss of life unconscionable, and doomed to failure." Cliff let his statement linger as he reached for a glass of water. "Senator Delamere's primary concern is the growing proliferation of guns in this country and that he will make this his signature cause. He is quietly working with the California Congressional representatives to fashion gun control legislation. The idea has lingered since President Kennedy's assassination and would deal, in the main, with a ban on mail order gun sales and gun registration. The debate over the proposal will be contentious and delay any action until next year. My guess is that the draft bill will die quietly in one of the many committees required to review the proposed legislation. A high-profile killing, whether it is gang or celebrity related, would change this and be disastrous for our cause."

"My sense is that Delamere will devote his attention to the Senate. His maiden speech exposed his proclivity, and debate would attract publicity. Before he can introduce a bill, he would have to do extensive research, and this trail would soon reveal the direction he intends to take. We must be vigilant. Let's alert, subtly, our sponsors and your new friend, Mr. O'Malley. Why don't we meet again in a couple of months?"

Cliff smiled. "We could meet in Idaho and pack into the wilderness for some fly fishing."

Boynton frowned.

20

FIRST LIGHT

1913-1967

Sumner Boynton hadn't strayed far from his alma mater. His home in Old Saybrook on the Connecticut coast lay an hour north of New Haven and its small airport. Frequent local trains connected his hometown to both Boston and New Haven, which provided an opportunity for an uninterrupted reading time. Boynton compartmentalized his life neatly into two areas: his work as a consultant to various weapon manufactures and his reclusive life in Old Saybrook. He organized both in infinite detail and rarely allowed one to encroach upon the other. The people he interfaced with in each part of his life knew nothing of his other activities. His time at home remained sacrosanct.

The hard times in 1932 had not affected the lifestyle of Sumner's family. Quite the contrary, his parents lived in a fashionable section of Boston, traveled in Europe extensively and could afford to send him to the Phillips Academy, an exclusive preparatory school in Andover, Massachusetts. His father worked for an old-line Boston bank and, it seemed to Sumner, spent his time talking about money and hobnobbing with his family's Beacon Hill connections. He and his father spent scant time together, rarely talked, and his father visited Andover only once in four years—Sumner's graduation. The sole content of his father's advice was to stay out of trouble, associate with respectable people and earn a good living.

Sumner loved his mother, Sanna, and always wondered why she had married such a vacuous person. She was pure Finn, blond and beautiful, with ice-blue eyes. Her father, Pappi Lukas, had immigrated at the turn of the century and brought with him exceptional lapidary skills and connections with the Belgian precious stone trade. Pappi Lukas lost his wife soon after arriving in the U.S. and redirected his devotion to his daughter and Sumner. They were an attractive family but scarcely tolerated by his father's side of the household. Pappi owned a fourteen-foot daysailor named *ILO, (Joy)* which introduced Sumner to his life-long passion for the wind and sea. Pappi kept his sailboat on a trailer which allowed him and Sumner to spend weekends visiting bays and lakes along the New England coast. Together they discovered Old Saybrook on the mouth of the Connecticut River. Lukas not only taught Sumner to sail, but he also provided Sumner with the council that should have come from his father.

In 1931, Yale accepted Sumner on merit, not connections. He fit in with the Ivy League image; made friends quickly, earned good grades with minimum study and joined a fraternity. Money seemed not to be a problem. His mother and Pappi Lukas occasionally visited; his mother admonished him on his feckless lifestyle but enjoyed the glances and attention of his friends. Pappi was more circumspect and attempted to focus Sumner on value and substance.

"Let's spend the weekend in Old Saybrook, Sumner. The weather is perfect for sailing."

"Gotta study, Pappi," he lied. "Maybe next month."

"Never miss an opportunity to add zest to your days. You will be sharper after a few days of salt air," his grandfather offered. His favorite gem was his grandson who needed to be frequently polished.

During the second semester of his junior year, something happened that altered his life. On a wet March morning, Sumner's mother telephoned him; something she had never done before.

"Mom, why are you calling? Are you alright?"

Her voice seemed far away. "I need you to come home, Sumner." Then, a long pause—an emptiness, before she spoke again. "Your father has had an accident."

Years later, looking back at this moment, Sumner remembered his emotion vividly. A coldness had swept over him causing him to shiver. He didn't ask what had happened and sat staring at the rain drumming on the window pane.

"Is Pappi with you?"

His grandfather came on the phone, his voice gravelly, and he sounded tired. "We need you. Come home soon."

Sumner packed one duffel bag, stashed his books in a closet and left a note for his roommates. It would be a three-hour bus ride to Boston.

Sanna's church arranged the funeral service, a brief affair attended by a few bank associates and immediate family. None were present at the burial. Suicides were considered a disgrace and friends, who were no more than acquaintances, quickly disassociated themselves from the sordid affair. Sumner watched the casket drop into the grave followed by two flowers and then dirt. The tombstone would announce nothing but his name and the span of his shallow life.

"Where's the gun?" Sumner asked his grandfather. "I didn't even know he owned one."

Lukas shuffled into Sanna's bedroom and withdrew the pistol from a box the police had used to return it. Sumner knew nothing about guns and had to study the short barreled weapon to find the maker's name: Smith & Wesson, model 627, a .357 Magnum used mainly for home protection. Someone had cleaned and oiled it, probably the police. Sumner sat for several minutes holding the handgun, his mind churning through questions about his father. The short barrel and light weight made it easy to conceal. The thought of his father placing the gun in his mouth and squeezing the trigger crushed him. Was his father's life so desolate that he wished to end it? No note. No farewell...nothing.

Sanna came into the room and watched her son balance the gun in his palm. "We're going to move to a place in the country, maybe closer to New Haven," she said evenly. Your father made some bad investments and lost our savings—Pappi's too."

Pappi had told him about the money. Most of it drained away in the stock market; some wasted on lavish living. "Where will you go?"

"We found an apartment in a small coastal town south of Boston, Duxbury. There's a beautiful bay where Pappi can sail plus he has a job working for a jewelry repair shop. You can sleep on the sofa when you visit."

"How will I pay for school?"

Sanna sat down next to Pappi and held his hand. "Your father's bank said it would loan a small amount and suggested that we ask the university for help."

Sumner had never thought about money; it had always been there for him when he needed it. His Yale friends had plenty to spend, and Sumner assumed that he would eventually be as well-heeled and live a prosperous life. Returning to a student's existence, studying an irrelevant mix of subjects would not guarantee the rewards Sumner wanted. Finishing school would come later, but at this moment he needed to find a job, and as important, an occupation that offered a prosperous future. He looked away from his mother and down at the metal object in his hands.

In 1933, it seemed that everyone was looking for a job. Sumner helped Sanna move to her little apartment, he sailed for several days with Pappi Lukas and then took the train to Springfield, Massachusettes to ask Smith & Wesson for a job.

By 1967, at the age of fifty-four, when he had taken Cliff Williamson for a sail to Block Island, Sumner Boynton had achieved his prosperous future. He had begun his career as a salesman for Smith &Wesson, eventually headed up their business with police departments throughout the country and by the time the Second World War started, he managed the company's military sales. The war and the country's obsession with weapons introduced him to most U.S. gun makers. In 1955, the larger manufacturers held a clandestine meeting to discuss ways to regulate their activities profitably. Sumner attended, and the industry hired him as a consultant. His job was to discreetly monitor the manufacture's relationship with their government and business clients. He supervised the arms industry's lobbyist, liaised with the NRA and frequently met with foreign entities seeking U.S. munitions. His members grew to respect his acumen and paid him handsomely.

Sumner's responsibilities left little time for a healthy life. His marriage lasted two years, ending soon after the birth of his son. Pappi Lukas passed away a few years after he settled in Duxbury; Sanna lingered there for another twenty years supported by Sumner. His job and thirst for money consumed him, depriving him of healthy relationships and what most people term "joy." Searching for a foundation for his existence and balance, Sumner purchased property in Old Saybrook and built a home overlooking the river estuary. He spent his time with boats, not people. There would be time for all of this once he had amassed more money, and this possibility loomed as he and Cliff Williamson worked the scheme. His father would have liked the money; his grandfather would have known the goal was hollow.

21

DISCOVERY

September 1967

Delamere had been in office exactly nine months. Squandered time, Bill mused. Settling into the Georgetown apartment, Madelyn's lack of enthusiasm for her new home, the endless rounds of meeting people and Capital Hill parties, had taken the wind from his sails. His office staff had increased by two, which helped alleviate the nuisance of visiting constituents with their requests and problems. The war in Viet Nam expanded, the body count continued, and anti-war protests occurred daily throughout the country. Bill had given his obligatory brief maiden speech in the Senate chamber, established himself as a critic of the war and worried his colleagues that he was a loner on a mission. Both parties became suspicious of his intentions.

The Republican whip, Bobby Steed, had recently barged into his office, unannounced. A gregarious man, now in his third term as a senator, installed himself in Bill's office as if they were old friends.

"Ah been 'meanen' to visit with you Bill," he drawled, "and apologize for taking this long. Time slips away in D.C. Are y'all settled in and pleased with your committee assignments?"

Delamere remained patient with Steed and answered his questions honestly until Steed began to zero in on guns. "My position is clear, Senator, and I look for your support. The war is appalling, and we must extricate ourselves. We should be cautious of our shipments of military weapons overseas, and the Senate has an obligation to provide this vigilance. I hope we can work together," Bill added in a tone that indicated the meeting was over. He did not want to talk about his growing alarm over the expansion of small arms sales in the country, and he knew that was the subject that Steed came in to discuss.

Cliff Williamson visited him twice. Both meetings were passive and led to no commitment on either side, but did result in a first name rapport. During the second meeting, Delamere queried Williamson on his relationship with the NRA.

"There's a buzz in the chamber about small arms and the NRA's interest in promoting them. I'm new and unfamiliar with the gang of lobbyists knocking on our doors, and I'm hoping you can straighten me out, Cliff, if you don't mind. Delamere gave his friendly smile. Do you represent the NRA?"

"It's confusing, Bill, I know. I do not represent them though I do keep in touch with their people in Fairfax. They have a new fellow who visits with Congress—I think his first name is Cobb. I work for the people who make weapons, and I do talk with members of Congress frequently."

"Is there anyone else in this chain of lobbyists?"

"Yes, there are some others. But I handle most of the well-known American gun companies."

The veteran, retired Senator, and the freshman from California agreed to keep in touch. Both felt they had extracted helpful information from their conversations. Delamere had a gut feeling that there was another person involved in the chain of command—a rung up, perhaps.

"Good morning, my young spies. You've been busy, and I have neglected you. We all have something to report so let's put it all on the table." Delamere sat back in his chair and cradled his coffee cup.

Holly noted that Senator Delamere looked ruffled and wondered if he needed to appear in public today. His necktie came from the previous decade, narrow and striped, and his suit tugged at the center button. Mrs. Delamere wasn't paying attention.

"Our project has three legs," Delamere continued. Let's leave the war for another day and begin with our supply of weapons beyond our borders. What have you discovered?"

"That subject belongs to Holly," Kasper offered. "Exciting stuff, I might add."

Holly placed a thin report before both Delamere and Kasper. "My findings are spelled out in this ten-page account. There are some surprises. The largest recipients of weapons probably are Israel, Egypt, South Korea, Pakistan and Saudi Arabia. Except for the Saudis, all use aid funds to buy weapons from U.S. companies.

"Who benefits?" Delamere asked.

"It's all in the report. I've listed the major suppliers and the states which are benefiting. What is more interesting is who is orchestrating this commerce in Congress. In the Senate, for starters, three Senators are regularly visiting the countries mentioned and to add spice, they usually meet with the same people.'

"A sinister cabal," Kasper said with glee. "Here they are on page three—three Republicans. The Nebraska Senator, Carlyle, is no surprise, nor is Bobby Steed, but Senator Jordan from South Carolina doesn't fit the image."

"If you know your history, South Carolina has elected obstreperous senators before," Delamere added. "The Senator from Nebraska is well known to me. I've chatted with him many times, here and in Lincoln where I went to school. He is a bright and attractive man and will pose a challenge for us. What's our next move?"

Holly glanced at Kasper who answered. "We would like to know who they are visiting in these countries and how they benefit, that is, if at all.

"Good, I agree. Now, Kasper, what have you been up to?"

"Here is a list of gun shops I've visited in Virginia, Maryland, and Pennsylvania. Most were helpful. Hunting rifles and shotguns remain well over half of their sales. However, they acknowledged that interest in handguns is increasing and that they were devoting more display space for it. Also, some were showing military type automatic weapons."

"Who are their customers?" Delamere asked.

"That question made them suspicious of my motives, so I backed off. Their stock answer was collectors wanted the power rifles. Some ranges are offering opportunities to fire AK-47s."

"Anything else?"

"Yes, one item. The NRA is pushing them to stock handguns."

Senator Delamere sat very still. He had a million questions, and his mind began to sort them into priorities. He turned to Kasper, "I'm not startled by your findings. Excellent work. See if you can find out who supplies the gun shops with handguns. Is there a wholesaler? Let's meet again in two weeks."

After Delamere had left the room, Kasper turned to Holly. "You need to gain access to one of those three senator's office."

"How do I do that?"

"Work for a temp agency that provides secretaries to Senators. There's one called "Senataries," which has most of the business."

"How can I do that, Kasper? I have a job—here."

"Take a leave of absence. You can craft some excuse. You'll need to change your name, and I happen to have a friend who can help you."

Holly walked to the room's single window and looked out at the alley below. "Good idea," she said, turning back to Kasper. "I'd like to become 'Melissa Savage.' Sort of sexy, don't you think?"

22

MANEUVERING

November 1967

Michael Carlyle looked like a Presidential candidate, tall and lanky with a cautious smile. Journalists obsessed on his thick hair, peppered with gray, heavy eyebrows and impeccable clothes. A retired fighter pilot, now in his second term as a U.S. Senator, Carlyle was the darling of Nebraska politics and the press corps and respected by his chamber colleagues.

His appearance and oratory seemed to mesmerize the press, a few of whom made him their 'darling' but overlooked his somewhat eccentric behavior. For example, his wife and children remained in Lincoln and rarely appeared at public events. Carlyle owned a D.C. home facing Lincoln Park, just far enough to offer jogging distance to the Capital Building. His spacious office and large staff appeared excessive considering he spent half of his time away. He claimed his committee responsibilities demanded travel abroad.

Senator Carlyle planned to remain in D.C. for the month of November to attend several Standing Committee meetings, a Defense subcommittee, and a Foreign Relations subcommittee, and to finalize his program to promote US weapons sales abroad.

On this Monday Carlyle rose early and drew the curtains in his apartment to let in the pale glint of dawn. He would jog to his office, he thought, shower there, breakfast in his favorite deli and arrive in ample time for the Chamber session. Today, they were discussing the sale of arms to friendly nations, and he planned to speak.

His secretary, Ms. Phillips, would be absent for several months on medical leave. She alone could anticipate his wishes and manage his inner sanctum. Training a temporary would be tedious. His office door opened, and Melissa peeked in.

"Good morning, Senator. My name is Melissa Savage, and I will be your secretary until Ms. Phillis returns. I have the instructions she left, but perhaps you would like to review them?"

Carlyle stood and came around his desk to shake Melissa's hand. He instinctively wanted a closer look at her beauty. Her dress revealed elegance in its simplicity, and the stride of her walk across the room carried confidence. "My concern over Ms. Phillips absence just evaporated, Melissa. Please sit down and let's talk about several important areas of your job. I dictate my letters and instructions into a tape machine. Are you familiar with this gadget?" he said pointing to a black metal box with a microphone attached.

"Yes, I am."

"Many of my letters are to foreign dignitaries, most of whom have titles. Some past letters are in those file cabinets," Carlyle said, pointing to the wall. A sliding door with a combination lock concealed the recessed file cabinets. "Others in the office do not have access to these files—so please be cautious and discreet."

"How will I access them when you are traveling?" Melissa asked.

"There will be no need for you to use the files when I am traveling, which brings up the other area I want to touch on. I am very particular of my travel arrangements. The airline selection, seating and desired departure times are important to me. Your job is to arrange my trips. Always give me the schedule before booking firm. Hotels and ground transportation are part of this responsibility. I know I sound like a school teacher but my time is precious."

"I see from the note that most phone calls pass through me, but some ring through directly to your other phone. Do I answer that phone when you are away?"

"No. I will collect the calls remotely from an answering machine. I'll be addressing the Senate this afternoon, so please hold all interruptions for an hour." He watched his new secretary smile; she closed her notepad and left the room quickly. *He needed to be cautious of this woman. She is striking and maybe a bit too smart.*

"Wilderman," Kasper said in a crisp voice.

"He hired me."

"Who?"

"Senator Carlyle. I'm his secretary for a month or more," Holly said in a low, excited voice. "I may get access to his confidential files."

"Listen, Holly. Be careful and cautious. Just do your job for a while and gain his confidence. That's important. Take your time; we have plenty of it. You're unbelievable; nice going girl!"

Kasper sat staring at the phone and felt the adrenaline racing through his body. This caper was his idea—a dangerous one. His nerves tingled. Carlyle would travel abroad soon and then Holly could snoop. How would they explain the source of their information to Delamere?

"Good morning, this is SRI. How may I direct your call?"

"This is Senator Delamere. I would like to speak with Kyle Norquist who I believe works for SRI."

"Yes, he does, Senator, but Mr. Norquist is out in the field this week. May I ask him to call you."

Bill Delamere had been thinking about his favorite student for weeks. The *Stanford Daily* had run a feature article on Kyle's heroics in Viet Nam and mentioned his injury. One morning Bill impulsively called Stanford and learned that Kyle had graduated from their engineering school and now worked for the Stanford

Research Institute, a reclusive research firm, run jointly by the University and the Federal Government.

Delamere suddenly decided to stretch his legs. He felt old and disconnected from the life he loved—teaching--and young people with thought-provoking ideas. Kyle had been one of the best at challenging. He missed him, other students too, and wondered when he would be able to return to the campus. Bill strolled out of his office, squeezed into a crowded elevator where everyone was talking at the same time. He headed aimlessly out onto C Street. The wind chilled him; he wished he had worn an overcoat as the easterly carried a dampness that penetrated his light raincoat. His body creaked. He had left middle age and he finally admitted to himself he needed to put his life into a higher gear. He required help and thought about the perfect person who could provide it. Kasper's surprising shrewdness had moved his secret project forward but Melissa's sudden leave-of-absence to help her ailing mother forestalled an essential ingredient of the project. Bill abruptly turned back toward his office building and walked with determination. There was much to do, and he hoped Kyle would call back soon.

Kasper's gun store network had expanded. Hunting magazines and industry newsletters introduced him to shops throughout the country. The profiles varied; some were large outdoor sporting goods stores with a gun section, but more were small and run by the owner. New ones were popping up in depressed parts of the major cities; some stores had no windows, just an entrance door.

During their last meeting, Senator Delamere had pressed Kasper for definitive data on the ultimate consumers. "Who are buying the pistols and for what purpose?" he asked. Kasper's sources in the field would shrug their shoulder and say—self-defense, I guess. Protect their home, was a typical response.

The flip side of the marketing channel intrigued Kasper. The gun stores were buying their supply of handguns from wholesalers. There were five that he knew of and their operations were remarkably similar: they sold only guns and related items, no visible salesforce, suburban location and innocuous ownership. It seemed to Kasper that the incentive came from the NRA and printed material; both told the shops where to buy. Colt, Browning, Jennings, Ruger, Remington, and Smith & Wesson were some of the makes on sale. *There is a common thread,* Kasper pondered. *Someone controls the connection. Why would the NRA promote handguns and not receive a reward—or were they?*

Kasper's mind bounced from enigmas to paradoxes. Melissa, the quiet analyst, had become undefined and free. *She is now living her real life. God, how did this happen? I need to move faster and find some answers.*

"Professor Delamere, this is Kyle. I'm so excited to be talking with you."

"Hello, Kyle. It's been too long, and we have so much ground to cover. I'm glad you returned my call quickly because I am planning to come back to Palo Alto for the Christmas holidays and I hope we can get together."

"Of course we can. Let's plan on a long lunch. Here's my number. You set the date, and I will be there. Give my love to Madelyn," and Kyle rang off.

This boy, no this man, if he would come to Washington and join me in the fight of our lives, he could provide the energy and command that we need. Delamere walked to his office door and peered out. "Mary Alice, please join me. I would like your help in arranging my trip home next month." He liked the sound of "home."

23

ACCOMPLICE

Old Saybrook
December 1967

T he slate-gray home perched on a precipice overlooking the
Connecticut River estuary, with the sea hazy in the distance.
The white trim accentuated the studied multi-level contours. A
landscaper had cleverly designed the natural grounds surrounding
the house and allowed spectacular views in all directions, yet the
house remained concealed from a view below. The stairways within
were like structural joists holding each room in place.

The house embodied Boynton's persona. Someone outside
couldn't see in, but Sumner could watch a car moving up the hill.
There were not that many visitors, mostly women, and they didn't
stay long. He preferred it that way, and after a few visits, his female
friends did as well. Educated, well read and always attractive, the
ladies were usually in their forties, and of course, alluring. The
women in his life would arrive discretely, bringing with them
something to heighten the occasion like food, wine, music or
hiking shoes. They all enjoyed sailing and Sumner's bed.

Sumner's son, from a marriage so distant his mind had erased
all details, rarely came to call. When he did, usually at Sumner's

insistence, his presence seemed invisible. He would disappear into town and reappear in time for dinner and afterward, retire to his headphones.

Lots of town wanna-be sailors were ready to crew on Sumner's sailboats, which were of a size that required two or three bodies when out on the sea. Pappi Lukas would not have approved of his blinkered and selfish life, his obsession with the process of making money, and the lack of family. Sumner Boynton was a loner, yet never lonely.

An early winter chill had settled on the Connecticut coast; the cold and the size of the sea swells moved any thoughts of ocean sailing to spring. Sumner spent his days hiking and working on his strategy for marketing handguns to retail outlets. The distribution would be his most profitable venture to date; the simplicity of the plan assured its success. He had recently watched the loquacious Cobb O'Malley captivate a talk show, explaining how the Second Amendment secured the right for a citizen to own a gun and how, during these troubled times, it is only common sense to keep one for self-protection.

Meanwhile, Cliff Williamson spent his time meandering through the halls of Congress, assuring the members that their constituents supported the Second Amendment and strong alliances abroad. Cliff had reported that the country was tired of the Viet Nam War and preferred that our allies assume greater responsibility for world security.

Sumner's five distribution centers, each with a separate name, supplied handguns to the gun stores. He had incorporated them separately in Delaware, and it appeared there was no connection between them. A Lichtenstein company, in turn, owned the corporate entities. The Lichtenstein bankers placed the administrative office on Jersey, an island between England and France, with the financial transactions occurring there.

An Englishman had created this elaborate network and for his creativity, held a minority ownership of the operation. The man, a Greek by birth, knew a great deal about the munition industry, had experience in sourcing guns, but operated this endeavor under the canopy of an ocean shipping operation. Sumner planned to spend Christmas week at his partner's farm in Surrey, about an hour south of London.

Boynton's overnight flight touched down at Heathrow as the sun rose in England. He cleared customs, collected his rental car and caught the M3 motorway to Surrey. Soon he turned dead south toward Guildford. He had been here before and knowingly used rural roads to skirt the city to the verdant farmland along the River Wey. The farm sat on a hill with a long gravel road leading to it. Nicholas Andropolis watched the car maneuver up the drive and stood by the circle to welcome his American guest.

"Welcome back, Sumner." They shook hands and Nicholas grasped Sumner's shoulder to emphasize his pleasure at seeing him. "It's good to see you again, and I'm looking forward to our usual conversations over good whiskey."

"Hello, Nick. A whiskey would put me down after a long flight. I need a shower and coffee. And, by the by, I am delighted to be here with you for the holidays. Your daily schedule should be first on our agenda."

After breakfast, Nicholas led Sumner down a steep staircase to his office, a room with no windows situated below ground under the farmhouse. Nicholas had an affinity for subterranean sites; his extensive wine cellar resided underground a short walk from the farmhouse. Sumner had been here before; it was an honor few people enjoyed. Sumner sauntered slowly along the wall showcases containing weapons, many long out of circulation. *What luck*, he thought, *to have accidently met Andropolis in a German gun show cafeteria. Fate perhaps?*

"I should send you some of the new American handgun models. My clients sense a large market emerging and they are being incredibly creative at trying to meet it."

"I'd like that. I'll let you know when one of my ships will call at a U.S. port. England has become rather stuffy about weapons." Nicholas switched the subject. "Tell me, how is our distribution investment progressing?"

"Excellent," Sumner said as he settled into a cushioned armchair. "We have five up and running, and sales increase each month. Here is a financial report." Sumner tossed it on the desk.

"Are the manufacturers questioning our method of moving their guns into the U.S. market?"

"No, they like it. So far it's clean and smooth; our operation removes the weapon companies from exposure to questionable sales practices at the retail level. And, we pay them promptly."

Nicholas threw a log on the fire and then turned back to face Sumner. "We have a week to discuss some ideas I have for our joint endeavor. In the meantime, there will be droves of people joining us, some interesting and some attractive. Many will want to spend the night. None, I might add, have an inkling of my hobby. I am a London Greek ship owner and you, my friend, operate several ship chandler companies."

Sumner sipped his coffee and watched Nick pour through the financial report. *He must be pushing fifty judging from the gray hair and distinct lines slanting from the corners of his mouth. His beard made a futile attempt to discourage the marks of age. But who am I to judge. I'm approaching fifty-five and dream of sailing, not love making.*

"This is excellent," Nick said with a grin. "I'm glad to be a part of your operation. What I have to propose to you will be more exciting, more profitable and more esoteric. My specialty is Africa, a continent stuffed with countries that require all kinds of weapons. Do you think your American clients would be interested?"

"Absolutely. I will need details. But first, tell me about some of the guests you are expecting.

24

LARCENY

December 1967

The four-star Palo Alto Greek restaurant was an old haunt of Delamere's and the maitre d' recognized Bill immediately.

"Ah, Professor Delamere, we have missed you. Now I should call you Senator, eh?"

"Hello, Macario. I can smell the lamb on the spit; nothing has changed. I'm expecting a young man to join me any moment, so while I wait, a table in the corner and the wine list would be a good beginning."

Kyle arrived at the table shortly after the wine. He and Bill embraced and then stood at arm's length surveying each other. Kyle's body had filled out and his hair was trimmed; he had traveled many miles since their last meeting. Bill's eyes rested on Kyle's left arm, which Kyle noticed and he lifted it in reply.

The two men sat quietly sipping the Tuscany Montebello and savoring their reunion. The conversation began with memories of the old days at Stanford, shared acquaintances, and their political science debates. Delamere subtly moved the discussion to Kyle's life, his work at SRI and then the war. "How do you like your job at SRI?"

"Challenging but not rewarding," Kyle replied, looking Delamere in the eye. "I'm a mechanical engineer, yet my projects deal mostly with chemicals. The Federal Government funds the operation with most of the money coming from the DOD. I'm not at liberty to tell you exactly what we are doing, but I'm sure you can guess that it's all about killing."

Bill wanted to know about the war in Viet Nam, not only what had happened there, but how it had affected Kyle's life after his injury. The roast lamb arrived, delaying Kyle's answer. His left arm hung motionless down to his lap. Others had asked the same question, and each time his reply had altered fractionally, taking on the nuances of time and acceptance.

When he began to tell his story to Bill Delamere; his voice carried a serenity that marked Kyle's acceptance.

"I didn't join the army carelessly—on an impulse. I had thought about it deeply for many years and could never quite reconcile my obligation to serve and my suspicion of the war's purpose and ultimate fate. The men I served with made the decision perfunctorily, and when wounded, they accepted that as well.

"I have changed fundamentally. Nothing now is simply black and white like it was before I went to war. The shades of gray are infinite. To face death daily, to watch someone die before you, to slice each day in small slivers, each presenting a different shadow of what was before and that which is coming, forced me to live in the moment. There was no time to think of what was before or the future. This sense of variance has remained with me ever since, impacts every aspect of my existence and, it seems, my life moves too quickly—like a movie projector on fast-forward. Now, nothing is entirely transparent; nothing is perfect, and everything is suspicious. When I find something with a foundation, something worthwhile, I stop and savor it, like this wine we're drinking."

Bill leaned forward, his arms resting on the table. "Come to Washington and help me, Kyle. What you've come to abhor is what I am fighting to prevent. You would be my chief of staff and direct my investigations."

"What subjects are you probing?"

"The proliferation of guns in this country, the sale abroad and, eventually, our withdrawal from Viet Nam," Delamere said with anguish. Bill finished his wine and continued. "I have a small staff embroiled in the investigation now, but they're over their head and need leadership." Bill let his offer reside in the moment and sat back in his chair. "What do you think?"

Kyle smiled and nodded his head. "Well, your proposal is interesting. I've thought about so many issues that need attention, both personal matters as well as ones that affect everyone, and like most, I do nothing. You've offered a chance to do something about an issue that has bothered me for a long time. Let me see if I can remove myself gracefully from the project I'm working on. If so, I'll be in D.C. as fast as I can wrap up my California life."

"Don't you want to know about the financial package?"

"I don't care," Kyle said firmly.

Before Senator Carlyle headed home for Christmas, he gave Melissa several assignments to complete before she could leave on her holiday. Two were intriguing. He gave her the name of a hotel in Zermatt, at which he wanted to be booked for five nights in January. Carlyle had smiled and mumbled something about getting away for a few days of skiing. He was specific on the dates and the flight to Zürich. *This meeting seemed out of context, she thought. Why is he going alone and who is he meeting?* Carlyle asked for no preparation material.

He then dictated a series of memos and letters dealing with the Senate Committee on Foreign Relations and its January agenda. The memos were to committee members recommending that they approve the sale of arms to a list of nations. The letters were to government officials in several of the countries under discussion.

On the morning before his departure to Nebraska, Carlyle asked Melissa about her plans. His eyes rested upon her face but revealed nothing. Before this, he had never displayed an interest in her or her life outside of the office.

"My secretary, Ms. Phillips, cannot return until sometime in February. I hope you will stay until then and even after that as well?"

Holly felt her blood rush and wondered why. He seemed suddenly interested in her—personally. "Yes, I believe I can stay on through February. We would need to check with my agency."

"Where will you spend the holidays?"

"I'll take off the week of Christmas and visit my family in California, but I will finish your correspondence before I leave."

"Your work is excellent, Melissa. I'd like you to stay on with me in some capacity. What are your commitments, both work and personal? You're not married, I gather?"

She responded too quickly. "No, I'm single and enjoying the freedom."

"Good," Carlyle said, still gazing at her. "I hope to get to know you better when I return. Here's my address in Lincoln. Send all of the memos and letters to me in a final form for signature. Address and stamp the envelopes." He turned his attention to a desk drawer and withdrew a small box. "Here's the key to my confidential file cabinets. I see no reason for you to require it, but in an emergency, you know where it is."

Just before lunch, Carlyle emerged from his office carrying his coat and briefcase, and stopped at Melissa's desk and casually rested his hand on her shoulder. "I'm off. Happy holidays and see you in a couple of weeks." He moved on, nodded to other staff members and left.

Later, Holly sat across from Kasper in a diner booth. Her stomach growled. She felt flashes of excitement and fear. *How close the two emotions are to each other, she thought.* She felt intoxicated.

"Well," Kasper said. "You've scored. Tell me everything."

The two conspirators talked for an hour. Kasper skillfully interrogated, extracting details Holly didn't know she possessed. Carlyle had written to some unusual characters, most of whom were influential second-tier government officials. Not one Israeli graced the list, but there were plenty of Arabs. The letters purported to assure the recipient that they could count on the Senate's support for their weapon wish list.

"I wonder who he's meeting in Switzerland," Kasper questioned. "Does he even ski? Let's check on how frequently he skies and where."

"I can't ask around the office. Carlyle's travel schedule is off limits and never discussed."

"I'll find out," Kasper said. "We need to look at his files. What would be the risk in borrowing a few for the weekend?"

"Are you crazy? Jail time for both of us would be my guess."

"Take a look at them tomorrow—should be easy. If the files apply to our project, I'll come over and photograph them."

Many of Senator Carlyle's staff had already left for their holiday. Holly was an accepted constituent, known to most and friendly with many. She could move in and out of the Senator's inner office with impunity and did so on the morning following her meeting with Kasper. Carlyle had telephoned from Nebraska so Holly knew there would be no surprises. No bells rang when she slid the desk drawer open. The box holding the key sat in the right front corner, something to remember. Holly opened the sliding door enclosing the two file cabinets and began to sift through the contents. *In the movies, the spy finds the document immediately. To read all of them will take me hours.* The files contained innocuous and routine business correspondence—nothing suspicious. One file drawer caught her attention because of the fine, hair-like string which was arranged nonchalantly across the top of the files. Holly measured its various positions from the edge so that she could place it back correctly.

The file names appeared to be city names—she learned later that they were and all from Nebraska: Omaha being the thickest, others were called York, Scottsbluff, and Ogallala and so on. She stood at the cabinet, transfixed, her eyes racing from one page to the next. Each dossier covered a shipment of weapons from the United States to a remote port, frequently in Africa. Kasper would need to photograph them this weekend, she decided. She then replaced the files in the order she had extracted them and returned the string to its guard post.

The following Sunday Kasper accompanied Holly to her office. Not a soul was working, not even the cleaning crew. Holly selected five files, and Kasper photographed the entire contents. They ran into the cleaning crew in the hall on the way out. The two cleaners smiled at Holly and headed for her office.

One of Kasper's friends, a professional photographer, developed the film without questioning what they appeared to be. "Now," Holly said, as she paced the room where they had reviewed the file contents, "how do we provide this extraordinary information to Delamere without revealing the source and our treachery?'

PART III

"Then pray that the road is long.
That the summer mornings are many,
That you will enter ports seen for the first time
With such pleasure, with such joy!"

Ithaca

C P Cavafy

25

TRAFFICKING

January 1968

Dark clouds covered the world; gloom enveloped the affairs of men, and ill winds blew havoc and death throughout the year. In America, three people fell from bullets; two fired from a rifle and the other from a revolver. Many grieved their untimely deaths—as all loss of life is mourned—the remembrance of two would last for generations whereas the third inflicted sorrow for his family and friends, but like most, the incident would become evanescent.

Senator Delamere arrived late to his office on this blustery January, Monday morning. Madelyn's chronic illness worried him. She rarely ventured outside and depended on Bill to handle chores. *I need help, both at the office and at home.* Mary Alice greeted him and motioned toward his office. "You have a visitor waiting. I'll bring you both coffee."

Kyle Norquist stood when Delamere entered the room. He grinned and reached out to shake Bill's hand. Delamere ignored his hand and grasped Kyle by the shoulders, almost a hug, and mumbled, "Heaven sent you and just in time."

"I'm here, ready and eager. How do I address you, Senator, Professor or Boss?"

"It depends on who is with us, but Bill would be my choice. Where are you living? You need to find an apartment before starting the grind that is awaiting you here. Mary Alice will help you settle in, and there is a young man who will work directly for you that seems to know about everything going on in this city."

Mary Alice brought Kasper to the Senator's office. "Kyle, meet my office sleuth, Kasper Wilderman. He'll work for you and can brief you on several of our sensitive projects." He turned to Kasper, "Kyle was one of my best students and is a close friend. He'll be my Chief of Staff and bring a fresh perspective to our endeavors. Why don't you two chat for a bit and then join me for lunch."

Kyle had not arrived unprepared. He and Delamere had spent long hours in Palo Alto talking about Kyle's employment. For appearance, he would work with Mary Alice to establish clear responsibilities for everyone in the California Senator's office. But Bill wanted him to focus on the gun issue. Although Kyle was only five years older than Kasper, he seemed more mature. The war had sapped away his blasé youth; when he spoke, it was measured and concise.

After Kasper had reported on his work in the field with gun outlets, Kyle asked him, "What about your colleague, Miss Saddler? She seems to have been absent for a long time. Are you in touch? Will she return?"

The dreaded moment for Kasper had arrived. Should he confide in this person? Holly was treading on a slippery slope, both her temporary employment under false credentials and here, where she had become incommunicado. She was on the cusp of securing additional essential information on the scheme to sell arms and had promised Carlyle she would continue working for him until February.

"Her mother has been critically ill," Kasper lied. "I'll track her down today and find out when she will return."

Washington's weather had also enveloped the Connecticut coast. Sumner Boynton sat at his desk, brooding, and idly watching the clouds obscuring his view of the river. His mind sifted through memories of his family, his father mostly, and their stifled relationship. His obsession with money, he admitted to himself, assuredly arose from his father's failures in life. *What am I doing with my life? My time is running out, and I have no one to tell my story.* Sumner turned his thoughts to the present and the challenges before him. Andropolis had arranged a meeting in Zermatt the third week of January. He wanted Boynton to meet an unnamed person who would be essential to their scheme to traffic arms to Africa and the Middle East. The mystery man was probably an Arab. Sumner had already invited Michael Carlyle to join them. The Senator's position on related subcommittees would be essential to the project's success. Cliff Williamson, the lobbyist, would not be included and Boynton hoped he would not become aware of this offshore operation. I need to focus on this now, he thought, as he reached for his phone.

Two weeks later, Sumner stood on the Visp rail station platform watching exultant skiers toting bags and equipment onto the electric train that would haul them up the mountain. *Why had Andropolis chosen a ski resort for this meeting, he doesn't even ski? I will, even if the others do not.* He had flown into Geneva and caught a fast train that skirted Lac Léman and then east through snow covered valleys to this small village. The cold, fresh air invigorated Sumner after his long trip. He expected Carlyle to join him here and they could travel the cog railway together. *The Senator would rent a car, which could delay him. I'll take the next train if he doesn't show soon.*

Holly had arranged Senator Carlyle's travel arrangements and had goofed. She was unaware that Zermatt did not allow cars and, additionally, had not considered the January weather conditions in Switzerland.

Boynton saw Carlyle walking toward the station. His clothes were appropriate for the mountains but looked new. Boynton chuckled.

"You'll have to park your fancy car in a garage for a week, Michael. You should have joined me on the train; beautiful scenery and the breakfasts beat anything you have in D.C."

"Hello, Sumner. Yeah, renting a car was a mistake. My secretary is new and probably has never been to Europe. The weather looks perfect. I'm planning to ski; are you?"

A sleigh and porter collected them at the Zermatt station and took them to a small, discrete hotel situated a street away from a collection of restaurants. An oak paneled bar sat next to the small lobby. Sumner accepted the hotel's elegance; Carlyle surveyed the rooms with delight.

The hotel manager appeared bearing a broad smile and an envelope for each. "Your rooms are ready. Mr. Muhsin left these notes for you and his invitation to join him for dinner. We will escort you to the restaurant at six this evening. Please call me if I can provide any further service."

"Has Mr. Andropolis arrived?" Boynton inquired.

"We expect him later this afternoon," the manager replied.

The packed restaurant exuded merriment and the aroma of garlic and lamb. *How will we carry on a conversation with all of this noise*, Sumner pondered, as the maître d' led them through the dining area to a room in the back. Seated at the round table set for four, was Nicholas and another man, who, when he stood to greet them, Boynton realized was short and thin in stature. His olive skin accented a gleaming smile.

Michael performed the introduction. "Sumner, I'd like you to meet Ahmad Abdul Muhsin, an old friend and our host in Zermatt."

When Sumner shook hands, he felt the strength of this small man. He then turned to Michael. "May I introduce you to Senator Carlyle who advised me that he is here to ski."

"Excellent," Nicholas said. "Ahmad is an advanced skier; good enough to take Egypt to the Olympics. We're in Zermatt because Ahmad spends most of the winter here, has a beautiful home and skis every day. He owns the hotel where you are staying, by the way."

The four men spent the evening discussing the wines they were consuming and exchanging routine background information on themselves. The subject of munitions never arose.

Later, in the hotel bar, Nicholas explained Muhsin's relationship to their meeting. "I have been working with Ahmad quietly and successfully for years. No one in my shipping operation is aware of him and our activities. He is my customer for most shipments to Africa, some of which are ultimately bound for the Middle East. Do not ask about his business. He won't tell you if you do ask."

"Why are we meeting?" Sumner asked.

"For several reasons" Nicholas replied as he raised his drink in a salute. "Payment will come from him to you. You'll need to examine this in detail, making sure it is practical and, ultimately, acceptable to you. He will provide you with a shopping list of weapons, a subject on which he is well informed. My part is to arrange delivery. And finally, he will ask you for copies of data verifying your government's intent and regulations that would allow us to do what we intend to accomplish."

Carlyle wheezed a heavy breath. "Shit, I didn't bring records like that. No one asked me to do so."

Boynton shrugged. "Call your office and have someone bring them here. We can ski for two days."

Carlyle returned to his room and sat on the edge of his bed thinking. *To have the files discovered in transit would be a disaster and I would be in deep trouble. A commercial carrier wouldn't make it in time. Which files do I need?* He let his muddled memory sift through his priority file cabinet, recalling that he had titled each related subject with the name of a Nebraska town. The one he needed was "Omaha." *I wonder if that temporary secretary could find the file and bring it to me.* Her face appeared in his thoughts, and he felt a rush. *Yes, she is the answer and is probably in the office right now.* He reached for the telephone.

"Melissa, this is Senator Carlyle. I have an incredible favor to ask of you. I'm in Switzerland and just discovered that I need a file from my office for this meeting. I need you to find it and bring it to me. Do you think you can do this?"

"I'm not sure, sir. Where are you—that ski resort—I'll look up the name from your schedule?" Her voice sounded husky.

Carlyle groaned. "I'm in Zermatt. Book a flight to Geneva and take a train to Visp. Get a travel agent to help you. Find a flight out today."

"I don't have the right clothes."

He groaned again. "Buy some. I'll pay you back."

There was a long pause before Holly spoke and her voice had become throaty. "Which files?"

"Get the key from my top drawer. The names of the three files I need are Omaha," and he named the others. "Do all of this quickly and do not say a word to anyone. Lock my office door and say you will be away for several days on a personal matter."

Another pause—he could almost hear her thinking. "I'll do it and call your hotel with my arrival time. And, Senator, you are lucky. I have a passport."

Carlyle cradled the phone and exhaled deeply. *I am lucky, and this girl is becoming intoxicating.*

Holly arrived in Zermatt the following day just after lunch. Nicholas was standing in the hotel lobby when Holly entered. He turned toward her as she lifted the large sunglasses from her face exposing the most startling hazel eyes he had ever seen. She dressed as a European; her tight ski pants tucked into boots fringed with fur, a white turtleneck under a waist length ski jacket and a stocking cap from which her abundant golden-brown hair flowed to her shoulders. She nodded to Andropolis and turned to the desk clerk.

"My name is Savage, and I have a reservation for two nights. Senator Carlyle made the arrangement."

"Welcome, Miss. Savage. Your passport will not be necessary since you are a guest of Mr. Abdul Masīh. Our porter will take your luggage to your room. Oh yes, you have a message from Senator Carlyle."

She glanced at the note as Nicholas approached bearing a sly smile under dissolute eyes. "Hello, Melissa," he said with a slight bow. I'm so glad you made the long trip safely. Michael will be pleased to learn you have arrived. He's skiing and should be back in an hour or so."

I bet he will, Holly thought, *but not so much that it deters him from skiing.* "Hi," she said with no flourish. "I'm exhausted and need a nap, but the Senator can call my room anytime."

"Would you like me to hold the files for his return and then you can sleep a little longer?" The tips of his sly smile disappeared into a dense beard.

Holly removed her stocking cap and combed her fingers back through her hair. "I brought a package for the Senator and prefer to give it to him myself," she said in a unpatronizing voice before heading for the stairway.

They all gathered at the Muhsin ski lodge, an expansive two-story wooden home nestled in a grove of trees that parted on the far side to allow a view of the Matterhorn. Ahmad greeted everyone expansively, introduced his young wife and then ushered them into the great room, all the time waving instructions to several Egyptian servants. There were other guests as well, Europeans, Holly guessed, and more women than men. She had purchased the perfect dress for this occasion, and Senator Carlyle would pay through the nose. She had charged it to his credit card account. Carlyle hung by her side; they circled the room chatting as if they were a couple until, finally, Carlyle drifted away. Holly drank her wine slowly and decided to sit with a Dutch woman who spoke perfect English and appeared interested in life in America.

The wine and hors d'oeuvres persisted, the chatter volume increased and a few, Holly observed, were tipsy. *You've come a long way, Holly-girl; from a small town in California to a high-octane crowd*

Stephen Pearsall

in the Swiss mountains. Finally, the now bubbly group moved to the dining room where a long, narrow baronial dining table awaited them. There were place cards; Carlyle had put his card next to Holly.

"Thanks, Melissa, for bringing the files." He swirled his glass of red wine and looked at her. "The twists in life are interesting. A month ago I wasn't sure you could take dictation, and now, here we are, drinking delicious wine together." Holly lifted her glass and touched his and watched him drain the contents. She surveyed the people sitting around the table. The women were young, all of them, probably under forty. She was the youngest. The men were attractive. They were smart, amoral, inventive and destructive men, selfish and greedy, emotionally cold and coolly attractive. She was aware of their glances. She could sense the wine toying with the blood in her veins.

After a waiter had cleared the plates, Carlyle turned to her, his eyes dissolute, and his hand settled on her knee and he began to make a slow pass along her thigh. Her instant reaction was electric—revulsion. Recovering, Holly firmly grasped his hand and placed it back in his lap.

"Not a good idea, Senator." People were beginning to move away from the table offering her the chance to leave. "I haven't slept for twenty-four hours; I think I will take my leave."

Andropolis sat on a bar stool in the hotel and watched Holly enter. "Come join me for a nightcap, Melissa. The others won't be here for hours."

Holly collected her key and then sauntered to the bar. It was empty except for the elderly man behind the counter. "I've reached my limit, Mr. Andropolis. I'm thinking of heading home tomorrow."

"Why? You just arrived."

"I'm a messenger, and my mission is finished. Besides, the opulence and attention makes me nervous."

"The Senator has an obsession with you and my guess is that's what makes you nervous. Join me for one small drink and let me order it."

"Franz, give us both some of your best vodka on the rocks."

Nicholas looked back at this attractive American girl now sitting on the stool next to him. He couldn't get enough of her hazel eyes, which now gazed at him unflinchingly. "My name is Nicholas. May I ask how old you are?"

"Old enough to know that I shouldn't be sitting on this stool. And you, Nicholas, do you have a family?"

"My family is farm hands and animals and some distant relatives on a Greek island." The vodka arrived, and they touched glasses. Nicholas began to talk, enjoying his proximity to Melissa. He described his shipping business and his farm in Surrey. Melissa, warming to the subject, egged him on.

"You never married? Do you prefer lots of women and no entanglements?"

Nicholas chuckled. "Yes and no. There was one lady some years ago that I wanted to have around. She was not interested in me and ran off with a South African who tragically died in a plane crash in Africa."

"What happened to her?"

"Don't know. She just disappeared. You remind me of her although she was blonde with summer-blue eyes. A very self-confident lady, like you."

"What was her name?"

"Samantha." Nicholas's eyes wandered, "Samantha Norquist."

"Scandinavian, I would guess," Melissa murmured.

"I seem to have an affinity for Americans, like you." He slid from his stool, drank the rest of his vodka and reached for Melissa's waste. "I never kissed Samantha and wish I had. And now I have another 'Samantha' before me, and I'd like to kiss you just this once. Would the stubble bother you?"

Holly reached for her drink, drained it, and moved off of the stool. *This is crazy,* her muddled mind said, *but what the hell, I'm leaving tomorrow and I've never kissed a man with a beard. Besides, I'm not decorous Holly; I'm sexy Melissa.*

Franz looked away as they lingered in their embrace. When they moved apart, Nicholas asked, "Was the beard so awful?"

"I didn't like the beard much, but the kiss was nice. Maybe we'll meet again—your farm perhaps." She left the bar quickly and in the morning, departed early.

26

THE COMMITTEE

February 1968

Kyle found a pied-à-terre in a large apartment complex near the capital buildings. The residents were young government workers, friendly and helpful to new arrivals, but vague on their exact employment. The morning bus ride resembled a library, whereas the afternoon return trip a social gathering.

A dull pewter sky greeted Kyle when he boarded the bus for work. His mind dwelled on the day before him, the complexity of the weapons project and Delamere's pressure for answers. Today, the enigmatic Holly would return, and Kyle pondered how he would approach the subject of her absence and adventure. He had been suspicious from the onset, especially when he could not locate her either in D.C. or Los Angeles. He had pressed Kasper and learned the truth. They were on dangerous ground and exposure would be a disaster for Senator Delamere. Snow had begun to dust the world, hiding its reality. When Kyle stepped from the bus, his long overcoat felt good.

The back office, a dusty library with one window, had become the sanctuary for the three-person committee investigating weapons. Others in the office knew it was off limits. Kyle stood by the narrow window watching the snowstorm grow in strength. When the door opened, he turned to observe his wayward colleague enter, along with Kasper. Kyle lost his breath as he watched Holly walk toward him. He had met her before, many times, in his imagination. He asked time to stop so that he could savor the moment, like eating a deliciously ripe peach. She seemed apprehensive; no, more like anxious. Her eyes glanced at his left arm briefly and then moved to Kyle's face, and she smiled.

"Hello, Holly, I'm Kyle Norquist. I've been looking forward to meeting you. Kasper and I have struggled with this project for a week, and he has filled me in with the details."

"Kasper just told me that he had spilled the beans. Am I in trouble?"

"Melissa has problems, but let's see if we can protect Holly." Kyle smiled as he sat down and began to shuffle his papers, acutely aware of her nearness. Kasper had relaxed under Kyle's seeming acceptance of his and Holly's escapade.

"Let's review what we know for sure. First, Senator Delamere must never become aware of your adventure. What you did is a crime. Stealing state secrets leads to prison. We must carefully review your two months working for Senator Carlyle and cover your tracks. When you returned from Switzerland, did you talk with anyone in Carlyle's office?"

"I came back on the weekend and went to the office on Sunday to collect my things. No one was in the office."

"So," Kyle said, "Melissa left Carlyle's office and disappeared into the ether. What about your identity data. You must have provided a social security number, address, and some background information?"

"I did, but it was all bogus." Holly had been sitting still in her chair, but now became animated. "There is one glitch that bothers me. Kasper and I never dreamed I would need a passport and when Carlyle asked me to fly to Switzerland, I had to use my authentic one."

"Ouch." Kyle groaned.

"But let's think about this," Kasper exclaimed. "Who would know except immigration?"

"As far as Senator Carlyle is concerned, he has no idea that you looked at his files and copied some, right?"

"There's no reason for him to think that I was interested. He thought I was a not too bright secretary with nice legs."

"But he must have asked himself why you departed Zermatt abruptly and left his office without a trace? Should we not assume that he will search for Melissa Savage?"

"My guess is that he won't do that. He attempted to become too friendly while we were in Zermatt. He would not want that revealed: to the press, his family, anyone."

"Wow," Kyle exclaimed. "This is like a movie. Kasper, make sure that your contact who prepared the ID papers, is well compensated and that he destroys all evidence. His memory loss must be permanent. You should do the same, Holly. And then we have the worry of someone recognizing you."

"Yes, that could happen," Holly said, "but it's not likely. I dyed my hair, used different makeup, and my clothes were flashy. I had no involvement with anyone in the office; they must have thought of me as strange and not worth knowing."

This announcement thrust the two men into a quietness that filled the room. Suddenly, the door burst open, and Bill Delamere strode in waving a newspaper. "This guy, Cobb O'Malley, is a whirlwind. He's everywhere, on TV talk programs, in the press and giving town hall speeches and he's never at a loss for words. Well, that's no surprise, he's Irish after all. Oh, hello, Holly. I came in to welcome you back. How's your mother?"

"She is recovering rapidly. Thank you, Senator," Holly stood to greet him.

"Glad to hear it," the Senator puffed, his substantial frame filling the doorway. "You will be pleased to hear that two colleagues and I are writing a draft bill that will regulate firearms, covering both owners and manufacturers. Here is a list of questions we have about the marketplace, and I'd like you to dig up some answers. We plan to present the bill to Congress in April." Delamere handed

Kyle the list and headed for the door. He paused and looked back at the committee of three. "I'm also working on a draft bill covering the sale of weapons to foreign entities. You will be busy."

Kasper perused the list and then handed it to Holly. "I can get most of the information asked for on this list. But I have an idea that would speed things along. Senator Delamere should visit the NRA headquarters and meet with the CEO, Rex Sloan, and convince him to support the bill. I understand he's considerate and pliable."

"Why would he cooperate?" Kyle asked.

"Make the proposed bill fat with restrictions and then negotiate away some onerous points in exchange for the key segments."

"Good idea. I will talk to the Senator today." Kyle turned to Holly. "Did you meet anyone at the ski resort that could help us with this?"

"Yes, I met several actors who were up to no good, but my exposure was brief. The host, a wealthy Egyptian, was probably the customer/distributor for the arms trafficking operation. I didn't talk with him. The meeting organizer, an Englishman who owns a fleet of cargo ships, handles the delivery and, I guess, the financial arrangements. These two would be of no help to our investigation. Carlyle you know and I think we should leave him alone for a while. The fourth person, an American, said little, ignored me, but I had the sense that he was important. We should do a background investigation on him."

Kasper laughed. "Where is the timid Holly I knew? You'll be working for the FBI soon."

"By the way, Kyle," Holly said, turning her attention to a man she wanted to know better. "The Englishman, Mr. Andropolis, told me a tale of a woman he knew and admired and her last name was Norquist. Do you have any relatives floating around Europe?"

Kyle looked at Holly intently. "My sister lived in London for several years. Did he mention her first name?"

"Samantha."

Kyle felt his heart thump. "Good Lord! Samantha now lives on an estancia outside of Santiago, Chile. She was a photojournalist in the early 1960s and exposed a gun-running caper in Africa. I'll track her down immediately."

"Samantha, this is Kyle, your brother. Can you hear me?" The phone connection to Santiago, Chile crackled and faded in and out.

"Hello, Kyle. What a surprise. I can hear you perfectly over the sound of my two son's yelling. It has been too long. Where are you? Are you coming to visit us? You will love the horses."

"I'm in Washington D.C. working for Professor Delamere who is now a Senator. I promise I will visit you soon, but first I need your help solving a situation we are working on. It's a sensitive case, and I can't reveal the details. We've found a person in England who interests us and may be involved in some illegal activities, and we believe you knew him a few years back."

"What's his name?"

"Nicholas Andropolis."

"Oh yeah, I know him. He's a Greek ship owner and lives on a farm in Surrey. Is he in trouble?"

Kyle hesitated and then dove into the conversation. "We're interested in an arms trafficking case, and his name has popped up."

"I'm stunned. Hold the phone—let me put the boys outside—I may have something for you." There was some shouting and banging of doors before Samantha returned. "My two-year assignment in Africa covered gun running. After the plane crash in which Brian and Dag died, there were several investigations in Rhodesia and South Africa, in addition to others in London and Stockholm. Suspicious characters disappeared or turned up murdered in Cape Town, and to my knowledge, the police and Interpol have kept the cases open. We all suspected that a European syndicate pulled strings and that well-placed people in Salisbury and Pretoria looked the other way. The police never connected the gun shipments with a ship. It seems to me that would have been easy. Andropolis runs a fleet of small, ocean-going freighters that ply the African coast. There could be a connection. Brian's father would know if the cases are still open and I need to call him anyway as we haven't talked in ages. Give me your address and I'll send you some pictures of Andropolis."

"Thanks, Sam. I think we will be talking again soon."

A swarthy man with a tailored mustache hiked up the path leading to the front door of Boynton's home. Sumner had been watching the man's assent from the moment he had left his car. His walk was methodical, slow and steady. Sumner opened the upper half of his Dutch door as the visitor reached the top step of the porch. He could now see the man's face, black eyes and thin lips; his mouth looked like an open scar that the mustache attempted to conceal. The man clenched a large envelope.

"I would like to speak with Mr. Sumner Boynton," he said with a Slavic accent.

"About what?"

"I am to deliver this envelope to him. If you are Mr. Boynton, I need to see some identification." No 'please' or pleasantry, just a deep voice, almost a growl.

Sumner accepted the thick packet, and the messenger turned quickly and retraced his path back to his car. Sumner scowled as he watched the car move up the front road, and then he headed to his office to view the envelope the importance of which required a messenger.

The bulk of the contents, maybe twenty pages, was a list of small arms and ammunition: automatic handguns and rifles, grenades, landmines, and bazookas, plus army gear for operations in the field. Boynton ran his finger down the list, his mind ticking off companies that could supply the item. He then turned his attention to a brief cover letter that reflected no date, address or name. It confirmed conversations held in Zermatt. Boynton's share of the endeavor included sourcing the materials and discreetly shipping to one of his distribution centers. There the arms would be created and carefully mislabeled and documented. When one of Andropolis' vessels had cargo for delivery to a minor US port, he would receive notice. Boynton snickered when he saw the shipping destination, Bremerhaven. The crates would never see a German port.

All of the financial arrangements would occur beyond US borders. He would arrange invoicing and payment to his suppliers. Lichtenstein was Andropolis' favorite off shore numberd account location, and he had set up an account there for Boynton as well.

The messenger would confirm the delivery of the instruction. Now, Boynton would be busy. For security reasons, he would deliver the orders in person to each supplier. He felt no joy or enthusiasm for the work before him. It simply was what he did and allowed him not to have to look life in the eye.

Carlyle sat at his desk clicking a ballpoint pen, his mind elsewhere. Melissa's abrupt departure bothered him for several reasons. She had gradually become an obsession; her face kept appearing before his eyes, her voice, her walk and that sly smile. He had exposed her to his partners in crime, which was reckless. If she were here, working in his office, under his thumb, he would feel in control and safer. *Why had she left in the night? Was his hand on her thigh so rash? Or was there some other reason?*

Carlyle reached for his phone and dialed his friend on the Senate Appropriations Subcommittee on Defense, the wily Senator Jordan from South Carolina. His crackly high voice came on the phone immediately.

"Did you ski?"

"I did and drank a lot of excellent wine."

"What about the people you met? Are you confident we can trust them?"

Carlyle didn't hesitate. "Absolutely. They are professionals and experienced. I was the rookie, in many ways," and he proceeded to describe his anxiety over Melissa's disappearance. "What do you think I should do?"

The southern drawl took over the Senator's conversation. "Do nothing and get on with your life. I'll send over a man who will know exactly how to handle this. He will ask for background information, and you will have to pay him out of your pocket." Carlyle heard a laugh. "You need me, Michael," and the Senator rang off.

27

TO REST

Spring 1968

Looking back on his selfish decisions, Bill Delamere admitted to himself that he had made a series of miscalculations. The life of a senator was strenuous and stressful, crowded with intrusions and long days away from home. The Georgetown apartment had not become a home for Madelyn nor did she take an interest in the garden. A gregarious woman, she gradually began to withdraw from her husband's life, rarely attended dinner parties and over the following twelve months spent half of her time with their daughter in San Francisco. She hated the weather, disliked Washington and loathed the politicians. Her life had lost meaning. The girl from Nebraska didn't fit, but not once did she suggest to Bill that they should return to California.

At the end of the first year, Bill and Madelyn returned to Palo Alto for Christmas. Their daughters joined them, and the family took long walks under a warm winter sun. Day trips to Monterrey and San Francisco invigorated Madelyn, deluding her into thinking that she was ready to return to D.C. When she did return in early January, a raw, cold winter greeted her, with endless dark clouds carrying occasional snow and rain. By February she began to experience chills and a mild fever, forcing her to remain in their apartment, usually wrapped in a blanket sitting before the always lit fireplace. Their doctor joked, "Welcome to winters on the Atlantic coast," and prescribed a steam inhaler to clear her lungs and Tylenol. As her condition worsened, Bill spent more time at home than in his office and in desperation, hired a nurse to spend days with Madelyn.

The nurse, a stern woman, now retired from a lifetime of working in hospitals, approached Bill after her first week of duty. "Senator Delamere, I'm very concerned about Mrs. Delamere's condition. Her illness is not a common cold. You just don't sit around waiting for it to disappear. Her shortness of breath and coughing are alarming. She should be in a hospital."

Bill called the Stanford Hospital and obtained an appointment with the leading pulmonary specialist. He then called his office.

"Mary Alice, please book an immediate flight for my wife and me to San Francisco. Pull some strings if necessary. I will be in later today to clear my desk. As usual, you'll have to take charge as I will be away for ten days or so. Make sure Kyle is in the office waiting for me."

Galloping pneumonia waits for no one. Madelyn's health declined rapidly. Each day in her hospital room, Bill sat with his thoughts, studying the face of the person who shared his life—his confidant, his love. She struggled for breath and slept fitfully. His world stood still, the future no longer clear. Their year in Washington D.C. had been a nightmare, his selfish dream an ordeal for his wife. Bill's heart was filled with remorse.

For one hundred years, the cemetery inhabited 160 acres of forested rolling hills east of Lincoln. The Lakota Indians called it Wyuka— "to rest"—and the name endured. Bill purchased a large plot near the top of one of the hills, close to a grove of Norwegian maple trees that faced west toward the University campus. Madelyn cherished her college years and the life she and Bill enjoyed teaching in a high school not far from the cemetery. The funeral had been in Palo Alto, so the burial in Lincoln was perfunctory.

"Mom will find peace here so close to the places she loved."

"Someday I will too," Bill murmured as he gazed at the grass near Madelyn's grave.

The warmth of the spring day comforted the Delameres. It would be a good day to fly. Bill would return to a desolate apartment and a demanding office. His life would never be the same and loneliness would enshroud it.

28

AN ESTANCIA

April 1968

Time tempers anguish as time passes. Kyle had met death in Viet Nam, yet Madelyn's surprised him; he had neglected her in his thoughts and selfishly focused on his life, and was unmindful of her declining health. Bill had allowed his life as a Senator to interfere with his personal life.

Delamere had called him from the hospital and obliquely asked him to come west and help as Madelyn's life was ebbing away. Kyle did not arrive in time. He found his friend and mentor heartbroken and surrounded by his family. Kyle helped with the memorial service and gave a eulogy. The following day, under dark clouds, he walked the Stanford campus—his mind brushing so many memories. On the third day, he returned to D.C.

He found the Capital in a state of shock over the assassination of Martin Luther King. Legislators were struggling again with the subject of guns and the second amendment. The assassin had used a rifle, transported it across state borders and the weapons' point of purchase remained murky.

In the back office, three files sat menacingly on the conference table awaiting Kyle's attention. Kasper and Holly had been busy but had reached a point in their research that they required a decision. They sat silently avoiding mention of Kyle's recent trip and Mrs. Delamere's death and watched him skim through the briefings.

Kyle turned to Holly. "You're being followed?" he said, more of an observation than a question. Her body language reflected no anxiety; she sat motionless, poised, studying Kyle like a cat before a birdcage.

"I think so," she replied. "I've seen the same man three or four times in locations where he looked out of place."

"Give me an example, and also, what does he look like?"

"He's short—well under six feet—stocky and wears clothes out of a 1930 movie. An overcoat and fedora, can you believe it? I would guess him to be well over fifty; he looks Italian. I noticed him in a café one evening, and again in a coffee shop frequented by young adults. Yesterday, in a department store, I saw him watching me. He surely knows I'm aware of his shadowing."

"Carlyle has panicked and hired a private eye," Kasper offered.

"Do we assume he suspects that you looked at his files?"

Holly nodded her head as she thought about this possibility; her auburn hair shimmered in a ray of sunlight that had found its way through the only window. "Yes, he must have. Why would he hire someone to follow me because I left—without saying goodbye? It's the info he thinks I stole, and I did read the files—and, he should be worried."

Kyle stood and began to pace the room. "Stop me if I'm wrong. He's been facilitating questionable weapon sales to foreign parties. His subcommittees never challenge the written authority Carlyle provides for the illegal shipments. He must be rewarded handsomely for taking these risks."

"Who are his customers and how do they pay him?" Kasper questioned.

"You will probably find your answers by checking out the men I met in Switzerland."

"You're right Holly, and Kasper and I will do that immediately. But I think it might be a good idea for you to disappear again. I'm worried about your safety."

"I don't want to go anywhere," she said, her eyes flashing. "I'm just beginning to enjoy this job." *And I'm enjoying being around you, Mr. Norquist.*

"You will like what I have in mind and its part of this investigation. We need to get rid of your shadow and find out what is most important to Senator Carlyle: your location or preventing exposure of his nefarious dealings."

"Where am I going?"

"You will need your passport and clothes you would wear on a farm in the autumn," Kyle said with a grin and then turned his attention to Kasper.

"Get me a list of every government body that looks at or approves the export of weapons. We will need to know which agency would ultimately interdict illegal shipments. I'm curious as to Carlyle's style of living, but we should leave that query for a later time. Let's meet tomorrow afternoon again."

Senator Carlyle rarely went into his office on Saturday, preferring the seclusion of his home study. But the detective had insisted on meeting in the Senator's office and said he would explain why when they met.

Carlyle left his inner office door open allowing him to watch for his visitor. Several others were working on this Saturday, and he didn't want them intruding. He saw the man enter, look around and when he spied the Senator, he marched up the aisle, entered the office and closed the door. Carlyle stood and began to move around his desk.

The stocky man said as he removed his felt hat and overcoat, "There is no need for us to meet formally. You know what I'm doing, and we should talk about it."

"That's fine with me," Carlyle said, returning to his chair. "What have you found?"

The visitor sat stiffly in his chair and handed a thin envelope to Carlyle. "Here is your missing secretary?"

Carlyle opened the envelope and studied the photographs. "Yes, this is Melissa. Who is she?"

"You are looking at Holly Saddler. She lives on Elm Street, works as a secretary for one of your colleagues, Senator Delamere, and has a clean and uninteresting past life. Do you have any idea why she posed as someone else and wanted to work for you?"

Carlyle continued to study the photos, remembering her well. "None whatsoever," he lied.

"As I understand it, she carried some documents from your office to Europe. Were they sensitive and is it possible that she looked at them?"

"Yes and no. The meeting in Switzerland was ordinary, and I asked her to bring some backup files I had forgotten. Mailing them would have taken too long. She could have looked but would have found them uninteresting."

"Show me where you keep the files in question."

Carlyle pointed to the wall cabinet.

"Why are they kept in your office?" the visitor asked. "They seem to be secure. Did she have a key?"

They explored the topic for another ten minutes, and the visitor left. He knew Carlyle was lying, but it was not his job to question why. This young woman had walked off with information that has set off alarms. Carlyle paid him $1000 in cash for his services so far and instructed him to keep an eye on Miss Saddler's movements, but to stay well away from Delamere. They agreed to meet again in one week.

Holly collected her duffel from the airport carousel, cleared immigration and stepped hesitantly into the throng of passengers heading to the terminal. A hand grasped her shoulder, and a deep voice asked with a slight accent.

"You must be Holly Saddler. I'm Ricardo, Samantha's husband." He grabbed Holly's duffel and pointed to a tall, blond woman wearing knee length riding boots and holding the hands of two small boys.

Samantha released her sons and stepped forward and greeted Holly with a broad smile and a hug. "We've been looking forward to your visit, Holly. Ric and I need to practice our English, and you will be on a horse before the sun sets today. Welcome to Chile."

"Hello, Samantha," Holly said in Spanish. "We'll trade languages as I'm rusty too."

Ric and Samantha's estancia sat in the middle of the grape growing region north of Santiago, nestled below the towering Andes Mountains to the East. Samantha's home was first a vineyard and second a horse ranch. Over the following fortnight, Holly would savor many new delights and pleasures which would remain forever in her life.

That first day in Chile, Holly slept until mid-afternoon. The yelling of the two boys pulled her from a deep, dreamless sleep. The autumn sun and coffee introduced her to the remainder of the day. The two boys, each holding her hands, pulled her across the yard toward a long, red barn. At the far end, in a corral, a Paso Fino stood saddled, sniffing the warm breeze. "This is your horse," they chattered in English. "Mamá and Papá will be coming soon."

Far off on the horizon, a cloud appeared, and it moved toward them with force. Two riders raced across the rim of the hill; the woman rode in front, but it was the man who captured Holly's gaze. His horse flew on the trail, yet the man sat straight in his saddle, showing no movement, just a grace that made him seem as one with his horse. It was surreal; the action—perfect and beautiful. The two riders rode with the wind at their back and Holly would soon learn that this was true in their life as well.

Later, well after sundown, they sat on the patio with their wine, watching a man season a leg of lamb and then place it on an open fire pit. While the boys helped with the cooking, Holly, Sam, and Ricardo chatted about wine, horses and Holly's life in America. Samantha asked about Kyle and how he coped with the loss of his arm.

"I've only known Kyle for a few months and can tell you very little about him. He arrived in January, took command of Senator Delamere's office, and I report to him. He's organized, energetic, and looks for solutions; the office already respects him. I like working with him because there is an absolute tranquility to him, a peacefulness that overrides ego and it envelopes those around him. I think you would say it's Zen-like. And, I might add that he's very good looking."

"Well," Sam said, "you seem to have fallen under his spell. I did too when we were kids growing up together. He reads a lot; did so when he was a boy. What can you tell me about his injury?"

"He doesn't talk about it. Long sleeves always cover his arm with just the hand part of the prosthesis visible. He moves his hand and arm naturally—authentically. Honestly, watching him use it is natural, and because it is so, I don't see it. It's part of Kyle. I wish I could tell you more. I didn't know my destination until Kyle took me to the airport and only then did he reveal that I would be staying with you."

"He was a good looking boy and a straight arrow. I bet nothing has changed'" Sam offered.

On the estancia, each day began with horses. Ric sometimes joined Samantha and Holly on morning rides, but it was Sam who wandered the stable inspecting each horse, their tack and guiding the men working there. Holly loved the physical nature of their activities: the smells of the barnyard, the sensual touch when grooming her horse after a ride, their conversation about immediate topics. She found the newness and excitement spiritual.

After riding, Samantha spent time with her children, ending with a mid-day meal and a short nap. In the afternoon, Samantha set aside an hour to talk with Holly. She began by discussing her background in Africa and how her experiences and contacts might help Kyle with his investigation. By the third afternoon, Holly had divulged her part in the story: her Melissa adventure, photographing the documents, and what transpired in Zermatt. She touched on Senator Carlyle's obvious but feeble attempt at seduction and her conversations with Nicholas Andropolis. It was the latter who interested Sam the most.

"It looks like you fell into a weapons trafficking scheme. I did too, seven years ago; the similarities are astonishing and having one character common in both stories ties them together."

"Mr. Andropolis mentioned that you spurned his infatuation with you."

"I bet he did," Samantha said, snickering. He likes fast women and a fast life; I didn't fit that mold, and I was dating a wonderful man, Brian Wellesley. At the time, I became involved in an assignment covering the Belgian Congo, just before it became independent, and discovered a wild scheme to smuggle guns into the southern province of Katanga. I never connected Nicholas to the subsequent terrible events. Wait, I have some photographs you will find interesting." Sam disappeared into another room and soon returned with a sheaf of pictures. "Look at these—our friend Mr. Andropolis."

Holly searched each picture slowly. "The farm is large. Did you see his animals?"

Samantha laughed. "I milked his cows and Brian and I swiped two horses and rode his forest trails. His home was rustic and beautiful"—she hesitated a moment and then returned to the present by adding, "Keep the photos and give them to Kyle."

Holly had been studying Samantha for the past few days. She was beautiful and a joy to be with, but in addition to all of this, she possessed an uncommon quality—an 'equanimity' and Holly realized that Kyle had it as well. Talking with Samantha about her brother had initiated a desire to see Kyle again and be with him more. "In addition to getting me out of town for a while, Kyle said you would know people in Africa who could help us in our investigation?"

"I've already talked with Brian's father in Cape Town. He was a respected barrister and South Africa's delegate to the United Nations. He quickly recommended two individuals, both with the police and involved with the gun trafficking in 1961. Here is their contact information. They are expecting a call from Kyle. Ian McQueen is the head of the National Police Commission and personally supervised South Africa's attempt to stop the vast illegal weapons trade. The guns were moving to rebel operations throughout Southern Africa. Jillian Pienar is the other contact. She is with Interpol and, apparently, still keeps an open file on the gun running incident that led to the shooting down of Dag Hammarskjöld's plane. As you probably know, Brian was on that plane." Sam's voice caught in her throat, and she turned away to collect herself.

"The head of the South African gunrunning syndicate was assassinated before the police could connect him to his superiors. Jillian is confident the gun operation mastermind is in England or Europe. She will be most interested in our Mr. Andropolis."

Holly and Samantha took a liking to each other. They talked endlessly, alternating between Spanish and English. When discussing Africa, Sam supplemented her remembrances with photographs. Holly wept when she listened to the story of Brian's death in the plane crash. Sam asked unending questions about the Peace Corp and Peru. "We are a lot alike, Holly. We must stay in touch."

This daily routine continued unabated. The day of Holly's return flight day arrived all too soon. Samantha's family had accepted her into their lives; the day-to-day activities were in a rhythm that Holly enjoyed, and it had changed her life. The two boys captivated her, causing her to wonder if she would have children. She felt relaxed and ready for a slightly refined version of her old life. She looked forward to seeing Kyle Norquist again.

29

ENTANGLEMENTS

June 1968

Two individuals followed every detail of the shipment to Egypt: Boynton knew the path and watched for complications; Kyle monitored each section of its progress—a revelation for both.

During the five weeks leading to the shipment, Kyle and Holly had researched every possibility, followed all clues and devoted every minute of their time looking for an illegal transfer of weapons destined for inimical buyers. They didn't know the source or the destination, but they were sure that the arms would travel abroad on one of the Andropolis ships.

Since returning from Chile, Holly had spent her working hours with Kyle in the back office. Her talks with Samantha about Kyle had created a curiosity, and as she admitted to herself, a persistent need to be near him. And now, working closely with him, her feelings were accentuated.

Kyle scanned the list of Andropolis's vessels and their existing deployment. There were eight ships, a modest fleet he thought, and he wasn't interested in the two tankers. The remaining six were small, multi-purpose cargo ships, around 40,000 dead weight tonnage (DWT) and old. A wealth of maritime information was readily available through government agencies, both in the US and in England.

"Holly, find a map of the world and let's pin it on the wall. We have six ships to follow. My guess is that one will soon head for a US port and it will be there that we'll find the illicit cargo."

"When will you inform the authorities?"

Kyle leaned back in his chair, cupping the back of his head with his right hand. The first time Holly had seen him stretch like this, it seemed unnatural and for Kyle, uncomfortable. Now it was regular and not noticeable. "There are so many government agencies that would be interested in our discovery. We have to decide which one before we go public with our investigation. The Customs Department for sure, and I suspect, both the Commerce Department and the FBI would be interested. My fear is that they would confiscate the consignment before we could track the source and establish the ultimate destination. Our intention is to quietly expose the people behind this business, probably your friends in Zermatt, and provide information to Senator Delamere that he can use to support his bill to stop the illegal sales of weapons abroad."

Holly slid an envelope across the table. "Here is a report from Jillian Pienar in Cape Town in response to your sister's inquiry. She has asked Interpol to review Mozambique and Angola port records from 1961 onward to see if they can connect any of Andropolis's ships to the time of a known illegal arms shipment. She says they should have done this much earlier."

"Good work, Holly. Let's keep an eye on those six ships. When one heads our way, we'll saddle up."

Sumner Boynton peered at a similar map although his depicted only the Atlantic Ocean and the ports along its perimeter. He too had to wait for the ship to announce its destination in the United States. He knew Andropolis was searching for a mundane product slated for the United States. Sumner prided himself on his patience.

His five distribution centers were operating profitably and efficiently. They were an unobtrusive cog in the connection between gun manufacturers and retail outlets. To render them even less visible, each was a distinct business, separately owned and operating under a different name. His pilot operation, Jupiter Industries, located in Virginia, supplied most of the East Coast. A subsidiary, Jupiter International, purchased all products destined for export and handled the packing and the multitude of required documents and licenses. The trading operation was scrupulous in every detail. Every aspect was above board; Boynton did not tolerate red flags.

The US government is a bureaucracy out of control. The various agencies responsible for inspecting shipments of weapons rarely talk to each other and are understaffed and underfunded. After scant review, they approve export documents and licenses so long as they reflect appropriate seals and signatures. If the port authorities looked in the crate, they would find what the manifest detailed. Red flags cause problems. And most importantly, none of the government organizations had his number. So far he had remained anonymous.

Boynton stopped his pacing and gazed out at the ocean. *It's beautiful,* he thought; *and today very blue and peaceful.* The offshore sailing weather had arrived, and he ached to spend time preparing his boat to sail.

Carlyle worries me. He's careless, greedy and egotistical—and any of these traits could cause a rupture in my plans. But for the time being, he provides an important element— accredited documents. Boynton returned to his desk, peered down at the map and then stabbed it with his finger. *Newport News would be the logical port and convenient for me.* He hesitated, and then moved his finger north along the coast, passing New York and Boston. *Portland would be perfect; small and off of the inspection agencies radar. We will soon know.*

The other thorn in the side of my grand scheme is Senator Delamere. He pondered this thought at length and ultimately admitted that he did not have a solution. Watching the Senator was Wilkinson's job. He made a note to call the lobbyist.

Six hours earlier, Nicholas Andropolis took the decision the two Americans, Norquist and Boynton, were patiently anticipating. Volkswagen's exporter had signaled that a load of automobiles was available for collection in Bremerhaven. The destination—New England—caught Andropolis's attention and he instructed his German office to quote a competitive freight rate. Portland would be the best port of call.

"A gentleman is waiting to see you, Senator, and he would not give me his name."

"Thank you, Miss Phillips. Please show him in. Carlyle expected the detective and was anxious to conclude his arrangement before leaving for Nebraska. His secretary returned with the poker-faced man who nodded to Carlyle and sat down without an invitation.

"Are there any new developments? Carlyle questioned.

"Nothing out of the ordinary. The Saddler woman disappears into Delamere's office in the morning and reappears in the late afternoon and heads back to her apartment. She periodically dines out with female friends and always returns home early."

"What about weekends?"

"Usually works on Saturdays along with two men, both about her age, both employees of Delamere. The younger one, Kasper Wilderman, took her to a shooting range in Virginia and then to dinner once. The other man, Kyle Norquist, is Delamere's chief of staff and a Viet Nam veteran. He and Saddler have left the building for lunch several times and, now recently, they meet for dinner. She lives an uneventful, uninteresting and unguarded life. It is as if she is an entirely different person from the women who worked for you."

"I find it astonishing that an amateur spy can plant herself in this office, gain access to privileged files, change her name and then work for another senator as if nothing was awry."

"I don't know that she's an amateur. Appearances can be deceptive."

Carlyle muttered to himself as his eyes continued to glance at the wall file cabinet. *What exactly had she looked at, if anything? I should immediately destroy some of the letters to my international contacts.* He looked back at his visitor's bemused face. "She broke the law, yet to pursue that would achieve little and cause me some embarrassment. I haven't discovered what she was after. Until I do, let's back off, give her some rope and see what develops."

"As you wish, Senator Carlyle. Senator Jordan knows how to reach me."

Carlyle pulled an envelope from a drawer and slid it across his desk. "This should cover your efforts to date. I wouldn't want anyone privy to our little exercise, even Jordan."

The man pocketed the payment, nodded and like a late afternoon shadow, disappeared.

For Washington D.C., June is the precursor for the congressional recess and depressing, humid weather. On this Saturday morning, Kyle's apartment complex was a beehive of activity; everyone seemed to be heading out of town, many with bikes attached to their cars. *This weekend is going to be long and dull. I need to exercise, plus, there are so many historical sites to visit nearby. I need a car. Maybe I should visit some car lots—no, I better make some decisions on Senator Carlyle's illegal weapon shipment.*

The ringing phone cut short his thoughts. "Hello, Norquist speaking."

"Good morning, boss. It's a beautiful summer day out there, and I bet you're sitting at your desk. I have no plans and thought I could help you with your homework and then, maybe, take you for a drive into the Virginia countryside."

Kyle was startled and felt a wave of pleasure sweep his senses. Holly had never called him. "Hi, Holly, your call is a pleasant surprise. As you guessed, I am at my desk, and I'm looking at your stolen documents with no idea of how to proceed. As for the drive in the country—I'm interested. Come on over anytime. Do you know where I live?"

Holly left his last question dangling. "I'll be over in an hour or so and will help you on our project. Let's head for the coast for a late lunch; Virginia might be too hot. See you in a bit." She rang off.

Kyle's mind drifted; thoughts became entangled. He had developed a crush on this beautiful woman with whom he worked, and it was not smart to mix infatuations with business. Persistent thoughts of her occupied his mind, and it was distracting him from his work. He and Holly had been dining together, at first once a week, but now they were spending many evenings together. They talked easily as each delved in the others past. They had quite suddenly become more than friends. Kyle knew that if he kissed her, the damn would burst.

Holly's impending visit finally compelled him to clean up his apartment. An hour would give Kyle time to make the bed, start the dishwasher and vacuum. He put on khaki shorts and pulled a long-sleeved tee shirt over his head. Leaving his mechanical arm visible, bothered him. He had long ago accepted his forfeiture, but it was a slight inconvenience compared to what others lost in the jungles of Viet Nam. There was no pain, and his dexterity allowed the accomplishment of most fundamental tasks. There were, however, some challenges.

Holly arrived dressed for the seashore. She looked like a young girl: radiant, sylphlike and beaming with the brightness of the day's prospects. When Kyle opened the door, Holly shook his hand and headed into the kitchen for coffee as if everything was familiar. Then she did something that Kyle would remember forever. They stood looking at each other next to the small desk piled with papers. She swept her arms out and said, "I never see you in casual clothes—always a suit. You look fantastic." Holly, then, stepped closer and gently grasped Kyles arm, the prosthesis, and held it casually. She looked at him, her hazel eyes searching for his acceptance. "It's not as thick as I thought."

Kyle shrugged. "I don't dwell on it much. I'm glad you're comfortable with my artificial arm, many are not, and it shouldn't be a distraction to our working together." He said this casually and as if to make a point, lifted a chair with both hands. "Sit here. Help me with two roadblocks and then let's head for the coast." They sat opposite each other and Kyle arranged the stacks of documents.

"Have you read the letters Kasper photocopied?"

"I did," Holly said, "actually, several times. They were innocuous."

"A perfect word," he said grinning. "No mention of weapons, deliveries or promises. I've run a check on the recipients: government officials, military officers, bankers. None are prominent people, but all could be influential. What interests me most is the location of the meetings. He visited a roll call of Arab capitals: Beirut, Amman, Cairo, and Riyadh, plus some quick stops in West Africa. More surprising are his frequent trips to Lisbon, Malta, and Cyprus. Why Portugal? Are they interested in US weapons?"

Holly had been taking notes and looked up. "Agents in Lisbon could be representing factions in Angola. Cyprus offers a less conspicuous place to rendezvous with buyers from the Middle East."

"How come you know so much? Most Americans don't know the capital of their state."

"My father taught history at our high school and during dinner continued his lectures. He loved world politics, geography, and European history. I absorbed it by osmosis."

Kyle studied her with renewed appreciation. "What did you study in college?"

"I majored in history with the thought of teaching one day. Languages came easily, and I studied Spanish and beginning French. I never told you that I attended one of Professor Delamere's classes. It was in his home and I remember it as being exciting."

"Yes, his home sessions were stimulating. I was studying engineering but yearning to enter politics and make the world right."

"And here you are."

"Tell me, then, where does Carlyle fit into this escapade? You've spent time with him, met his clandestine confidants, set his appointments and congressional meetings—what's your take on him?"

"Want more coffee?" she asked, heading for the kitchen. She returned with the pot, filled their cups and remained standing behind her chair as if it were a dais. "Carlyle's a puppet, Kyle.

Someone controls him, and I suspect it's Boynton. I bet he runs the program, needed someone tight with the right congressional committees and agencies, and influenced Carlyle to join him with money—lots of it. Boynton supplies the products and controls the money flow. Carlyle assures a problem-free export and deals with the customers."

"Then why the meeting in Zermatt?"

Holly returned to her chair. "The business got too big and dangerous. They needed help."

"Where does the Egyptian fit in?"

"Ahmad Abdul Muhsin? I was not around him very much. His English was good, but he used French when talking with Andropolis. They're old friends and, I gather, have been trafficking guns together for years. Ahmad is the broker; he supplies the customers and takes Boynton and Carlyle out of the picture. They're still dirty, but safer."

Kyle adjusted his prosthesis, fiddled with the straps on his shoulder, hidden by his shirt, and returned his attention to this remarkable woman on the other side of the table. "This is too big for us, Holly. Involving Bill Delamere would do him a disservice. It should be turned over to a law enforcement agency, but which one?"

"What are our choices?"

"Carlyle uses the Department of Commerce and, of course, there is the port authority. The FBI would love to get their hands on this as their business is 'crime.' But part of this offense is occurring overseas. And I worry about their ability to keep a secret. We need an agency that operates at the delivery end and can coordinate the investigation with other countries. I have an uncle who would know what to do."

"Where does he work?"

"At the CIA."

Holly headed east toward the Chesapeake Bay and arrived in Shady Side, a small bayside town, in slightly more than an hour. They had not paused to eat at Kyle's and were ravenous. Down the street from the marina, they found a seafood café offering a deck with a view of Pirate's Cove. A laughing and boisterous crowd gathered on the sun-kissed deck to celebrate the arrival of summer. Kyle, holding Holly's hand, maneuvered through the tables and found a perfect spot along the railing. He felt a glow of happiness, an unknown joy that had not touched him for too long. Viet Nam haunted him; memories persisted to impinge on his daily activities, sapping any pleasures offered. But Holly Saddler's unexpected arrival on his stage had evoked his old sense of exuberance. They ordered beers and sat gazing at the busy harbor and each other. The cold beer quickly infused them, slowing down thoughts, bringing them to the moment. After finishing the beer, Kyle ordered a bottle of chilled white wine.

"Take a gander at this menu," he said. "I want it all. What should we order?"

"Crab cakes, of course." Holly smiled. "What about you?"

Kyle returned her smile with a twinkle in his eyes. "Here's my suggestion. We'll start with a plate of oysters, then have the crab cakes and finish with shoofly pie."

Holly held his gaze. "Aren't oysters an aphrodisiac?"

"Yes, they are," he smirked. "Let's order one large plate, and we'll share it."

They talked about many things during lunch, mostly about their early lives, families, and travels. Between the crab and pie, Holly asked Kyle about his wound, how it happened and the aftermath. People thought the subject to be too sensitive and skipped around it in conversation. Kyle liked her directness and related the entire experience. He described the scene, the grenade explosion, and his vague recollection while on the helicopter.

"The army field hospital surgeon removed my shattered arm from just below the elbow. I was unconscious. Later I learned that a less skilled doctor might have taken the entire arm, but this guy removed the shrapnel and repaired the upper arm well enough that all the central army hospital in Saigon needed to do was to clean the arm stump and stabilize possible infection. They never consulted me concerning the amputation. When I woke up, my arm was gone. I remained in Saigon for a few days before they evacuated me to an Hawaiian hospital. My father and mother came to Hawaii during my recuperation and helped me learn to use my new prosthesis."

By mid afternoon the heat had reached its zenith. Kyle and Holly strolled to the marina to check out the yachts and stopped on one of the piers stretching out into the water to watch the equipping of a sailboat. "My Dad and I sailed together a lot," Kyle offered as he pointed out several riggings to Holly. "We kept an E-boat at our Wisconsin home, which bordered a lake. In fact, everyone in the family sailed and raced on weekends. Our summers together were momentous. My siblings and I competed, argued, told stories and laughed together; we bonded, as families should. Let's drive down the coast and find a beach. I need to walk."

It didn't take long to find an open stretch of shoreline, although rocks dominated the beach. "Park up there," Kyle pointed to a motel lot facing the beach access. "Looks like there is ample room and later we can sit on their café deck."

It was tough walking. Apparently, others had given up on this beach for the path soon ended at an outcrop of larger rocks, boulders-size rocks, which prevented hikers from proceeding at high tide. "Let's sit here for a bit and then head back to that café," Holly suggested. They found a resting place sheltered from the merciless sun high in the west. She had quickly realized how much more she wanted to know about Kyle.

"How did the war, the killing, and your injury change your life or were you able to return home, somehow blot it out, and continue as before?" Holly was sitting next to him on the rock, in a lotus position, turned so that she could see his body language when he answered.

Kyle gazed at her, searching her eyes for intent and watch her hazel eyes surrounded by honey now shifting to flecks of gold. Her eyes consumed him, and his mind meandered. Finally, he looked away and began to assemble his thoughts. "Everything changed, Holly—everything. In the hospitals, I had time to contemplate my life, my existence before and which path I wanted to follow in the future. Strangely, my life before entering the army seemed imprecise and, in many ways, irrelevant. Yes, my childhood was immaculate, school rewarding and my family and friends important. It all looked like the galaxy I watched as a boy, beautiful and significant but distant and complex. This is tedious, isn't it?"

"Keep going; I want to know everything."

"My conclusion, at least, philosophically, was that life would only become vivid in its immediacy. I wanted to slow everything down and scrutinize the passing time and to pay close attention to what I was doing and to the people in my life. I had to do this for the repose of my soul." Kyle looked back to her eyes and then noticed her lips, slightly parted. He looked away.

Dropping from their perch, they cut through the brush and up the embankment to the road where they could walk more easily. They turned into the motel access road that ran in front of the cottages.

"They're booked," Kyle observed, noticing cars parked in front of each of the freshly painted beach houses."

"There's one that appears empty. Let's take a look." Holly marched up the stone steps leading to the deck, impetuously tried the door and then peeked in the large window. "There's a kitchen. They're little bungalows with a view."

Kyle looked in the window too, and as he did so, Holly turned to face him, and their bodies touched. He kissed her, ever so lightly on the lips, lingering, hoping for a response. Her eyes, contemplative and very gold, came up to meet his.

"Let's stay here for the night," Kyle whispered, more as a statement than a question.

She wrapped her arms around Kyle's neck and leaned toward him searching for another kiss. "Yes, I want to."

"You're lucky," said the proprietor, a large woman with gray hair dangling from an untidy bun on top of her head. "We've been booked for weeks, but these people just called to cancel for one night, so it's yours, but you gotta be out by eleven. Oh, yes, there's a bottle of wine in the fridge and some toilet articles in the bathroom."

"What about dinner?" Kyle asked, sitting on the edge of the bed.

"I'm not hungry. I only want you, all to myself, in this crazy bungalow by the sea." She lifted the bottom of his tee shirt and slowly pulled it from his head and arms. Kyle said nothing and felt her unfasten the harness from under his right shoulder which allowed her to pull the prosthesis gently away from the arm stump. Without asking, she retrieved a towel and wrapped it before placing it on the table near the window. Kyle stood, undressed and waited for Holly to come to him. When she stood before him, naked, she hesitated, and then reached up and pulled his face to hers. They kissed slowly, letting their tongues touch, and she felt his arousal. Unable to control her desire, she pushed Kyle back onto the bed and moved next to him. She giggled, and murmured, "Remember, you had an aphrodisiac for lunch, so be gentle."

Hours later, the rain pelting the roof awakened them from their love sleep. Kyle caressed her breasts with his good hand and then let it move to her bottom. Holly moved her legs and arched so he could enter her, and they began again. This time their lovemaking was less frantic and more thoughtful. When they parted and lay entangled and exhausted, Holly whispered, "Is this a fling or could it lead to something more?"

Kyle turned to rest his head on his elbow and scrutinize his bedmate. "I know about flings, and this is not a fling," he assured her. "You and I have a mountain of time yet to spend together, but let's spend it cautiously, thoughtfully and allow it to take us wherever it will. There will be something more, for sure, but tomorrows are not a promise."

30

FERRETS

July 1968

"Kyle, this is your Uncle Arne, returning your message. I apologize for taking so long. I was abroad in an area where telephone calls were difficult to arrange."

"Is this my favorite uncle? When you didn't return my call, I became concerned. How are you?"

"Gosh, it's been so long since I heard your voice. I remember our long chats at the lake and how you introduced a grounded lawyer to the galaxy. We should do that again—time is getting away from me. How is your father?"

Kyle and Arne chatted comfortably for a time, mainly concerning family and mutual friends and Kyle's battle experiences in Viet Nam. Arne was a senior officer with the CIA and about to retire.

"How can I help you?" Arne asked. "Is it something we can discuss openly on the phone? I know you are working for Bill Delamere. He's a good man; we need more senators like him in D.C."

Kyle began to explain his predicament carefully. "Senator Delamere asked me to develop background statistics to support his campaign to monitor our weapons sales to foreign customers. In doing so, I inadvertently uncovered criminal activities involving some prominent politicians, US citizens, and foreigners. A responsible agency should handle this, and I called you for your suggestion."

Arne didn't hesitate. "It would be best if someone from here visited you. I'll ask Mike Stein to call you this morning. He'll know what direction you should take and help make the arrangements. Say hello to my brother and promise me you will come to Langley for a long lunch with your old uncle. Talk to you soon."

Michael Stein had called Kyle immediately after Arne hung up and now, late afternoon, he sat in Kyle's office pouring over a sheaf of documents. Stein did not explain his position at Langley, but in his brief discussion with Kyle, revealed he knew his way around Washington and the bundle of intelligence and law enforcement agencies. Kyle guessed Stein's age to be about forty, and his accent and clothes placed his origin and education in the East, probably New York.

Stein finished his reading and sat back and studied Kyle. "Your report is precise on intended criminal activity and what's about to happen, but vague on your source of information. How the devil did you gather all of this material about Senator Carlyle, for example, or the Egyptian? This dossier contains serious stuff."

Kyle had prepared for this inevitable question. "We accidentally stumbled on much of it, and when we connected the dots, we knew we were in over our heads. Some of the information was provided in confidence, and I hope you will not press me for answers. It's our thought that if the right agency follows the trail, they will develop more than enough information on all of the involved parties. Senator Delamere's office must remain uninvolved."

"I can't promise that, but let me discuss this with Mr. Norquist, who I gather must be a relative. My guess is the Department of Justice will be keenly interested in this scheme, and, of course, the FBI would jump on it as would the US Customs Department. But my thoughts keep returning to a small agency burrowed obscurely within the Department of Commerce that would be ideally placed to oversee the investigation."

"What's its name?"

"OEE," Stein replied. "The Office of Export Enforcement is not well known. Whatever happens, my office will follow this case as well."

By the end of the week, Kyle had not heard from anyone. He, Holly and Kasper watched with concern the pin on their map, representing one of Andropolis ships, leave the Baltic and head into the North Atlantic. "It's coming our way," Kasper announced. "Now what do we do?"

"Which one of his ships is it?" Holly asked, squinted at the map.

"It's the *SS Argo*, a 38,000 DWT freighter, a perfect size for small ports. The name is a Greek myth, I think," Kyle said.

"Dead on, Kyle," Kasper announced. "Jason was the captain and they were looking for the Golden Fleece. This time, the ship is coming for weapons."

Kyle made his decision. "One of you locate the *Argo's* port of call—I would assume it's along our east coast. Then return to your study on handguns and the NRA involvement. We need to brief the Senator before his Judiciary Subcommittee forum. I think I'll pay a visit to Langley and ask for their help with our adventure."

Mike Stein ushered Kyle into a small windowless meeting room at Langley and introduced him to three people. "Al Shafer is Deputy Director of the US Customs Department. Since our investigation will begin on his doorstep, I felt Customs should work with us from the beginning. Bill Leland heads up OEE, and Doris Carlson runs their operation along our northern Atlantic seaboard."

Kyle settled into his chair, accepted coffee and nodded to the three faces looking at him intently. "I must say I'm relieved that you are involved; your assistance is essential. Where should we begin?" Kyle said, looking at Stein.

Carlson answered the question immediately. "We know the *Argo* is scheduled to arrive in the Portland, Maine outer banks in nine days and will sit until a dock becomes available. The cargo is automobiles, which will take two days to unload. Before that, the port will receive goods scheduled for shipment on the *Argo*."

"Do you have a manifest?" Stein cut in.

"Not yet," Shafer said. "The shipping company knows what it's picking up, but we only find out when the cargo arrives at our dock. We thoroughly check the cargo documents and randomly inspect the contents. My guess is that the load we are looking for will be easy to identify by its packaging, its destination and the identity of the shipper."

"Here are my concerns on confiscating the shipment too early," Kyle said, looking at Stein for approval to continue. "My bet is that the documentation will be immaculate. The shipper will be an ordinary company with an unblemished record of export shipments and, most important, the customer will be legitimate and an approved known entity. If we expose our hand prematurely, most of the individuals we are seeking will disappear into the woodwork. I think you should quietly follow the *Argo* and find out who receives the shipment."

"Do we know where it's going?" Leland asked.

Stein smiled. "Not yet, but we will when it departs from Portland. I would guess Africa, either the Mediterranean coast or the Atlantic coast. Al, you will recognize the 'package' when it arrives on your dock. Give it your usual attention. Doris, please scrutinize the documents, make copies, and call me." With that, Stein stood, thanked each of the three with a handshake and they departed.

"This couldn't be their first shipment," Kyle said, as he moved to the door. "I am most curious about the shipper. Will you let me know?"

"I'll keep you informed on all aspects of this case," Stein replied.

31

RAGE

August 1968

Chairman: "Good morning on this hot August day. Please be seated so that we may begin this meeting."

The ruckus abated as chairs scuffed and the packed room settled in for the much-anticipated debate. Three members of the Senate Judiciary Committee sat on either side of the Chairman, each backed by their staff. Bill Delamere sat to the left of the Chairman, Kyle behind him and Holly in the rear, taking notes.

Chairman: "My colleagues and I, representing a quorum of the Senate Judiciary Committee, have assembled here this morning to address and, I hope, rectify certain clauses that have caused a stalemate in the Senate and a temporary halt to our draft of the Gun Control Bill. Guns, and by that I mean long guns and handguns, have been a part of this nation's history, beginning before the Revolutionary War, to our terrible Civil strife and the movement westward for exploration and settlement. The intent of the bill is not to take away the right of citizens to own and in certain situations carry weapons, although the firearm classification might someday necessitate revision. It is apparent that the overwhelming majority of Americans want laws governing the sale and use of guns. The assassinations of Rev. Martin Luther King and Sen. Robert Kennedy this year have heightened our awareness of the lack of reasonable firearm laws. Today we meet to do something about it. The seven members of the 'Committee' may debate the bill among themselves. We have invited four individuals, as our guests, to participate in our conversation. They each bring divergent views on the issues before us, which could alter our opinion of thorny segments of the bill. The press is welcome to listen and report, but should not ask questions during this session. And so, without further comment, let us begin."

The guests sat, along with the press, in a pit-like area below the seven senators. A rectangular wooden table sat in the center of this space, the surface empty except for three microphones. A well-dressed man with a seemingly large head walked to the table and stood alone behind the center chair.

Chairman: "Thank you for joining us this morning. This gathering is for an informal discussion; an oath is not in order. Please be seated and state your name and occupation."

O'Malley: "Good morning, Mr. Chairman. My name is Cobb O'Malley. I am the Executive Vice President of the National Rifle Association and Director of Development. Our President, Rex Sloan, asked me to participate in your discussion." O'Malley's eyes were a cold gray, belying his deferential face.

Chairman: "Are you familiar with the Gun Control Act draft bill?"

O'Malley: "Yes, I've read it through several times."

Senator Bobby Steed: "Before we get to the bill's details, I'd like to know more about you and the NRA. Briefly, what is your background?"

O'Malley: "I grew up in Missouri where my father taught me to hunt, mostly upland game. He smiled as he spoke and made eye contact with Steed. I have an undergraduate degree in Government, a law degree, and as a Marine Officer, I experienced battle in Korea."

Steed: "The country thanks you for your service. I would judge that you are familiar with most types of handheld firearms, which is a perfect background for our discussion. Tell us something about the NRA's activities."

O'Malley: "In three years we will celebrate our centennial anniversary and, of course, during this time, many of our undertakings have changed. Essentially, today, we are a nonprofit organization dedicated to the safe and intelligent use of firearms used in all types of hunting and target shooting."

Delamere: "How do you educate your members?"

O'Malley: Cobb had been thoroughly counseled and briefed on Senator Delamere and was ready for rigorous questioning. "Well, we publish several magazines which include articles on firearm use and safety."

Delamere: "Do your magazines include ads for guns?"

O'Malley: "Yes; they are a source of revenue, which helps to cover our publishing costs."

Delamere: "Wasn't the rifle used to assassinate Martin Luther King purchased from a mail-order firm's ad in your magazine *American Rifleman*?"

O'Malley: *I knew this dumb-ass senator would get to this.* "Yes, I believe that is correct."

Delamere: "I know it's correct. What else does the NRA do?"

O'Malley: "Throughout our history, we have focused on the use of guns for hunting: safety, maintenance and competency. We work with gun clubs to monitor the health and sustainability of game birds and the culling of game animal herds to assure their proper health and populations. Also, we sponsor target shooting matches for young adults."

Chairman: "You do the same for the skeet shooting enthusiasts and, if I'm not mistaken, you are involved in the recruiting and sponsorship of Olympian shooters."

O'Malley: "That's right. We are particularly proud of our work with youth organizations."

Delamere: "All of what you are describing has pretty much to do only with rifles. Explain to us where you stand on the promotion and use of handguns?"

O'Malley: *Shit, here we go. I knew he would eventually zero in on pistols. I must be careful.* "Public enthusiasm for handguns is relatively new; a lot of it comes from Korean and Viet Nam vets. We are promoting the same rigorous safety procedures for pistols as we do for rifles."

Delamere: "You say you are the NRA's Director of Development. What exactly does that entail?"

O'Malley: "I spend almost all of my time in the field working with gun clubs, sporting goods outlets, hunting conferences and our youth target shooting safety programs."

Delamere: "Are you also calling on members of Congress?"

O'Malley: "I do, periodically. We would like our elected officials to be aware of our good work."

Delamere: "The NRA, as I understand it, is an officially accredited lobby organization. Why would you spend your member's money to entertain politicians and finance their activities?"

A buzz spread through the spectators and the Chairman rapped his gavel.

O'Malley: "I'm sure you are aware, Senator, that our membership is expanding and that the mood of the country supports our endeavors. Our liaison with members of Congress is to assure their support for the Second Amendment. In doing so, we speak on behalf of our membership. We are not a lobby for the munition industry; I believe there are several lobbyists, Cliff Williamson is probably the most respected."

Delamere: "Rifles are the stuff of your history, but why the obsession with handguns? What is your purpose to promote the proliferation of handguns? Do the citizens of America need to possess pistols?"

O'Malley: "There are violent and sick people roaming our streets threatening good citizens. Our members want handguns for their protection."

Delamere: "One provision in the bill we are discussing covers gun registration which would prevent the sale of a weapon to a felon or a mentally defective person. Licensed dealers would be required to screen buyers. Would the NRA object to a law providing these requirements?

O'Malley: "I assume the A.T.F. would oversee the enforcements. I have to take your question under advisement, but I might add that our members are troubled over the federal government's infringement of our freedoms."

Delamere: "Except target shooting, what is the ultimate purpose of a handgun?"

O'Malley: "Well, as I just said, we encourage our law-abiding members to carry a gun for self-defense."

Delamere: "I thought that is why we have law enforcement agencies. But going to my question, my definition of a gun is that it is a tool used to kill."

Chairman: Time is running away from us, Bill, perhaps you could wind-up your questioning of Mr. O'Malley, which would allow us to break for lunch.

Delamere: "Mr. Chairman, with the limited time remaining, I would like to summarize my position on the various gun issues facing not only Congress but our country. As you know, I'm a college professor at heart, and this term as a Senator is a hiatus from school. My students taught me many things, one of which was that every quarrel has several points-of-view. I gather from our discussion this morning that the National Rifle Association's main concern is government's encroachment on the rights of gun owners. Which rights are we worried about? To own a pistol is one thing but to carry it in public places is another? I believe that is the central concern of the American public and they are not alarmed by hunting and skeet shooting. To settle an argument using a pistol is a frightening thought. Rage is a common emotion, and it is now more evident with the growing complexity of our lives. Road rage, gang disputes, marital arguments are examples of situations that could lead to tragedy if a loaded gun was readily available. A ready supply of handguns will aggravate this situation.

"Additionally, I see the NRA becoming a subsidiary of the gun industry; a virtual lobbyist, if you will. It is spending less time protecting the freedoms of its membership. Soon the gun industry will be free to sell all types of firearms, including military assault weapons, to the public. If left uncontrolled, I forecast that within a decade we will have more guns floating around this country than there are people. Our streets will become battlegrounds. Our police will come under fire.

"Our forefathers never dreamed that the Second Amendment would produce this social dilemma. They were worried about arming their militias. The British, however, are no longer coming.

"The Gun Control Bill we are debating is a small single step to protect our citizens and help our law enforcement agencies by licensing gun dealers and restricting some categories of firearms. I urge my colleagues to consider these concerns and agree to pass this important bill on reconsideration.

"Thank you, Mr. Chairman, for your patience and Mr. O'Malley for his tolerance of my passion on this matter."

32

RESOLUTIONS

September 1968

The conspirators orchestrated their gun trafficking scheme with perfection and the fact that no one person knew every aspect of the plan made it brilliant. The cabal members knew each other but never questioned the other's activities or competency. The Argo shipment exemplified their perfection.

The demand for American-made weapons began to escalate in the late 1960s. Small nations fought their neighbors, political factions within a country battled, and it seemed that every tribe in Africa needed to settle a grudge with a gun. The US munitions industry offered advanced and sophisticated weapons in a variety that was attractive to people at war. And America's bureaucracy and obsession with its war in Asia provided unhindered avenues for the guns to travel.

Egyptian history was replete with nefarious activities in African and Mid-Eastern countries. Geographically well positioned, governed by a military junta and blessed with the Suez Canal and sea-lanes to the world, Egypt offered an ideal location to broker trafficking operations. Ahmad Abdul Mahsin's family reached back over a century to trading endeavors, both in goods and humans.

Ahmad's connections were vast within Egypt and Africa. He knew who wanted weapons and whether or not they could pay for them.

Money, it seemed, was not a large problem for his clients. They robbed, exploited and stole what they needed and foreign entities interested in their success would often provide funds. Even US Aid found its way into dirty hands.

Ahmad had the contacts but needed help in three connected areas to assure success for his undertaking: unfettered access to US weapon manufacturers, assurance that the US government would not hinder shipments, and a means of distribution. When he met Nicholas Andropolis at a London party, he solved the delivery problem.

Kyle took the call from Michael Stein in his office. "Good morning Mike, any news?"

"Three forty-foot intermodal containers arrived on the Portland dock yesterday. Jupiter Industries in Fairfax, Virginia is the shipper of record. I can probably see them from my window here at Langley. We are checking them out as we speak. Doris Carlson, whom you met in my office, opened one container—a routine duty. Now, are you ready for this? Wooden crates occupied about two-thirds of the cubic space, yet the container weighed 50,000 lbs. Jupiter's documents correspond exactly to the Argo's bill of lading; both stating clearly that the contents of the crates include weapons and ammunition."

"What kind of weapons," Kyle asked.

"Now the story becomes fascinating. With a few exceptions, all crates contain the same quantity of items such as assault weapons designed for military use, 45 mm semiautomatic pistols, ammunition, and grenades. A few of the crates housed landmines. The paperwork for the other two containers declares they are the same."

"Who is the consignee for all of this stuff?"

"The Egyptian Army Military Police Corps is the listed recipient, and the port of delivery is Alexandria. Oh yeah, one of the stipulations is that the containers must be housed in the ship hull, not on the open deck."

"I wonder why?" Kyle said, his whole body tense with excitement and curiosity from the drama developing. "What government agency authorized this shipment of weapons to a foreign destination?"

"That's strange as well. The State Department signed off on this, not the Department of Defense. We're going to let the shipment sail and see who these guys are and who gets the arms. The FBI won't like not being in charge, so we'll let them know just after the ship departs. The Argo will arrive in Alexandria in twenty-two days. During that time we'll check out Jupiter Industries." Stein paused and then added, "I know Senator Delamere is working on a draft bill covering this sort of activity. Please make sure he uses the stuff we have developed judiciously. Cheers."

The press reported on Delamere's interrogation of Cobb O'Malley in unabridged detail. O'Malley had called Cliff Williamson seeking direction and Cliff had then telephoned Boynton. *This mad professor from California and I are working on the same two endeavors except our intent is different. He wants the government to restrict both, and I am in the business of expanding them.* Sumner idly reached for the phone and then placed it back in the cradle. *How do I make the Senator go away? He's squeaky clean and bellowing banality. He planted one of his clerks in Carlyle's office, and exposure of that deceptive act would be to his embarrassment, but it would also cause awkwardness for Carlyle.* Sumner decided to wait a few days before doing anything about Delamere. *When the Argo is on the high seas, he would know half of his business was moving smoothly. He needed to talk with Nicholas; he would know what to do.*

"A jolly good morning to you, Sumner," Nicholas's voice came through the trans-Atlantic call, clear and crisp. "I hope your morning weather is breaking as fine as our day just finished. I can smell autumn."

Boynton plodded to the kitchen in his slippers, retrieved his mug of coffee and then headed to his desk. "Hello, Nicholas. Glad you called. We have much to discuss."

"Before you start on your list, I'm pleased to report that the Argo left port unhampered and is on the high seas. The crew is unloading the containers and replacing the arms with something of similar weight. Once the ship leaves Alexandria, delivery will span three weeks. Our customers will wire payment to our Cayman account. Have you instructed our bank on disbursement?"

"Yes, they already have Jupiter's statement, which is identical to the one included with the documents at the point of shipment. Jupiter will pay the weapon manufacturers and retain a small profit. The entire transaction is clean and standard."

"Who owns Jupiter?"

"A Delaware Corporation," and Boynton added, "which in turn is run by a Luxembourg company."

Andropolis cogitated before committing to his next statement. "Wire my share to Liechtenstein as before, and I'll take care of our Egyptian friend. Carlyle is your responsibility. I'd like to pause before we accept new orders. I sense some rumblings in the bush which make me nervous. Someone is investigating me; I think it probably is Interpol and stems from an African activity back in 1961. I'm quite clean, but I do have some competent people checking for me. Now, tell me about your Senator Delamere."

Boynton drained his coffee mug as he watched the small crafts leave the marina and point toward the ocean. *It looked choppy; white caps and formable waves.* "Delamere is the most outspoken and strident voice in the Senate on two draft bills, both dealing with weapons. Both houses of Congress are dragging their feet on gun issues and are overwhelmed with civil right legislation and concerns over our involvement in Southeast Asia. He is like a terrier, he won't let go, and it appears he will bring both bills to a vote next month. His actions will force the government to supervise more carefully our weapon exports. He has five more years in the Senate. I wish there was a method to make him go away."

Andropolis waited for Boynton to continue, hoping for a suggested solution, but only static prevailed. *This business has become too complicated, too fraught with danger and repercussions. The fascination of trafficking guns is gone, and I'm no longer interested in the outcome of small, armed conflicts in the subcontinent. I have everything I want—life is good—I should retire. I'm too old for this.* These thoughts flooded his mind as he waited for Boynton to offer a solution. Finally, and he was surprised at Boynton's indecision, he offered a difficult but effective solution. "He should be eliminated. You choose the time, the place and provide the weapon and I will send an executor. He will require assistance on logistics and a library card."

"A library card!" Boynton exclaimed.

"He likes to read during his down time."

33

KILLING

October 1968

M ike Stein stood on the other side of the security barrier in the CIA headquarters' lobby waiting for Kyle to clear. Together they walked to the elevator and ascended to the third floor. A middle-aged man in a gray suit stood at the far end of the conference room, his eyes surveying Kyle as they entered the room.

"Kyle Norquist, meet agent Robert Gieg from the FBI," Stein's introduction was without embellishment. Kyle had always been observant, of things and people—and the galaxy too—and he could find no unique feature in this man from the Bureau. He was a man one would not recognize a week after meeting him. Gieg shook hands, offered a hushed greeting and sat quietly waiting for Stein to take charge.

"I have briefed Robert on the Argo shipment, and the FBI is willing to work with us until we determine the destination of the arms and the people involved in the delivery. Your exposure, Kyle, is peripheral. The FBI has agreed to neither acknowledge nor include your office in the ongoing investigation. We both wanted to express this to you in person so that when you leave here today, the door will close on your participation." Stein turned to Gieg. "Have I stated our position correctly, Robert?"

"We wouldn't normally do this," Gieg said evenly, "but we're not willing to expose Senator Delamere's office to the fallout from an investigation that will take some time and might become nasty. We expect Congress to sign the Foreign Military Sales Act this month, thanks to the leadership of Delamere, and this case could emerge as the first victim of the law. Mike and I have agreed that his people will continue to monitor related activity on foreign soil and report to me. Once we have sufficient evidence, the Bureau and the Attorney General will take charge."

"Did the Egyptian Military Police take possession of the containers?" Kyle asked.

"They did. The police delivered the containers to their cadet compound near Cairo where the contents of metal furniture, mostly barrack beds, was unloaded without fanfare."

Kyle looked at Stein with astonishment. "What happened to the crates of weapons?"

"They're still on the Argo, which is docking in Benghazi, Libya as we speak."

"We have many questions," Gieg added. So far, every entity we have investigated has been above board and forthright with its response. The arms manufacturers are well-known, old-line American companies who delivered against proper documents. Jupiter is one of five gun distributors owned by a Delaware Corporation. A small British shipping company owned by a Greek family owns the Argo. It's an intricate network of evil which we will unravel."

"Thank you," Kyle said. "I have one favor to ask. Senator Carlyle is involved in some way. I hope you can keep my staff completely separate from your inquiries."

On October 22, 1968, President Lyndon B. Johnson signed into law two Acts: The Gun Control Act of 1968 and the Foreign Military Sales Act of 1968. Both were moderate in scope but recognized the need for the Federal Government to take stronger measures in controlling the sale of weapons at home and abroad.

> Upon signing the Act, President Johnson said:
> "Congress adopted most of our recommendations. But this bill—as big as this bill is—still falls short because we just could not get Congress to carry out the requests we made of them. I asked for the national registration of all guns and the licensing of those who carry those guns. For the fact of life is that there are over 160 million guns in this country—more firearms than families. If guns are to be kept out of the hands of the criminal, out of the hands of the insane, and out of the hands of the irresponsible, then we just must have licensing. If the criminal with a gun is to be tracked down quickly, then we must have registration in this country. The voices that blocked these safeguards were not the voices of an aroused nation. They were the voices of a powerful lobby, a gun lobby that has prevailed for the moment in an election year."

Bill Delamere stood smiling in the foyer of his office greeting well-wishers. The two gun bills were now laws and the press had given Delamere credit. A wave of appreciation from the general public muted the NRA membership outcry. *The public would move on, but the NRA would not forget,* Kyle thought, as he navigated the crowd with a bottle of Champagne. President Johnson's congratulatory note lay under glass on a table near the temporary bar. The guests trickled away by late afternoon along with the office staff, leaving Kyle, Holly and Mary Alice to supervise the cleaning crew. The senator's perceptive secretary had observed the developing relationship between Kyle and Holly but resisted a comment.

"Kyle, do you plan to travel with Senator Delamere to Nebraska next month?" Mary Alice asked.

"I offered, but he wanted to make the trip alone. He plans to spend several days in Lincoln visiting old friends and, of course, Madelyn's grave site. I suggested he continue to California and take a few weeks off. He's exhausted."

"He will give a major address to the University on November 7th. The press anticipates an indictment of the war in Viet Nam," Holly added, "but it's not about that at all. I'm still editing the speech."

"I bet it's a world full of guns," Mary Alice offered.

"No, it isn't at all. The Senator's subject is complex, yet beautiful when you listen carefully to his ideas. He talks about 'understanding': appreciating other people's ideas and opinions, truly understanding our convictions and recognizing that the world is interconnected and our place in it is infinitesimal."

As Kyle listened to Holly, his mind drifted back in time to when he was a student and had fallen under the spell of Bill Delamere's wisdom and foresight. *He was even then way ahead of his contemporaries and so right. He's a sage.* "It's a wake-up call. Good night, Mary Alice." Kyle opened the door for Holly, and the two headed for an Italian café near his apartment.

Sumner Boynton had reached two conclusions; both of which would alter his life inexorably. The decisions were emotional, not cognitive, and he instinctively knew in his gut that the time had arrived to make both. He paced about his Old Saybrook home, pausing to touch something, a chest here, or a book there, things that preserved a memory. This house was his, every board and brick, he built it and only he had lived in it. He loved it like he had his grandfather, so long ago, and like everything in life, the house would become a memory. He was, by any standard, a wealthy man. He lived simply and frugally and had squirreled away his savings in remote nests.

He had decided to involve Cliff Williamson in his consulting arrangement with the weapons manufacturers. He would make it sufficiently lucrative to prevent Cliff from rejecting the offer. His Delaware Corporation would continue to receive a share of the fees and Cliff would manage the distribution centers. He would explain that he needed to take an extended leave of absence, provide no details, and simply disappear.

He had a lot to do, and quickly: sell the house, the boat, and the car. Close bank accounts, cancel credit card accounts and pay a technician to expunge everything on his computer. He had some reserves in the Cayman Islands, but he held most of his cash assets in a numbered account in Luxembourg. Sumner Boynton knew where he would spend the rest of his life. The authorities could search the Caribbean and the Mediterranean to their heart's content, but they wouldn't find him. They would never track him down. And best of all, he had a home, just like the one he was sitting in, already built and waiting for him. Pappi Lukas would be smiling.

Andropolis had made the other decision for him, and Nicholas's man would arrive on Sumner's doorstep within the week. This man would enter and leave the country like a shadow, question nothing, travel discreetly and carry out his task. He would need money, mostly small bills, and Boynton had $5000 ready in his desk drawer. And the irony of the plan was that he would need a gun. Boynton stopped his pacing in front of the antique chest and unlatched the double doors. The box containing the Smith and Wesson 45mm semi-automatic and a cartridge clip rested on a shelf. He had purchased the pistol off the street. The filed serial number prevented tracing it. Andropolis had given him no warning on what weapon the assassin preferred. Always thorough, Boynton had also procured a standard Remington rifle, a model 700, 30-06 with a 26-inch barrel, and a telescopic sight. Its size would make it harder to carry in public. The rifle offered pinpoint accuracy at 400 yards. He had painstakingly removed its serial number also.

Two days later, the same man that had delivered documents a month before arrived mid-morning on his doorstep. This time he used the driveway and parked his car below the stairs leading to the deck. Boynton noticed the mustache and thought he had the features of a Slovak. Again, they did not shake hands, but the visitor agreed to sit on the porch for their discussion.

His dark eyes poured over Boynton's face. "I arrived this morning and rented that 1967 model Ford," he said, pointing down the steps. I'm unfamiliar with American cars. Do you think it will make it to your west coast?"

"If you drive with caution, it will make it. How did you pay for it?"

"Someone in Europe prepaid all the charges. I can turn it in at any airport and walk away."

"Perfect," Sumner murmured. He couldn't refrain from staring at the man's lips when he talked. They were thin and moved awkwardly. "I have several items for you. Do you prefer a pistol or a rifle?"

"I would like a long barreled, centerfire bolt-action rifle with a good scope and a simple tripod. The rifle can be American, but the best scopes come from Germany. I'll need a box of cartridges so that it looks like I'm a hunter. There must be a store in your village that sells hunting clothes." His accent was slight and noticeable only if you hung on words—Serbian maybe.

Sumner led the man with no name into his house. The Remington lay assembled on a table. His visitor studied it in silence and then began to take it apart with precision. He was obviously comfortable with weapons. He packed the gun parts in a black carrying case and placed the scope and ammo in a separate grip. Sumner then retrieved the money from his desk and stacked it on the table. The man from nowhere zipped the bills into a pouch without counting.

"I have several more items for you. Here are some newspaper clippings, with pictures. The lecture is to occur at the University next week. Also, I have a layout of the cemetery and have marked the grave site. Naturally, I did not make any accommodation arrangements for you. I do not wish to know your travel plans. You and I have never met. I do not know you."

The stranger gathered his cases and headed for the front door. Sumner felt a chill sweep his body and stood rigid watching the departure. His voice surprised him when he spoke. "Here is a fake residence card you can use to access the library. I assume you have a passport."

Lincoln, Nebraska lay straight west of Old Saybrook, Connecticut; the driving time was around 23 hours. The Serb chose the northern route, fractionally longer, but it would offer him time to hone his skills in driving on U.S. highways, and I-90 would have less traffic. The weather provided pleasant driving as he headed north before turning west across upper New York. He stopped for the night in a town near Buffalo because he saw a large sporting goods store along the frontage road. He purchased boots, an American visor hat, a woodsman shirt, a tarp and a pair of inexpensive binoculars. He settled on a motel up the street, had supper in a diner, and returned to his room and fell into a deep sleep. He was still on European time.

The toll road I-80 took him rapidly along Lake Erie, around Chicago, across the Mississippi River, and into the Great Plains. At the end of his second day of driving, the silhouette of Lincoln, NB appeared on the horizon. The lecture would be in two days which gave him plenty of time to reconnoiter and settle in. He had studied English in Serbia, could read English with skill and had selected a history book of Lewis and Clark's expedition west. He would not use the library.

The next day he drove directly to the cemetery northeast of town. The Serb was surprised at its size as he drove around the perimeter. There were two gates, both open, one guarded by an office building. The road in the cemetery meandered which required him to backtrack several times. *He would need to memorize every detail of the route,* he thought. He found the grave site he was looking for on a knoll, forty feet from the road. The hill became steep on the far side of the site offering an unrestricted view of the countryside and a glance of the city to the west. Scattered bushes and a few small trees, recently planted, framed two sides with a wooden bench angled to face the grave and view. The Serb turned toward his car and surveyed the hill on the far side. It was an ordinary cemetery with footpaths wandering among the tombstones on the open slope. His eyes fastened on the top of the hill where a thicket of maple trees stood looking like a head of hair.

The road became steep and led to a small circular parking stop on top of the hill. There were no gravesites, just a few benches facing the view of the city. He walked into the trees on the north side, slipped several times on fallen leaves until he found a small opening in the trees and brush that offered a view of the gravesite on the little knoll about 400 yards below. Taking his binoculars, he studied the entire area carefully. He had remained alive because he was careful, prudent and patient. The trajectory was steep enough so the car would not block his shot. It was morning, no activity, so he decided to retrieve the tarp and establish a firing position, one that offered an open shot. After two hours of studying both his selected location and the gravesite knoll, the Serb felt satisfied and returned to his car and drove into Lincoln.

Senator Delamere had arrived several days earler according to the local newspaper and had spent his time visiting friends and giving lectures at the University. Tonight he would give his speech and leave for San Francisco the following day. The Serb called several airlines that served this route and found two flights: one at dawn and another in the early afternoon. The Serb felt confident his target would make a trip to the cemetery before leaving on the afternoon flight.

The following day arrived, misty with slate gray clouds low in the sky threatening rain. Good, thought the Serb. People would be reluctant to visit gravesites on such a gloomy day. Wearing his hunting clothes, he checked out and drove to the unattended rear gate of the cemetery and headed up the hill. There were no visitors, and the wind had abated. He found his secluded spot, assembled the rifle and scope on the tarp and then sat down with the binoculars to watch for his target.

At 10:23 am, a sedan stopped beside the knoll. The Serb moved quickly to the tarp and lay down next to the rifle. No one emerged from the car. *Is this his target? What if he is not alone? No, he would travel alone and turn in his vehicle at the airport.* He heard the slam of the car door and watched a slightly stooped man with wild white hair trudge slowly onto the knoll. He wore a dark raincoat and carried a handful of small flowers which he meticulously placed on the one grave. Then, he stepped back and stood at the foot of the grave; his head bowed as if meditating.

An average human heart beats about 42 million times a year. Delamere's heart had probably pulsated close to two and half billion times. Although his heart grieved in memory of his beloved wife buried before him, it was still robust and full of the love of life and ambition. The bullet defiled this perfection. It entered the Senator's back, missed the spinal column and punctured his left lung before passing through the center of his heart. Death was instant. He fell face down at the foot of Madilyn's grave, his arms outstretched as if he wanted to hug his wife as his soul broke free.

34

MAIDEN SENATE SPEECH

March 1969

"Mr. President and my Senate colleagues, I offer my warm welcome to those of you who braved this morning's inclement weather to be here for my maiden speech. This singular opportunity envelopes me with humility and a touch of trepidation for I am a member of this chamber through the confidence of one vote, the Governor of California. Except for a vicious act of violence, my teacher, mentor, and friend, William Delamere, would be standing at this lectern discussing the issues close to his heart.

"My responsibilities are clear: to represent the desires of my constituents in California, to exemplify worthiness of the trust given me by Governor Reagan and to accept the challenge of the issues begun by my predecessor. Senator Delamere was first and foremost, Professor Delamere, a brilliant and inspiring teacher of philosophy and history and these two ingredients and his service to this country during the Second World War, brought him to the conclusion that war and killing solves little.

"America is once again at war, squandering precious young lives and draining our treasury. The purpose of this conflict escapes me as it does many others, and I can tell you first hand that it is a dirty war headed for disaster. To understand that, one has to have been in the Viet Nam jungle, endured the incessant rain and exposure to death, and then, only then, would you know the ineffable sorrow and futility of war. It will be part of my mission to convince this august body to cease our involvement in what is a domestic dispute. Many of you will resist this point of view, particularly from an apprentice Senator, but I ask you to consider the long-term ramifications of our involvement. I believe you will find it ill-conceived, a terrible waste of human life, an unwinnable endeavor, and immoral as well.

"The Viet Nam War benefits very few, certainly not the Vietnamese nor, if you think about it deeply, this country. There are a small number of individuals and organizations rewarded by conflict; the munitions industry is a classic example. This inequity is worthy of the Senate's monitoring and regulation. I hope to present more on this in the coming months.

"By tradition, a junior senator's first speech should be non-controversial and brief. I probably have aggravated the first but to make amends; I'll now thank you for your generous time and will take my seat."

35

THE INVESTIGATION

April 1969

S enator Kyle Norquist sat at his desk thumbing through the morning newspapers. He had developed a knack for skimming and identifying news items relevant to his sphere of interests. Already politicians up for election in 1970 were scurrying for support and positioning themselves to survive in the troubling Nixon term. On page five of the *Post*, he spotted the headline: 'Nebraska Republicans Begin Search for a Senate Candidate.' His heart thumped as he read the article. Senator Michael Carlyle, influential two-term Nebraska senator, announced in a press conference held in his hometown of Lincoln, that he had reluctantly decided to retire from politics to devote his attention to his long-neglected family and other interests. "Life should be a blend of experiences," he said, "and this is the perfect time for me to move on. My colleagues might object, but I have always thought that my job as a senator was not a career. I feel it is a citizen's duty to help the commonwealth and so it is time for someone else to take my place."

Kasper Wilderman leaned on the doorjamb. "Good morning, boss. Did you see the article on our friend Senator Carlyle?"

"I've just read it for the second time looking for inferences. What do you think?"

Kasper smirked. "He's shitting in his pants and wants to escape Washington before he's investigated. And, as we suspected, he has stashed his illegal gun running profits somewhere."

Kyle found Agent Gieg's calling card and dialed the FBI. His call passed through several secretaries, and he finally left a message for Gieg to call him. "Holly is still troubled by the thought that Carlyle or one of the other men she met in Switzerland will involve her in the investigation. I'll be happy when they all move on; one way or another."

"Senator Norquist, this is Robert Gieg returning your call."

"Thanks for calling back. I see Carlyle is bowing out. Will he escape your net?"

"I'm very pleased that Reagan appointed you as a senator. Very smart and I sense you are perfect for the job. I read your maiden speech—it was right on." Gieg paused briefly. "Say we meet this evening for dinner? Mario's Italian Café is my favorite, and you can buy."

"No one will notice us here," Gieg said looking around the crowded restaurant. "Politicians rarely dine here, just guys who respect good food—like us." A bottle of Sicilian red arrived, and the two men perused the menu.

"I called you instead of Mike Stein because Carlyle presents a domestic issue. Will you pursue him to Nebraska?"

Gieg ordered grilled pork loin and then turned his attention to Kyle. "Stein is gone. Langley sends people out into the ether without a goodbye. I'm wondering if you would mind calling your uncle and find out who is handling this case?"

"I'll do that tomorrow, but Arne's tough to track down."

"Our position concerning Senator Carlyle is to propose a trade. We want to know all about the people he worked with, here and abroad, and other senators involved one way or another. Also, he has a lot of money that doesn't belong to him. It will take a while, but in the end, he will answer all of our questions. And if he does, we'll be lenient."

"What about the men who ran the export business?"

"Now it's becoming interesting," Gieg said. "The exporter, Jupiter Enterprises, is clean. It legally buys arms from US makers and ships according to official government documents. The nefarious activities occur once the guns leave our borders. Jupiter is one of five weapon wholesalers in the country, a major supplier to gun shops. Their handgun business is exploding—but that's another subject. The CEO is Cliff Williamson; a well-known retired US Senator and the principal lobbyist for the munition industry. The man he replaced, Sumner Boynton, operated in the murky shadows and now, suddenly, has disappeared. He sold his assets, parked the funds in a Delaware trust and overseas and left the US on a one-way ticket to Zurich."

"How does all of this relate to Bill Delamere's murder?"

"Delamere was assassinated by a professional. Someone feeling the heat of our investigation brought the killer into the country to dispose of Delamere. My guess is he has left our shores for good. We have developed small bits of information in Lincoln. The groundskeeper saw his Ford sedan at the cemetery, and we traced it to a motel. They think it had a Massachusetts license plate. We have a general description of him from the employees of a nearby café. Haven't found the rifle—a Remington 700—thousands of them in our country. We think he headed to the west coast and, as a long shot, we have alerted airport car rental agencies."

"What should I ask my uncle?"

"Is Mike Stein still working on this case? What are they doing about the Greek ship-owner and have they any idea where Boynton fled to? I could contact Langley, but you'll get a better answer."

They stood and shook hands. "Next time I'll buy," the FBI agent said, smiling for the first time.

36

THE EMBASSY PARTY

May 1969

The April drizzle had worked its wonder on the Washington cherry trees. Verdant gardens exploded in color, and exuberated floral shapes brought a sense of *Bonne Vie* to the drones of government. Spring is a season of embassy parties, and an invitation to the Embassy of the United Kingdom's usual extravaganza is the most coveted in the Capital.

Mary Alice placed the off-white linen textured envelope in front of Kyle and stepped back to observe the senator's reaction. Kyle eyed the gold relief crown on the upper edge and the title 'Esquire' after his name. He looked at his all-knowing secretary and asked, "Will it be black tie?"

"I believe it is. It's one of the social events of the year attended by diplomats from the world, prominent officials from our government, celebrities, and a few lucky Senators."

Massachusetts Avenue had become embassy row, and the British Embassy was the first and one of the largest. Situated in the compound facing a manicured garden surrounded by stands of mature trees, the ambassador's residence resembled an English country manor. Off to the side, welcoming visitors, a statue of Winston Churchill stood, his arm raised in the V for a victory salute.

The gentle evening breeze moved the floral scent around the garden and into the chanceries, where the ornate ballroom, already crowded at 8 pm, burst with the chatter of many languages. An enormous table laden with food sat under one of the chandeliers at one end of the long rectangular room. The waiters moved smoothly through the throng with silver trays of Champagne and hors d'oeuvres.

Kyle arrived late and by taxi. He knew few diplomats but was eager to blend with the guests and observe. He wandered the perimeter of the room, stopping to watch people and attempted to guess their nationality. He was tall, trim and the black tie emphasized his good looks. Women glanced surreptitiously. His artificial arm appeared normal in the tux jacket; only the black glove was out of place.

"What happened to your arm?" a military officer asked, stepping in front of Kyle's abstract watching. His eyes moved from the black glove to Kyle's face; he offered a tight smile and his hand. "Allan McFadden."

"Hello, Colonel. I'm Kyle Norquist. I see you were with the 4th Infantry Division. Were you in Viet Nam?"

"I was, off and on, through the sixties. I guess you were there as well and lost an arm."

"Half an arm. A grenade while on patrol near the DMZ." Kyle looked at back the crowd. "Are you now involved in diplomacy?"

"I teach counterinsurgency at the War College up the Hudson. My superior couldn't attend and suggested that I would enjoy the spectacle. What about you?"

"I'm a new senator trying to find my way around the Capital. I don't know a soul and was thinking about heading home."

"Now I recognize you, Senator Norquist. I knew your predecessor, Senator Delamere. What a terrible loss. Have they found, he hesitated, the assassin?"

Before he could answer, Kyle sensed an electric energy drawing him into it. He cocked his head slightly, looking over McFadden's shoulder, and through clusters of people holding glasses and laughing, his eyes rested on the beautiful face of an Asian woman who was staring at him. McFadden turned and followed his gaze. "Old friend?" he chuckled. "I hope we run in to each other again, Senator," and he headed into the crowd.

Catherine Lee floated through the crowd, her eyes glued on Kyle, no hint of emotion, just intent. She seemed taller than he remembered; probably high heels hidden by her long black evening dress. As she came closer, he felt the same energy and vitality he had experienced in college. And then, suddenly Catherine stood before him, her gorgeous light-brown eyes studying his face.

"I've been looking for you, Senator Norquist."

"Hello, Cat. I had no idea you were in D.C. I suppose it wouldn't be appropriate to embrace you in front of the many eagerly watching eyes."

"Maybe later," as her brilliant smile surfaced. She reached for his left arm and held it in both hands. "Do you remember our conversation on the Bergen Wharf? You were agonizing over the war and what you should do. There is so much I want to know about you; the jungle, the killing, and your injury. And the full story about that wonderful man, Professor Delamere, murdered at his wife's grave. You Americans and your guns!"

Their earlier conversations flooded his mind. He missed Cat's incisiveness, curiosity, and knack to avoid the mundane. "Two men are watching you, Chinese I'd guess."

"Unfortunately, my government feels I need security. They're careful men and remain in the shadows."

"So, Cat, dare I ask what you do?"

"I'm still doing what I learned to do when we bummed around Europe together, only I'm better at it, and the game has become dangerous. I'm a director of an SID section."

"You work for the Singapore Security and Intelligence Division if I remember correctly." Kyle nodded to her two watchers, took her arm and guided Catherine onto the balcony and down the sweeping steps to the garden. They found a bench and settled next to each other.

They sat without speaking, enveloped in each other's aura. "Are you married, Cat?"

"I was, but it didn't last long. I'm busy, travel too much, can't talk about my activities and have no time for children. My husband couldn't handle the baggage and an alpha wife. Asian men still place women a rung or two down. I like what I'm doing and its purpose. I'll probably never marry again. What about you?"

"I'm involved with a lady named Holly. We live in sin but have not committed to a long-term relationship."

Catherine looked around for her escorts and then at her watch. "I'm flying to Tokyo early tomorrow and have a lot to do tonight." She touched Kyles' hand and said, "I would have liked to spend a week with you at the sea shore, like the old days, but of course that is now but a memory. But maybe there is something I can do about Professor Delamere's killer. My small organization is perhaps the best in the world in dealing with gun traffickers. What can you tell me about the people involved?"

Kyle told her what little he knew about the assassin. But he had more information on the man he believed arranged the murder—Sumner Boynton. "The FBI says he disappeared with a lot of money."

Catherine stood and faced Kyle. "I'll have someone visit your office and collect any information and photos you have on Mr. Boynton. I will catch him, and then you will have to decide what should be his sentence."

"Will I see you again?"

"I'll find you when I come to D.C." Catherine reached up and wrapped her arms around Kyle's neck. "You are destined," she whispered, "for great things, my love. I will always be watching you." Catherine turned and without glancing back, strode toward the street exit, followed by her watchers.

37

FAMILY

September 1973

The mellow early morning sun brushed the yellow corn stalks along the highway. The fields of unharvested corn stretched to the horizon; a solitary tree seemingly lost from the woods broke the rows' symmetry. The air wafted pungent farm aromas: animals, earth, vegetation—the essential ingredients of life.

"This sure is a change from D.C.," Kyle said, his face glowing with pleasure. "Look at the farms, Holly. Red barns and white houses, one after another."

"It must be lonely out here in the winter. What do these people do to keep their sanity?"

"Feed the animals, drink brandy and make love," Kyle replied, chuckling, as he turned their rented Buick onto a rural road. The corn fields yielded to pastures, fenced homes for black and white dairy cows. "When I was four, and Europe was on the brink of chaos, my father and mother piled our family into the old station wagon, and we headed north from Elmwood to Wisconsin. I think, deep down, we wanted to escape from reality, but our excuse was to find a lake on which to sail and a spot of land to build a lodge away from the world's noise."

Holly had heard the story before, but this time they were visiting the memory, and it was vivid. Holly turned away from the rural scenery, her hazel eyes large and contemplative, and watched her husband's excitement build as he talked on about his family's history. *He is the most positive person I have ever known: kind, loving and posesses profound equanimity. How lucky I am.* "What led you to Emerald Lake?"

"The locals all agreed that this lake would be perfect for our dreams." At that moment the road topped the hill, and their first view of the kidney-shaped lake appeared. "Our lodge is on the far side, about five miles past the town at the west end." Now they began to pass small vacation homes surrounded by venerable red oaks. The village surprised Kyle for it had expanded since his last visit, adding shopping malls and parking lots. The golf course, no longer a clean break in the cornfields, now appeared smothered with homes along the fairways and the clubhouse was no longer visible from the road. They drove on in silence until Kyle announced, "See that narrow road ahead on the right? That's where my father had an epiphany. I guess he saw the grove of trees, was attracted and turned in." The entrance lane had not changed much; it still was not paved, and as it meandered through the woods, it reminded him of the freshness from the old days—a thing of beauty. They drove slowly through Gunnar's farm; the road still separated the house from the barnyard. "I worked here during the summer, and it was here, with Gunnar, that I learned about plants and animals." *And, I vividly remember French kissing too.* The lake greeted them when they crested the final hill, blue, choppy and full of sailboats.

"We are the advance team," Kyle said. "Quinn and Samantha and their families arrive tomorrow. I wanted you to meet the lake lodge quietly, on your terms, before the onslaught of children and noise. Arriving before the others will provide an opportunity for Dad and me to sit on the patio under the stars and chat, as we did so often when I was young."

Kyle and Holly strolled, arm in arm, around the side of the lodge and immediately spotted a sleek sailboat heading toward the dock with Lars manning the tiller and Erik on the main sheet. Kyle watched his father secure the E-boat and then drop into the skiff, which Erik rowed to the long L-shaped pier. He felt the special nervous tingle from his youth when confronted by his older brothers. It was different now, no need for showing-off; each possessed an accomplished life and the stretch of years brought them closer together. Kyle left Holly and walked toward the pier as Lars and Erik headed up the path. Kyle hugged his father with his good arm while their eyes absorbed each other's countenance. "Gosh, it's good to be with you, Dad. Are you ready for the entire family?" Turning to his brother, "Hello, Erik, are you still the best E-boat skipper on the lake?" They too hugged and laughed. The three men turned to watch a handsome woman talking with Holly and then she waved. *She must be Carla, Dad's flame.* When Kye came closer to Carla, he could appreciate her beauty. She greeted him with a warm smile and hug. "So, I finally meet the youngest and smartest."

"When does the rest of the gang arrive?" Kyle questioned.

"They trickle in tomorrow, in the afternoon, I believe. Come in; I have lunch waiting. Joyce and Erik's children are coming over later."

And so, the long awaited birthday weekend commenced.

Kyle and Holly were married in October 1970. They found a one-room church, a relic from the previous century, now no longer in use but well maintained by the village ladies who offered it for small weddings. The church sat proudly on a hill, suspended in time, and surrounded by wild flowers, which seemed to bloom in all seasons. The village, mainly a provisions center for wealthy farmers and ranchers, offered a lodge with a celebrated kitchen.

Lars, Elizabeth, Erik, and Joyce journeyed from Elmwood together, spent several days touring the nation's capital and then settled into the lodge. Holly's father and mother came from California. It was a casual wedding, which had caught Quinn off guard and on an extended trip to the Far East. Elizabeth was frail and failing and a year from her death. She hung on Lar's arm but insisted on joining every party—her last fling. Kyle and Holly's friends trooped in for the long weekend and booked the entire lodge. To everyone's surprise and the great joy of Lars, his brother, Arne, and his wife were there.

On the morning of the wedding, Arne cocked his head, signaling Kyle to meet him on the side porch. They sat in rocking chairs, cradled their coffee cup and looked out on rolling farmland.

"This is total peace," Kyle said. "I'm thrilled that you came; so is Dad."

Arne nodded and turned to face Kyle. "I apologize for taking so long to respond to your phone call. I had no information for you until recently. Gun trafficking is not a high priority for the Agency. It belongs to any number of international law enforcement organizations. We did find one ingredient that triggered our curiosity—the ultimate customers! So far the trail has led us to disgruntled minor tribes, militant elements of despotic governments, and a vast array of incipient terrorist groups. Some of the shipments ended in the hands of European corporations operating in Central Africa and, of course, mercenaries. The Egyptian and the Greek ship owner's connections to troublemakers exceeded our wildest expectation. We are working with our European friends, moving carefully, and following each clue to its end."

"I'm astonished. How long before you arrest the brain trust?"

"We don't arrest people," Arne replied. "We'll keep digging and learning. Eventually, England and Egypt will bring them to justice. But it will take a while. There are old mysteries that may unravel."

"Thanks, Arne. I guess my office can close our file on this escapade."

"There is one remaining item which might interest you. The Finnish police reported on a dead man matching the description of Mr. Boynton. They found him dead in his sauna in a village north of Helsinki. They suspect no foul play as it appears the lock on the sauna door malfunctioned, trapping him inside and the heat caused heart failure.

Kyle closed his eyes. *I never issued that sentence. I'm thankful for my exclusion.*

It was to be a Norquist weekend. Rarely did all members of the family attend a gathering; this was special. Lars would turn seventy, not a particularly significant age, but he had called the clan together and had something unusual to share. With the expectation of perfect weather, on Saturday evening, a long oak table, with ten place settings, would rest on the patio. Lars had raided his sunken wine cellar for perfect companions to the caterer's renowned culinary delights. And, of course, there would be the toasts.

Well into the night, the Emerald Lake Lodge rocked with laughter and activities. Holly had never known a family that was so full of energy, so much fun and so competitive. Her acceptance into the family was absolute. She quickly learned that her adroitness at chess, croquet, darts, and sailing needed honing.

PART IV

"…Ithaca has given you the beautiful voyage.
Without her, you would never have taken the road.
But she has nothing more to give you.

And if you find her poor, Ithaca has not defrauded you.
With the great wisdom you have gained, with so much experience,
You must surely have understood by then what Ithaca means…."

Ithaca

C P Cavafy

38

THE LAST SUPPER

Erik

Erik stood; his expression serious, and raised his glass as he looked at his father. "As I am the eldest sibling, it is incumbent upon me to launch the first salute of the evening, and I must admit to you that I do so with trepidation." A reticent smile softened his face and a nervous chuckle quickly followed. "That first line was written by the love of my life, the woman who has put up with my eccentricities and bad behavior. She has survived all of this looking more beautiful each year. I salute Joyce first for she is my avatar.

"And then, there is a man among us who is my inspiration. My father supported my every endeavor: football in high school, tennis at Northwestern, flying jets off of carriers and, perhaps the highlight, he taught me to love woodworking as he does and as his father did. One doesn't always appreciate one's father until later in life, and for some, sometimes never. I discovered my dad during my journey to desolation, an awakening from that gave me the strength to survive. When I returned, shaken and humiliated, it was my father who greeted me with warmth and understanding. He gave me a job and helped me find meaning in my life. I've never expressed this to you, my family, and I never will be able to thank my Dad adequately.

"One thing all Navy jet pilots agree on is that the moment of truth is when you approach the aircraft carrier steaming in rough seas. It is then that the pilot needs total focus as a miscalculation will cost not only his life but also those standing on the deck directing the landing. I stand here tonight with that same focus, knowing this is my chance to tell my two brothers and sister how important they are in my life and to toast my father and tell him I love him. Please raise your glass and join me in this toast of love."

Quinn

Quinn sat midway down the dining table between two blondes; his Norwegian wife, Mette, and his sister, Samantha. They both turned toward him suggesting it was his turn to speak. In his early forties, Quinn looked younger, bolstered by his fitness and relaxed nature. When he finally stood to speak, the intensity of his thoughts, with red wine swirling in his glass, added to the suspense.

"I have you all at a disadvantage because I know something you do not. I'll not reveal my secret except to tell you it is explosive and will impact all of our lives.

"As you know, I believe in the teachings of the Buddha. I spent a little time in an Indian ashram and many months studying Zen in Japan. I practice Zazen, a simple way to meditate. My discipline to do this has waned because of my travel schedule, demanding children and a beautiful wife who deserves my attention. I believe that there is no such thing as luck. People create their lives, and the source of that creation exists within each. Have a sip of wine and follow me.

"If that is true, explain this. I am of northern European extraction, male, born in this opulent and marvelous country to parents who were loving, thoughtful and attentive. We lived in peace; we never were threatened, and we enjoyed an elite education. Did I create this or was it luck. I've thought and thought about this conundrum for a long time. Contemplation and meditation have not provided me with an answer. For some unknown reason, my path eluded suffering. But what I have and what I am, I owe to a great part to my father. In fact, we all can admit to being humbled and grateful for our family, especially to the man responsible for this family. My father's insight and helpful hand have guided me through difficult decisions. He is an inspiration, and I raise my glass in a salute to this man, Lars Norquist, my father."

Samantha

Sam pushed her chair back and placed her hand on Ricardo's shoulder while she stood collecting her thoughts. Allowing her hand to remain touching Ric seemed to present a togetherness in what she was about to say. Her beautiful and tan face, thick blonde hair cascading over her shoulders and her fit body all delivered the picture of youth and energy belying her forty years.

"Last week," her voice caught in her throat, "a friend of ours was shot and killed on a Santiago street. The Chilean army, for no known reason, assassinated Victor Jara, a well-known singer and playwright. Victor would frequently visit us and join in camping trips in the hills. He was the face of love and peace; our children adored him. Darkness has enveloped Chile; politically, socially and economically. The law no longer protects its citizens. Chile is now not a place where we wish to live, and we have decided to move to the United States.

"For eight years Ricardo, our two sons and I have lived an idyllic life among our vines and horses, with the magnificent Andes looking down on us. Our joy distracted us from the growing political turmoil which has ravaged most of our country. Law and order have disappeared. Years ago I saw the same oppression and cruelty in Africa. I lost people I loved to its malevolence.

"I've waited until tonight to relate this story for several reasons. For the past six months, we have been moving our horses to a friend's ranch in Argentina. We sold our hacienda just before flying here, and we're thinking about buying a small ranch in Montana. We will become Americans.

"The move is an enormous change for us. We are excited about the challenge and being nearer to you. All of you are family, and you and we deserve being smothered in each other's love, so tonight let us begin. I offer a toast to my father. You know the old saw, fathers and sons compete, fathers and daughters have a unique relationship. After roaming the world, I've come home, and I want to spend time with the man who supported me on every crazy adventure, provided wise counsel when asked and gave my brothers and me a bedrock foundation for our lives.

"Lars Norquist, you are an amazing man, my mentor and inspiration and the best of fathers. I love you. Please, everyone, join me in this toast."

Kyle

Kyle stood and walked to the end of the table where his father sat. Kyle looked every inch a Senator in his height, stature, and bearing. He let his eyes rest briefly on each person and smiled when he looked at his wife. Where Kyle stood, he could not easily make eye contact with Lars, but their propinquity provided something more important. He began to speak, at first slowly, the timbre of his voice demanded complete attention.

"To know one's father takes a lifetime. As a boy, I was clueless, and my dad was just around. As a young man, I squandered endless opportunities to know my father better. I was the last to leave home which gave me many chances to talk with my father, and my mother, as well; to dig a little to find out what they thought about life. I wanted to know about their parents and their youth. Our conversations were pleasant but superficial. I learned little and soon left home on my adventure.

"When I was in the jungle just sitting and listening to the incessant rain clatter on my poncho and helmet, waiting, always waiting and knowing that danger lurked around the corner, it was then that my thoughts returned home to my family. I made a commitment to myself that I would explore and converse with my dad. I wanted the dialogue with him that would lead me to a better and deeper understanding of him, and through that, myself. And, perhaps, maybe allow him a better understanding of me."

Lars looked up at his youngest son. His eyes were large and moist. Kyle's good hand remained on Lars's shoulder.

"And so an extraordinary thing happened. We connected and began to talk to each other. Our conversations occurred right here on this patio and usually under the stars. Dad told me about his father, his youth, his disappointments and successes. We talked about the war, killing, friendships, love, sailing, and even the hereafter. He lectured me on morality and dedication. And guess what, we became good friends!

"We are here to celebrate Lars Norquist's seventieth birthday. Something from T. S. Elliot comes to mind:"

> *...and the end of all our exploring will be to arrive where we started and know the place for the first time.*

"Please join me in a toast to an extraordinary man and the father we love. May his new adventure provide pleasure and reward. And may his life be long and vigorous."

Lars

Lars released Carla's hand reluctantly. His children had spoken, and it was now his turn. Some turned their chairs to face the head of the table, and all awaited the long anticipated moment. Lars turned and discreetly signaled for the wine he had so carefully selected for this moment. Large wine glasses appeared along with three imposing magnums of red wine. With the ten glasses filled, Lars rose, buttoned his jacket and gave a respectful smile to his family.

"I've had many love affairs in my life." And like an actor working the pause, he let his comment sit a moment. "With wine, of course!" The table gasped and chuckled. "And tonight for this grand occasion, I want to introduce you to my latest infatuation, a Barolo Riserva from Piedmont. Enjoy its bouquet and prepare to be taken in by it.

"This place where you are sitting is hallowed ground. Erik and Quinn will remember the day we discovered this piece of land, and even before Gunnar agreed to sell it, we were designing the lodge, planning the pier and dreaming about sailing. To watch my family grow here has been magical. Your mother's memorial plate is on a large rock in that grove of trees," he waved his hand to the darkness of the night, "and I'll be there someday. We lived during good times in this country, we were fortunate, and I think that is what we are telling each other this evening.

"I've loved two women, your mother and, as I'm sure you know, this lady by my side. After ten years, Carla has returned, and we plan to spend the rest of our lives together."

"I will drink to that with great pleasure," Samantha announced. All at the table took their first sip of the Barolo and concurred that Lars's latest love was exquisite.

"During her time away, Carla finished her medical training and moved to a remote village in Brazil to practice medicine and improve her Portuguese. She ran a rudimentary medical center, confronted every known tropical disease, delivered babies, performed appendectomies and became known as Doctor Carla. She has already begun her 'giving back' process.

"In all of your remarks, you said we have been lucky. It took me a long time to understand the difference between luck and responsibility. Now, Carla is my inspiration. Kyle presciently prodded me to move on to new pastures, travel new paths, and Quinn has patiently helped me organize my new life. I want to do something with what few skills I have to improve the lives of others. I've made enough money. I can afford to put it to good use.

"Your presence and affection have overwhelmed me on my birthday. Turning seventy is nothing special; eighty is a loftier goal, so why not commit the next decade to a new adventure? Carla and I have decided to do just that.

"And what is old Lars going to do, you ask? Hold on to your chairs. Next week, Carla and I, with Quinn as our guide, fly to Singapore. After a few days of rest, we take a steamer to Sumatra, and then a riverboat up the Sungai Kampar River to a village named Kota Palawan, our new home."

"What are you going to do there?" Erik blurted.

"Carla will be in charge of a medical facility there which, I understand, is barebones and run by a midwife. The nearest doctor is thirty miles upriver. The medical supplies and equipment we have ordered should be there when we arrive.

"I plan to install a woodworking mill, a smaller version of the one my father started in Elmwood. Surrounding the village are vast areas of virgin hardwood, meranti, mersawa, and teak. Those valuable woods are being inappropriately logged and sold without any benefit to the villagers. I plan to teach them how to mill the wood into valuable items, maybe even furniture. The Sumatran government has begun the construction of the factory building. Quinn's influential friends have ordered the machinery."

Ricardo joined in for the first time. "What an exciting idea, Lars. I'm already planning a trip to visit you. I hope some of the locals speak English?'

"Quinn has a friend, Marla, who grew up in Sumatra, was educated in the US and has taken a leave of absence from her job with the UN. She is already in Kota Palawan looking for a house for us.

"During the next few days, I will be happy to answer all of your questions. Allow me now to describe some crucial decisions that will affect our lives.

"The ownership of the millwork has been placed in a trust with rights equally divided among my four children. Erik will manage the mill and he will have a contract spelling out his responsibilities and salary. He is imminently qualified to operate our factory.

"Our Elmwood home is on the market, and the proceeds will fund Carla's and my endeavor. You are welcome to take anything you desire from the house; the rest will go to a charity. And finally, this lodge by the lake will remain in my name until I die and then will pass in trust to my children. My hope is that it will stay in our family forever.

"I've asked Marla to find a house large enough to accommodate visitors. A trip from Singapore to Kota Palawan presents an adventure, and I expect all of you to visit.

"Our journey together has been on a straight road, paved with health and surrounded by abundant nature. We should be thankful. But life changes quickly, and we must be ready to adjust. I urge you to continue to seek the pleasures of new ports. Learning is life's aphrodisiac. Enjoy it. Ithaca will loom all too soon."

Lars raised his tulip of wine. "I can only hope that you agree with Carla's and my decision to leave. My actions always had your best interests at heart. I trust that you appreciate what I have arranged for our family. I drink this beautiful wine to celebrate my love for Carla, for you, my children, and your families and to the days ahead. I wish you all safe passage."

EPILOGUE

Lars Norquist never returned home to the United States. His millwork in Kota Palawan flourished and became the envy of other lumber towns in Sumatra. Both Carla and Lars achieved surprising fluency in Malay; Lars did not use an interpreter in the factory. Teak wood became his passion, and eventually, the mill specialized in furniture bringing profits to every family and improvements to the village. In 1981 Lars contracted a virulent form of dengue fever, struggled with the infection for a month under Carla's care and passed away while sleeping in the medical center. The villagers insisted that they bury some of his ashes on a hill looking over the river. The plaque said: *Tuan Lars, Village Chief.* Carla took the remaining ashes down the river and across to Singapore where she met Quinn, and they continued to Wisconsin. The entire family gathered at the lake and buried Lars Norquist in the grove of trees next to Elizabeth. Carla accepted this, spent time with everyone, including her two sons, and then returned to Kota Palawan. The medical facility depended on her, and she spent her time absorbed in her work. She remained for eight more years before her death. The entire village attended her memorial and burial next to Lars near the river. Her life had been a long, interesting and selfless journey.

Samantha's family didn't make it to Montana. They discovered Buellton, a town in the Santa Ynez Valley, which offered a treasure trove of attractions: horse ranches, vineyards, the Spanish language, endless sun and good schools. They purchased a property, which included a small stable, paddock, several acres of pasture and forty acres of vines ready to harvest. Ric quickly became an aficionado of Pinot Noir. He lived up to his promise to Lars, and he and Sam visited Koto Palawan the following year. Sam dusted off her camera, documented Lars's endeavor and sold the story to <u>National Geographic.</u> She was back in business.

California enthusiastically elected Kyle to a second full term as a US Senator. Pictures of him and Holly with their son and daughter frequently appeared in the press with the usual buzz of his suspected Presidential aspirations. Both sides of the isle admired him and sought his support.

Throughout the country, handgun sales increased rapidly, with limited, restrictive laws. And Americans continue to kill each other at an ever-increasing rate.

AUTHOR'S NOTE

Ithaca is a work of fiction. Most of the names, characters, and incidents in this novel are the product of the author's imagination. The dialogue between portrayed authentic historical people and fictitious characters never occurred. The creation of the conversations accommodated the unfolding story.

Gnossienne. French composer Erik Satie in the late 19th century probably coined this exotic word for use as a title for several of his piano compositions. These works employed free time and introduced innovative forms. The word derivation may be from the Greek word *gnosis* (knowledge.)

The sport of biathlon began in Norway in the eighteenth century as a military exercise involving skiing and shooting. In the next century, it became a sport, and the Norwegians and Swedes competed in earnest. Soon most of Europe joined the competition. The sport disappeared after WWII because it resembled a military activity. The excitement of watching incredible athletes racing across a challenging terrain on skies and periodically dropping to the ground and firing a rifle resurrected the sport on the European scene, and ultimately it became a men's Olympic sport in the Winter Games of 1960 held in Squaw Valley, ten miles from Holly's home.

This book is the last of the Norquist trilogy. The gaps in historical narration in this novel require the reader to return to the earlier books in the trilogy. The first chapter in *Counterpoint* occurs at the point where *Ithaca* concludes. The stories provide full circle for Lars, the patriarch, and each of the three books details the life of Lars's three children: Quinn, Samantha, and Kyle. Erik's story may come later.

As in my three previous books, my wife, Marianne, provided the glue which held the novel's development together and the encouragement to keep writing. She polished the final manuscript, and her suggestions are replete. Once again, brother Hank gave the story a critical and sometimes humorous edit. A good friend, Marty Noll, patiently and skillfully edited my manuscript and suggested countless improvements which yielded a smoother syntax. Mimi Komito's scrutiny is an exercise in proofreading 'plus.' Her grasp of English is amazing because it's her second language.

Marianne and I continue to live in Crystal Bay on the north shore of Lake Tahoe. Our dear English Springer, Jasper, recently crossed the great river and now, following the same hiking paths and swimming the cove near us, we have Chester, another Springer.

Made in the USA
San Bernardino, CA
12 April 2018